American Made

New Fiction from the Fiction Collective

AMERICAN MADE

edited by

Mark Leyner
Curtis White
Thomas Glynn

with an introduction by

Larry McCaffery

FICTION COLLECTIVE

NEW YORK   BOULDER

First Edition

Library of Congress Cataloging-in-Publication Data

American Made

  1. Short stories, American. 2. American fiction—
20th century. I. Leyner, Mark. II. White, Curtis.
III. Glynn, Thomas. IV. Fiction Collective (U.S.)
PS648.S5A45 1986   813'.01'08   86-4459
ISBN 0-914-59098-7
ISBN 0-914-59099-5 (pbk.)

Grateful acknowledgment is made to the following magazines in which these stories first
appeared: *Agni Review* for "The Fish" by Russell Banks; *North American Review* for
"Passion?" by Jonathan Baumbach and "March 11" by George Chambers; *San Diego
Magazine* for "The Dirigible" by Jerry Bumpus; *Washington Review of the Arts* for
"Crocheting" by Moira Crone; *The Noble Savage, New American Review, Shank-
painter,* and *Ithaca House* for "Whispers" by B.H. Friedman; *The Carleton Miscellany*
for "The Seersucker Suit" by Marianne Hauser; *Fiction* for "The Ruth Tractate" by
Fanny Howe; *Fiction International* for portions of "The Zippo Stories" by Steve Katz
and "At This Very Instant" by Ronald Sukenick; *Guest Editor* for portions of "The
Zippo Stories" by Steve Katz; *Missouri Review* for "Rumors" by Norman Lavers;
Between C And D for "Ode To Autumn" by Mark Leyner; *The Massachusetts Review*
for "Tattoo" by Clarence Major; *New York Arts Journal* for "Prognosis" by Peter
Spielberg.

Published by Fiction Collective with the support of the Publications Center, University
of Colorado, Boulder; assistance from the National Endowment for the Arts; and the
cooperation of Brooklyn College, Illinois State University, and Teachers & Writers
Collaborative.

Grateful acknowledgment is also made to the Graduate School, the School of Arts and
Sciences, and the President's Fund of the University of Colorado, Boulder.

Manufactured in the United States of America.

Designed by McPherson & Company.

CONTENTS

American Made

LARRY McCAFFERY

Introduction

To a greater or lesser degree (but this is only a matter of degree) all of us today live *in* language—that is, our lives, and our perceptions about our lives, are controlled and processed by the words and linguistic systems that surround us. This has always been true to an extent, for the human experience has always been intimately related to (perhaps even produced by) the words and the stories which allow us to communicate and make sense of our lives, but never to such extremes as in today's information culture. Every day we are literally bombarded with (and hence manipulated by) words, sounds and images that reach us, often without our consent, from a myriad assortment of televisions, radios, tee-shirts, word processors, politicians, ghetto blasters, sky-writing planes, and personalized license plates. Even our cars talk to us nowadays when we need an oil change or leave our keys in the ignition. The extreme nature of our current life-in-language produces a situation in which words have enormous potential significance—and an equally enormous potential for being debased, trivialized, commercialized. Such extreme circumstances demand extreme measures from our serious fiction-writers, for it is their duty to rescue words from trivialization, deflect them from predictable trajectories, reshape them into stories which will encourage readers to re(dis)(un)cover the meanings and energies that lie locked within language.

Unfortunately, just at this moment when our society most

needs the kind of fresh perspectives and alternate insights that vital fiction can provide, it is becoming increasingly difficult to find such fiction in our bookstores and magazine racks. The reasons for this "death of intelligent writing" (as Richard Kostelanetz has termed it) are enormously complicated and unlikely to change: they involved the takeover of the publishing industry by multinational corporations, the Walden Book Syndrome (which encourages the stocking only of mass-market books that are likely to sell large quantities), and the disappearance of first-rate editors willing to support quality fiction and damn the accountants. This situation certainly makes the appearance of the following anthology of stories by Fiction Collective authors an event that is both heartening and exciting. The collection is comprised of authors anxious to explore fictional possibilities, to counter the public "truths" (which are usually fictions of the most immoral, self-serving sorts) with freely invented ones, to open-up the communication network and maybe have some fun in the process.

That these nineteen stories are all written by authors who have published books with the Fiction Collective should not lead readers to assume that the anthology is the product of a unified aesthetic sensibility. Indeed, since its inception in 1974 the Collective has consistently had to battle the misconception that it represents a "Movement" or favors a specific kind of experimentalism; in fact, the Collective is composed of a heterogeneous group of writers of widely varying backgrounds and aesthetic inclinations who share mainly the conviction that since serious fiction is rarely being published by the big publishing houses, an alternative outlet needs to be maintained. This eclecticism is certainly evident in the variety of themes, voices, and formal approaches found in this anthology. With each story we are placed in contact with a highly individualized sensibility which is articulating the particularities of a certain kind of verbal experience *not* within the confines of some familiar ready-made formula (the staple of nearly all mass-market fiction) but within a structure which, above all, defines *itself*. Thus we find some stories here that retain at least the surface features of realistic fiction (as with Peter Spielberg's "Prognosis," George Chambers' "March 11," Jonathan Baumbach's "Passion?" and Moira Crone's "Crocheting"), others that present the fabulous in ways that seem akin to fable or allegory (Russell Banks' "The Fish," Curtis White's "Howdy Doody is Dead," Marianne Hauser's "The Seersucker Suit," Ursule Molinaro's "Apocalyptic Flirtation"), metafictional tales which simultaneously highlight story and the fiction-making process itself (Ronald Sukenick's "At This Very Instant," George Chambers' "March 11," Raymond Federman's "Report from the World Federation of Displaced Writers," Norman Lavers' "Rumors") and some pieces that largely dispense with character and plot in the interest of redirecting the reader's interest to other processes (as with Mark Leyner's "Ode to Autumn," Clarence Major's "Tattoo," Harold Jaffe's "Pelican," B.H. Friedman's "Whispers," Fanny Howe's "The Ruth Tractate," and Steve Katz's "Zippo Stories").

This kind of formal inventiveness does not at all prevent these stories from investigating issues that concern us deeply (issues that are inevitably betrayed or trivialized in most fiction). More than half of these stories, for example, explore relationships between parents and children (Bumpus, Spielberg, Lavers, Crone), husbands and wives (Baumbach, Chambers, Jaffe, Howe), or lovers (Molinaro, Hauser). What distinguishes the way these authors handle such relationships is their refusal to reduce their characters and situations to an easily defined set of cliches that can be conveniently manipulated to achieve a comforting sense of resolution. Thus both Ursule Molinaro (in "Apocalyptic Flirtation") and Marianne Hauser (in "The Seersucker Suit") startle us out of our familiar responses to female victimization by inventing surreal situations which retain powerful emotional associations. In Molinaro's story, an aging woman film-maker and a young man struggle to maintain some semblance of a loving interaction while their passion ebbs and their egos clash; but this interaction must endure the occasional takeover of his body and spirit by the "cyclotaur" (akin to other creatures of split psyches—the centaur and the Minotaur—the cyclotaur is half-man, half-motorcycle). As we watch this male creature crash heedlessly into her affections, patching-out over her emotions, and leaving her often "pinned under a primal motorcycle," we are also observing the way men's love and tenderness so often are transformed into hatred and destructiveness. Similarly, in Marianne Hauser's "The Seersucker Suit" what begins as a familiar he-done-left-me blues lament suddenly veers into a bizarre nightmare in which the metaphorical saying "all men are dogs" is literalized. Now lonely and abandoned, the narrator of this haunting and amusing tale reminisces about the "halcyon days forever gone" when she shared her little room with her lover R, whose "furry chest" she could rest her head upon for days and nights in utter bliss. Predictably, though, she still longs at odd moments for the child that will fulfill her, and eventually she gets her wish when R provides her with a playful, loveable dog-child named Karl. The events that follow, presented in Hauser's typically brilliant, lyrical prose, should not be revealed here; but suffice it to say that the story illustrates the message which the narrator's father ("a gay dog" himself) used to convey whenever he would leave wife and family, nattily dressed in his seersucker suit: "Life is an endless chain of departures."

Hauser and Molinaro's ability to probe human relationships without robbing them of their mystery or reducing them to a predictable set of conventions illustrates why so many of our best contemporary writers have abandoned traditional realistic approaches, which suggest that peoples' lives can be "captured" (a revealing metaphor) and presented in a well-made plot. In real life, as we all know, events rarely lead to climaxes and resolutions, people's personalities change and the sources of our passions and emotions remain maddeningly ambiguous—which is why a number of these stories undercut the notions that people have stable personalities and that actions have definable results. In Jonathan Baumbach's "Passion?", for instance, a narrator's story about the breakup of a marriage becomes the "displaced occasion" which gradually sheds light on his own troubled relationship with his wife. Although ostensibly this narrator is a kind of detective who means "to separate the knowable evidence from unwarranted conjecture," he also eventually acknowledges that no matter how many details of the situation he presents, an ultimate mystery remains. This mystery results partly from the undecipherability of people (he says of his friend's wife that "we can enumerate her qualities with no strong sense of knowing the person who is the sum and substance of them") but also from the fact that, as he admits, "What I think one moment ceases to be true the next." Like a modern day Oedipus, then, this "detective" becomes an element of the riddle whose solution he is seeking. What we experience in this story are the pain and confusion that emerge from our passionate involvement with others, and the desperate need we have to try and explain these emotions which control our lives—emotions which finally lie beyond our powers of articulation. Norman Lavers' "Rumors," on the other hand, deals with the problem of personal and metaphysical uncertainty from a different angle (significantly, the story's epigraph is Boswell's famous description of Johnson refuting Berkeley's idealist doctrine by kicking a stone). Convinced that he is receiving counterfeit letters from his wife, son and daughter (letters he assumes are forged by a staff member of the asylum where he is being kept), this story's narrator begins to play verbal games with his alleged correspondents to help remove himself from his obsessions and worries (which chiefly revolve around the pack of hyenas, whom he claims lurk menacingly outside his barred windows) and to involve himself actively in artistic creation (he regards these letters as "poems" or a "group novel"). Privy to all their correspondence, the reader, like the narrator, is trapped within an endless play of conflicting signifiers which may or may not represent anything outside themselves. By deftly balancing all possibilities—is the narrator sane, the letters forged? the letters forged, the narrator insane? other combinations?—Lavers produces an amusing and occasionally terrifying variation on Nabokov's great theme: the reality of appearances.

Other stories in this anthology attack the problem of falsifications implicit within traditional story-telling methods

more directly. George Chambers' oddly touching story, "March
11," demonstrates that authorial self-consciousness doesn't
necessarily lead to academic abstraction or pedantry. "March
11" opens with the words, "My wife asked me to write a story,"
and what follows is a description of Chambers' efforts on this
specific day (the "March 11" of the story's title) to write the story
that we are reading. Chambers is well aware that most stories,
including the one he is trying to write, are produced out of a
fundmental "urge to lie, to paint this up a bit, to provide some
allure, to hint at some *dark theme* to keep you attendant."
Resisting such urges, he decides that, "A better story would be
very close to some record of the day," so that what we observe
are passages such as the following:

> *Husband and wife.* (Switch on the FM Radio—a diver-
> timento by Mozart.) (The cat, not the kitten, is howling in
> the kitchen. I feed her.) What I would like to record is
> something about us, *this* husband, *this* wife. (Ooppps! A
> great ladder-backed woodpecker is backing down the
> hackberry toward the feeder! He's at it now, a very cautious
> bird. Gone.) I'd like to record the precise quality of our
> happiness, the exact nature of what we share and what we
> don't share. I'd like to present some of our more outstand-
> ing arguments. I would like to discuss *her*: her capacity for
> joy, her way with this world.

Gradually, Chambers draws us into the rhythms of his day, into
the recesses of his creative imagination where he can admit his
secret fears of inadequacy ("In the past you may have trusted my
stories about the pains of human relationships. But these were
lies, I think"), his fears about death and growing old, his sense
that the "secret happiness" he shares with his wife is closing his
heart to the pain and sorrow that most fiction demands. What
emerges finally is a presentation of the "nothing specialness"
that constitutes, for Chambers as well as for most of the rest of
us, the source of our deepest joys, our most profound sense of
satisfaction. Although the story moves forward without regard
to the usual sense of "progression" and shapelessness, it becomes
its own justification, a proof to Chambers that he is moving

towards something as both an artist and as a man. Likewise in Ronald Sukenick's "At This Very Instant" the composition process becomes part of the story in order to show that artistic creation has very real powers and effects. Thus we witness Sukenick freely inventing a fiction about escorting some friends from Poland around New York; Sukenick had met these friends during a trip he made to Poland to track down his own family roots, and during that visit he discovered that people in Poland were not free to do even many ordinary things that we take for granted. "At This Very Instant" becomes a space in which these Polish people and Sukenick can meet, interact, play out their fantasies so that they can *really experience* what is forbidden them at the very instant that Sukenick is composing and his Polish friends are reading this story.

Although these writers share a distrust of easy formulas which pretend to be able to explain a world which seems increasingly surreal, ambiguous, and disjointed, they certainly all seem interested in producing a verbal experience which somehow captures a sense of the many textures, moods, and sounds of contemporary life. The wildest and funniest of these interactions can be found in Mark Leyner's prose, with its crossed wires of free association that put us instantly in touch with the frantic, speeded-up world-gone-mad that touches all our consciousnesses:

> as nearby, at james dean memorial hospital, nurses use cold
> bottles of milk to cool the perspiring brows of
> surgeons who are engraving ideas into the smooth
> tabula rasa brains of fetuses
> an idea being that which exists at the moment a flyball
> pauses at the apex of its flight and bids the sky adieu...
>
> that moment is pregnant
> perhaps at that moment, in an s&m bar in plymouth,
> massachusetts, the 50 ft. woman straddles your face
> and defecates 17,000 scrabble letters fertilizing the
> fallow fields of your imagination...
> and a new american style is born

Or listen to Harold Jaffe's precisely rendered re-creation in "Pelican" of a young woman's speech rhythms as she describes a sexual encounter between her and her husband and another couple:

> In the past I had always been kind of turned off—scared, I guess—by wheelchairs, but I didn't feel that way about Roy. Still Burt and I were surprised when Rory say on his lap and they started necking. After a bit Rory got up and suggested we go into the sun-room, a lovely glassed-in room with plants and pretty rugs and cushions. Rory helped Roy undress and laid him on one of the rugs on his back. He had a pretty nice body, a little soft maybe, but nice skin. He didn't at all look paralyzed. He was hung okay too, about average. He had a nice broad chest. The crazy thing of it was that while I was watching how gentle and easy and sensual Rory undressed him and helped him onto the rug, I got turned on.

Through Jaffe's choice of details and his control of the nuance, pacing, and inflection in this presentation, the reader is soon put in touch with the healing, nurturing nature of this encounter without the usual authorial intrusions (Thomas Glynn achieves a similarly penetrating presentation of personality-through-speech patterns in his "The World's Most Amazing Prophet, a.k.a. Wallace Mumford Amazon Polleau"). Likewise, "Whispers (the first three)," B.H. Friedman's concretely rendered collage of impressions about executive life in New York City, supplies a remarkably revealing glimpse into one man's love affair with the densely layered textures of a city:

> I love what critics hate: executive dining rooms of Wall Street Banks, big legal offices with rows of CCH reports, the patterns made by teleregisters, and the way necktie stripes move up to the left among men who move to the right. The towers should be connected by bridges. I go down only to refuel—i.e., when not eating at some cloudy club. Down there, I like those filling stations in the mid-forties—Christ Cella, Pietro's, the Palm, places where they cut meat the thickness of lumber—and the French ones farther north where fish swim in sauce. . . . I like them

because the food is good and cheaper than the places that cost money. New York is almost free, if you love your work. (Once I saw a guy ask a cab driver for a receipt).

Such passages are good examples of what the writing in these stories does—engage us in a verbal process that resensitizes us to language's possibilities and opens up perceptual alternatives that sharpen our responses to the world around us.

In developing these perceptual alternatives, several of the best stories here rely on the principle—utilized by Kafka and, more recently, by the magic realists—that if a writer describes a dream (or a nightmare) matter-of-factly enough and with sufficient precision, he can make us believe in that dream-work so thoroughly so that when we return to our own world we can discern that dream-world which always lurks just beneath the surface of the ordinary. Often this technique involves taking a familiar situation or element and exaggerating it until it is pushed into the realm of fantasy—a push that paradoxically often serves to reconnect us with the truly marvellous aspects of the familiar. At times this approach has the flavor of fable or allegory, as with Russell Banks' story "The Fish," in which a fabulous, free-spirited fish miraculously escapes a series of attempts to kill it by officials who fear its power to engender in the community a sense of unity and spirit. As the fame of the fish spreads, it becomes an emblem of peoples' stubborn belief in the ineffable and in the existence of beauty in a world torn by strife and brutality (set in an unnamed Oriental country, the story has reverberations that extend to Central America as well). The story also illustrates the way the genuinely miraculous can be manipulated and used by authorities so that the sources of its life and vitality eventually evaporate, leaving behind only a bloated corpse (as I write this sentence, it is Elvis' birthday. . .).

Conversely, our society's marketplace mentality often transforms that which is trivial and ugly into an illusion of value and beauty. In Clarence Major's hallucinatory "Tattoo," a black narrator on his way to a Chicago Loop tattoo parlor observes his old friend Anita scratching desperately with "long, brown consuming fangs" at a shoestore display window. The object of

Anita's fascination is a pair of semi-high heeled white shoes, which have undergone a metamorphasis by the deceptive daytime neon lights so that they appear "sparkling, so breathtaking, so flesh-like, so resplendant that they might any minute flat up and walk on air, pure, light, weightless, shimmerings in eternity!" This simulation of life, Major emphasizes, directly contrasts the sensuous vitality of that black experience which is not sold out to "these decent, upstanding, smart-looking proficient assassins" who make enormous profits from our inner fears and desires. The narrator, soon joined by another acquaintance, Hilda, attempts to dissuade Anita from wasting her time wallowing in this "possessive lust." Soon the scene has turned into a comic nightmare: while Anita "nibbles without restraint" at the plate glass, Hilda is attacked by a murderous mob of men with UPPER INCOME stamped on their stylish white shirts. With its peculiar mixture of jive talk and symbolic gestures, "Tattoo" illustrates the way our society "tattoos" its citizens with marks of its own greed and confusion. Illusion is thus made an indelible part of the world around us.

Another wonderfully resonant fable is Curtis White's "Howdy Doody is Dead," a story which resembles Hawthorne's foreboding allegories in its complexity, precision of development, and tone. Subtitled an "Apocryphalyptic Fairy Tale," White's tale traces the tragic rise and fall of Howard ("Howdy") Doody, whose destiny is linked with the loss of a certain kind of American innocence somewhere during the time between the premiere of Howdy's own tv show in 1947 and those fateful days in 1960 when he is undone by the dastardly deeds of a woodenheaded impostor, carved out of flawed wood by the toysmith narrator. As his dark story unfolds, White recreates the feel of America in the 1940s and early 50s with an unerring eye for significant details that create a very realistic backdrop for the fantastic events that take place.

But all this is sounding much too stuffy and abstract—and in making these introductory comments, I realize that I'm surely guilty of the same reductionism and facile category-making that the following stories so carefully avoid. Certainly I hope that in calling these stories "non-traditional" or "experimental" I'm not putting readers off or intimidating them. Rather, I've hoped to suggest that these stories are "different" primarily in the fresh way they approach the art of designing essential narratives out of language. Really, the very best advice I can offer potential readers is simply to take the plunge here and open yourselves to the very real, particularized experiences these authors are presenting. You will find yourself soon drawn into absolutely unique verbal worlds with their own rules, voices, textures, and ambiguities—worlds, in short, which are continuous with experience and which help revitalize our relationship to the language which is our life.

RUSSELL BANKS

The Fish

When Colonel Tung's first attempt to destroy the fish failed, everyone, even the Buddhists, was astonished. On the Colonel's orders a company of soldiers under the command of a young lieutenant named Han had marched out from the village early one summer morning as far as the bridge. Departing from the road there, the soldiers made their way in single file through the bamboo groves and shreds of golden mist to a clearing, where they stepped with care over spongy ground to the very edge of the pond, which was then the size of a soccer field. Aiming automatic weapons into the water, the troopers waited for the fish to arrive. A large crowd from the village gathered behind them and, since most of the people were Buddhists, they fretted and scowled at the soldiers, saying, "Shame! Shame!" Even some Catholics from the village joined the scolding, though it had been their complaints that first had drawn the Colonel's attention to the existence of the huge fish and had obliged him to attempt to destroy it, for pilgrimages to view the fish had come to seem like acts of opposition to his administration. In great numbers the Buddhists from other districts were visiting the Buddhists in his district, sleeping in local homes, buying food from local vendors and trading goods of various kinds, until it had begun to seem to Colonel Tung that there were many more Buddhists in his district than Catholics, and this frightened him, which he regarded as no accident. Thus his opinion that the pilgrimages to view the fish were acts of political opposition, and thus his determination to destroy the fish.

Shortly after the soldiers lined up at the shore, the fish broke the surface of the water halfway across the pond. It was a silver swirl in the morning sun, a clean swash of movement, like a single brushstroke, for the fish was thought to be a reincarnation of Rad, the painter and an early disciple of Buddha. The soldiers readied their weapons. Lieutenant Han repeated his order: "Wait until I say to fire," he said, and there was a second swirl, a lovely arc of silver bubbles, closer to shore this time. The crowd had gone silent. Many were moving their lips in prayer; all were straining to see over and around the line of soldiers at the shore. Then there it was, a few feet out and hovering in the water like a cloud in the sky, one large dark eye watching the soldiers as if with curiosity, its delicate fins fluttering gently in the dark water like translucent leaves. "Fire!" the lieutenant cried. The soldiers obeyed, and their weapons roared for what seemed a long time. The pond erupted and boiled in white fury, and when finally the water was still once again, everyone in the crowd rushed to the shore and searched for the remains of the fish. Even the lieutenant and his band of soldiers pushed to the mud at the edge of the water and looked for the fish, or what everyone thought would be chunks of the fish floating on the still surface of the pond. But they saw nothing, not a scrap of it, until they noticed halfway across the pond a swelling in the water, and the fish rolled and dove, sending a wave sweeping in to shore, where the crowd cried out joyfully and the soldiers and the young lieutenant cursed, for they knew that Colonel Tung was not going to like this, not at all.

They were correct. Colonel Tung took off his sunglasses and glared at the lieutenant, then turned in his chair to face the electric fan for a moment. Finally, replacing his glasses, he said, "Let us assume that in that pond an enemy submarine is surfacing at night to send spies and saboteurs into our midst. Do you have the means to destroy it?" He tapped a cigarette into an ebony holder and lighted it. The lieutenant, like the Colonel, a man trained at the Academy but rapidly adapting his skills to life in the provinces, said yes, he could destroy such an enemy. He would mine the pond, he said, and detonate the mines from shore. "Indeed," the Colonel said. "That sounds like a fine idea," and he went back to work.

From a rowboat, the soldiers placed into the pond ten pie-sized mines connected by insulated wires to one another and to a detonator and battery, and when everything was ready and the area had been cleared of civilians, Lieutenant Han set off the detonator from behind a mound of earth they had heaped up for this purpose. There was a deep, convulsive rumble and the surface of the pond blew off, causing a wet wind that had the strength of a gale and tore leaves from the trees and bent the bamboo stalks to the ground. Immediately after the explosion, everyone from the village who was not already at the site rushed to the pond and joined the throng that encircled it. Everything that had ever lived in or near the pond seemed to be dead and floating on its surface—carp, crayfish, smelts, catfish, eels, tortoises, frogs, egrets, woodcocks, peccaries, snakes, feral dogs, lizards, doves, shellfish, and all the plants from the bottom, the long grasses, weeds and reeds, and the banyans, mangroves and other trees rooted in the water, and the flowering bushes and the lilies that had floated on the surface of the pond—everything once alive seemed dead. Many people wept openly, some prayed, burned incense, chanted, and others, more practical, rushed about with baskets gathering up the unexpected harvest. The lieutenant and his soldiers walked intently around the pond searching for the giant fish. When they could not find it, they rowed out to the middle of the pond and searched there. But still, amongst the hundreds of dead fish and plants, birds and animals floating in the water, they saw no huge silver fish, no carcass that could justify such carnage. Then, as they began to row back toward shore, the lieutenant, who was standing at the bow, his hand shading his eyes from the milky glare of the water, saw before them once again the rolling, shiny side of the giant fish, its dorsal fin like a black knife slicing obliquely across their bow, when it disappeared, only to reappear off the stern a ways, swerving back and suddenly heading straight at the small, crowded boat. The men shouted in fear, and at the last possible second the fish looped back and dove into the dark waters below. The crowd at the shore had seen it, and a great cheer went up, and in seconds there were drums and cymbals and all kinds of song joining the cheers, as the soldiers rowed slowly, glumly, in to shore.

The reputation of the fish and its miraculous powers began to spread rapidly across the whole country, and great flocks of believers undertook pilgrimages to the pond, where they set up tents and booths on the shore. Soon the settlement surrounding the pond was as large as the village where the Colonel's district headquarters was located. Naturally, this alarmed the Colonel, for these pilgrims were Buddhists, many of them fanatics, and he, a Catholic, was no longer sure he could rule them. "We must destroy that fish," he said to the lieutenant, who suggested this time that he and his soldiers pretend to join the believers and scatter pieces of bread over the waters to feed the fish, as had become the custom. They would do this from the boat, he said, and with specially sweetened chunks of bread, and when the fish was used to being fed this way and approached the boat carelessly close, they would lob hand grenades painted white as bread into the water, and the fish, deceived, would swallow one or two or more whole, as it did the bread, and that would be that. Colonel Tung admired the plan and sent his man off to implement it instantly. Lieutenant Han's inventiveness surprised the Colonel and pleased him, though he foresaw problems, for, if the plan worked, he would be obliged to promote the man, which would place Han in a position where he could begin to covet his superior's position as district commander. This damned fish, the Colonel said to himself, may be the worst thing to happen to me.

It soon appeared that Lieutenant Han's plan was working, for the fish, which seemed recently to have grown to an even more gigantic size than before and was now almost twice the size of the boat, approached the boat without fear and rubbed affectionately against it, or so it seemed, whenever the soldiers rowed out to the middle of the pond and scattered large chunks of bread, which they did twice a day. Each time, the fish gobbled the chunks, cleared the water entirely and swam rapidly away. The throng on shore cheered, for they, too, had taken the bait— they believed that the soldiers, under the Colonel's orders, had come to appreciate the fish's value to the district as a whole, to Catholics as much as to Buddhists, for everyone, it seemed, was profiting from its presence, tentmakers, carpenters, farmers, storekeepers, clothiers, woodchoppers, scribes, entrepreneurs of all types, entertainers, even, musicians and jugglers, and of course the manufacturers of altars and religious images and also of paintings and screens purported to have been made by the original Rad, the artist and early disciple of Buddha, now reincarnated as the giant fish.

When finally Lieutenant Han gave the order to float the specially prepared grenades out with the bread, several soldiers balked. They had no objections to blowing up the fish, but they were alarmed by the size of the crowd now more or less residing on the shore and, as usual, watching them in hopes of seeing the fish surface to feed. "If this time we succeed in destroying the fish," a soldier said, "the people may not let us get back to shore. There are now thousands of them, Catholics as well as Buddhists, and but ten of us." The lieutenant pointed out that the crowd had no weapons while the soldiers had automatic rifles that could easily clear a path from the shore to the road and back to the village, "And once the fish is gone, the people will go away, and things will settle back into their normal ways again." The soldiers took heart and proceeded to drop the grenades into the water with an equal number of chunks of bread. The fish, large as a house, had been lurking peacefully off the stern of the boat and now swept past, swooping up all the bread and the grenades in one huge swallow. It turned away and rolled, exposing its silver belly to the sun, as if in gratitude, and the crowd cried out in pleasure. The music rose, with drums, cymbals, flutes joining happily and floating to the sky on swirling clouds of incense, while the soldiers rowed furiously for shore. The boat scraped gravel, and the troopers jumped out, dragged the boat up onto the mud and made their way quickly through the throng toward the road. As they reached the road, they heard the first of the explosions, then the others in rapid succession, a tangled knot of bangs as all the grenades went off, in the air, it seemed, out of the water and certainly not inside the fish's belly. It was as if the fish were spitting the grenades out just as they were about to explode, creating the effect of a fireworks display above the pond, which must have been what caused the people gathered at the shore to break into sustained, awestruck applause and then, long into the day and the following night, song.

Now the reputation of the miraculous fish grew tenfold, and busloads of pilgrims began to arrive from as far away as Saigon and Bangkok. People on bicycles, on donkeys, in trucks and in oxcarts, made their way down the dusty road from the village to the pond, where as many of them as could find a spot got down to the shore and prayed to the fish for help, usually against disease and injury, for the fish was thought to be especially effective in this way. Some prayed for wealth or for success in love or for revenge against their enemies, but these requests were not thought likely to be answered, though it surely did no harm to try. Most of those who came now took away with them containers filled with water from the pond. They arrived bearing bowls, buckets, fruit tins, jars, gourds, even cups, and they took the water with them back to their homes in the far corners of the country, where many of them were able to sell off small vials of the water for surprisingly high prices to those unfortunate neighbors and loved ones unable to make the long overland journey to the pond. Soldiers, too, whenever they passed through Colonel Tung's district, came to the pond and filled their canteens with the magical waters. More than once a helicopter landed on the shore, and a troop of soldiers jumped out, ran to the pond, filled their canteens and returned to the helicopter and took off again. Thus, when Lieutenant Han proposed to Colonel Tung that this time they try to destroy the fish by poisoning the water in the pond, the Colonel demurred. "I think that instead of trying to kill the fish, we learn how to profit from it ourselves. It's too dangerous now," he observed, "to risk offending the people by taking away what has become their main source of income. What I have in mind, my boy, is a levy, a tax on the water that is taken away from this district. A modest levy, not enough to discourage the pilgrims, but more than enough to warrant the efforts and costs of collection." The Colonel smiled slyly and set his lieutenant to the task. There will be no promotions now, he said to himself, for there are no heroics in tax collecting.

And so a sort of calm and orderliness settled over the district, which pleased everyone, Colonel Tung most of all, but also Lieutenant Han, who managed to collect the tax on the water so effectively that he was able without detection to cut a small percentage out of it for himself, and the soldiers, who felt much safer collecting taxes than trying to destroy a miraculous and beloved fish, and the people themselves, who, because they now paid a fee for the privilege of taking away a container of pond water, no longer doubted the water's magical power to cure illness and injury, to let the blind see, the lame walk, the deaf hear, the dumb talk. The summer turned into fall, the fall became winter, and there were no changes in the district, until the spring, when it became obvious to everyone that the pond was much smaller in diameter than it had been in previous springs. The summer rains that year were heavy, though not unusually so, and the Colonel hoped that afterwards the pond would be as large as before, but it was not. In September, when the dry season began, the Colonel tried to restrict the quantity of water taken from the pond. This proved impossible, for by now too many people had too many reasons to keep on taking water away. A powerful black market operated in several cities, and at night tanker trucks edged down to the shore where they sucked thousands of gallons of water out, and the next morning the surface of the pond would be yet another foot lower than before and encircling it would be yet another mud aureole inside the old shoreline.

At last there came the morning when the pond was barely large enough to hold the fish. The Colonel, wearing sunglasses, white scarf and cigarette holder, and Lieutenant Han and the soldiers and many of the pilgrims walked across the drying mud to the edge of the water, where they lined up around the tiny pool, little more than a puddle now, and examined the fish. It lay on its side, half-exposed to the sun. One gill, blood-red inside, opened and closed, but no water ran through. One eye was above water, one below, and the eye above was clouded over and fading to white. A pilgrim who happened to be carrying a pail leaned down, filled his pail and splashed the water over the side of the fish. Another pilgrim with a gourd joined him, and two soldiers went back to the encampment and returned with a dozen containers of various types and sizes, which they distributed to the others, even including the Colonel. Soon everyone was dipping his container into the water and splashing it over the silvery side of the huge, still fish. By midday, however, the sun had evaporated most of the water, and the containers were filled with more mud than moisture, and by sunset they had buried the fish.

JONATHAN BAUMBACH

Passion?

"Everything remains to be done."
—*Jean Luc Godard*

1

A man I know, a long time sometime friend, recently left his wife and three children because he had fallen in love with another woman. Such news has a disquieting effect on our crowd. Henry is the most domesticated and repressed husband among us, the most devoted of fathers. If Henry, our moral light, is capable of such anarchic behavior, it strikes us that almost anything is possible. Surmise, however, is not the business of this report. What I mean to do here is to separate the knowable evidence from unwarranted conjecture. I mean to investigate the mystery of Henry's inexplicable act as though I were a detective tracking down a criminal.

2

Henry was barely twenty-four when he married Illana. They had met at college, had started going together when Henry, who was a year or so older, was in his sophomore year, though they had known each other casually (or such is the story one pieces together) from childhood. There were times, says Illana, when each was the other's only real friend. Her remark is not surprising. Henry and Illana had always seemed, to those of us who thought we knew them well, exceptionally close. They had grown over the years of their marriage to seem like mirror images of one another. One breathed in, we supposed, and the other breathed out. They saw themselves, and we tended to confirm that view, as a perfect couple.

3

The year before he married Illana, Henry, then a Rhodes scholar, started work on a novel about a young intellectual affianced to his childhood sweetheart who falls in love during a summer abroad with a French woman twelve years his senior. He wrote 126 pages of this book before giving up and the manuscript apparently still exists in its first and only draft. It was, insofar as anyone knows, Henry's only attempt at prolonged fiction.

4

In the second year of their marriage, their first daughter, Natalia, was born. Henry and Illana were extremely serious about the responsibility. Shortly after that, Henry, an up and coming editor, moved to a job in another publishing house that paid twenty dollars more a month. Illana also was working and they had a live-in maid to look after the child. Henry announced, we all remember, that Illana's working was a temporary arrangement, that it was the preference of both of them that she stay home with the child. Illana said that she and Henry on that matter were in thorough agreement. She made this assertion, as I remember, with surprising passion.

5

Henry was under a great deal of pressure at work and went into therapy to avoid, as he said, breaking down altogether. He had a dream—his therapist had been after him to write down his dreams—in which his father, whom he hadn't seen in ten years, came to him and said that there was evidence that someone was shooting at him and he wondered if it were Henry. Henry said that he admitted to being angry at his father for having walked out on his mother but that he had no recollection of trying to kill him. The father said if thoughts could kill, Henry would have to be the number one suspect. Thoughts don't kill, said Henry. Well, how do you explain the bullet in my stomach? said the father.

6

About that time Henry reported to friends that he and Illana were reading to each other in bed at night. "We are going through the entire canon of Dickens," said Illana, "one chapter a night." "How long will it take to do all the novels?" someone asked. Henry, figuring to himself, a private smile on his face, said nothing. "We'll do it until we decide not to do it," said Illana.

7

Illana had written a children's book in her spare time. Henry agented it for her, showing it to children's book editors at two other publishing houses, avoiding his own as a matter of moral discretion. Illana and Henry had always taken impeccable moral positions. And though they didn't presume to judge others, one sensed a certain discomfort with the unscrupulous or overween-ingly ambitious. Illana withdrew the book at some point, indicating that she had no great desire to make her work public.

8

I spoke to Henry at the hospital after the birth of his second daughter, Nara. He said, although he and Illana had wanted a boy, they were not in any way disappointed. Illana said the same thing to my wife in almost the same language, impressing on us (was it meant to?) how together they were, how intimately allied. A week later, when we visited them at home, Henry in Illana's presence made the same speech. When we got home my wife said, "Perhaps they protest too much," and I said, no, I thought they meant it. "It's the same thing," she said.

9

We all admired the seeming ease with which Henry rose in his chosen profession. What was most impressive was that his ambition, which evidence suggests was considerable, was never aggressively displayed. He had never, not to our knowledge at least, advanced his career at the expense of someone else. We had almost never heard a bad word of him. Yet at the same time we felt that Henry's full capacities were not being realized. What we meant by that was not at all clear.

10

What do we know about Illana? When friends of Henry's and Illana's get together, the question tends to come up. What has she had to say for herself in all the years we've known her? We thought of her as taciturn, though not unfriendly, a bit formal in manner, a woman who spoke her opinions as if they were national secrets. She had a way of looking after her children— this was when Henry was there to help—without making it seem, as do some mothers, that the job was overburdening her. We can enumerate her qualities with no strong sense of knowing the person who is the sum and substance of them.

11

This is Henry's story mostly. It is Henry who announces one day, Illana sitting at the kitchen table with the baby on her lap, that he has fallen love with someone else. "You have?" Illana is imagined to have asked. "What does that mean in terms of our marriage?"

"I don't know," said Henry. "It's too new to me."

"You don't know?" The question asked with some manner of skepticism. "What do you want to do?"

"What do you want me to do?"

"Well, naturally," Illana said softly, "I'd like you to break it off if you can."

"Out of the question," said Henry.

"I didn't realize that it..." said Illana, a small crack of panic in her usually impassive face, swallowing her words as though ashamed of their inadequacy.

"It happened," said Henry. "I didn't mean it to, but it did. I'm terribly sorry."

12

After that first confession, Illana becomes a tacit partner, an accessory after the fact, in Henry's double life. Henry works out a regimen, accommodating both worlds. He has dinner with Illana and the children, helps put the children to bed, leaves afterwards to spend the night with Patricia, returning by taxi at 5 AM to be present when the children awake. It is important to him to have the children perceive their world as intact. (Also important perhaps to keep up appearances in front of himself and Illana, a way of deflecting awareness.) "I want you to do what's best for you," Illana is reported to have said to Henry. "I don't want to leave you and the children," said Henry, "and I can't give up Patricia." If this assertion wounds Illana, there is no visible evidence for it. After breakfast, Henry takes the older daughter, Natalia, to school, as he has always done before going off himself to work.

13

The Vice-President of the government foundation at which Henry now worked had been having an affair with the wife of one of the Board of Directors and word of it—one wondered why the news had taken so long—finally reached that lady's husband. Scandal ensued and the notorious administrator had no choice but to resign in favor of a slightly higher paying job at another foundation, leaving in his wake a vacancy at the top. It was rumored that Henry was in favored consideration for the post. Who knows where such rumors start? Henry, at the time, was the youngest and ablest associate director at the foundation, and it was more than possible that his well-wishers, wanting the rumor so, presumed its likelihood. Henry, taking nothing for granted, went to see the president of the foundation to indicate his interest and availability. Whatever Henry's boss said to him—the account given to me was notably short on specifics— Henry appeared hopeful in his guarded way. "Frankly," he said, "I have no reason to expect anything."

14

Illana said, out of Henry's hearing, that she thought Henry was setting himself up for a fall. "You think he won't get the job?" asked her confidante, who in this case was my wife Genevieve. "I think his chances are not as good as he thinks they are," said Illana, according to my source. "Of course he deserves the job," she added. "I just don't think he's in line for it." Something odd was going on between them, we thought. Why hadn't Illana, who was the epitome of loyalty, offered this perception to Henry?

15

One day my wife asked me if I found Illana sexy? Sexy may not be the word she had used. "Attractive" or "beautiful" is more likely. I don't remember what I answered. "Uhnrr," perhaps. Something that cancelled itself out, I suspect. What's that about? I thought, though let it slide by at the time. About a week later, something else bothering me, I asked her why she had asked about Illana. "Oh," she said, "someone else was saying, I don't remember who, that Illana was the most beautiful woman of his acquaintance and I wondered if you thought the same thing." I said I didn't even think Henry thought that. "That's an odd thing to say," she said. "Well, she's beautiful in a conventional way," I said, "but there's something glacial about her as if she weren't quite alive."

16

Why do I remember my wife's question about Illana and my answer, and what do they have to do with the larger question under investigation in this study? I think we both felt that there was something invisibly wrong with Henry and Illana's perfect marriage, though we were not in touch with that perception. And why should we have been? Why should we have thought of Henry and Illana at all? I don't know the answers. I ask the questions merely to ask them. Illana was not the issue of my wife's question as it turned out, merely the displaced occasion. I had heard the question she had asked, but not the unspoken confession it contained.

17

Two days after Henry's son was born, he got word that the job he had coveted, had come in fact to count on, had been given to someone else. The news arrived, as it tends to in government agencies, by way of rumor, and Henry, as angry as he ever remembers himself, went to see his boss to check it out. "Don," Henry said, "I've heard some disturbing news." Don took his glasses off to listen, lit a cigarette, though he had given up smoking a week ago this day. "Well, what have you heard?" he asked. (His tone suggested, Henry reported, that there wasn't any rumor around he wasn't prepared to deny.) "I had heard," said Henry, "that you had made a decision on Calvin's replacement." "Oh that," said Don. "You said you would let me know as soon as you came to a decision," said Henry. "Did I say that?" said Don. "Frankly, I don't remember making any such promise. The feeling was, and as you know I queried opinions from all directions, that you could have done the job adequately—no one had anything negative to say about your capabilities—but that ... " Henry had no recollection of how the sentence was completed.

18

Henry, it was reported, took his disappointment with extraordinary grace, which was our idea of Henry. "That's the way it goes," he said, defending the qualifications of the man chosen in his place. "What I have to do is reevaluate my commitment to my job." Illana seemed emotionally drained. We perceived it as a form of loyalty to Henry and admired them both—this special couple—all the more.

19

The following account has been confirmed by two sources and so it is included here despite my own tendency to disbelieve it. The time was about four weeks after Henry learned that he had been passed over for the promotion he had anticipated. The affair with Patricia, if it had already started, was some two months shy of becoming public news. Henry and Illana were at a party hosted by Henry's employer. It was a cocktail party held in some east side apartment to honor the grant recipients of that year and the living room was crowded to the walls with the mostly uninvited. Some bearded middle-aged composer, congenitally sour, took it into his head to assail Henry over the granting policy of the foundation which had just passed Henry over for promotion. Henry was polite at first, said he was not responsible for the choices of committees on which he hadn't served, then proceeded, which is typical of Henry, to defend the foundation's policies unequivocally. The composer kept after him, finding fault with one choice after another. When he could take no more—one can imagine the complication of his feelings—Henry turned his back on him. Illana, who happened to be on the periphery of the small group listening in, was heard to whisper to Henry, "Why didn't you answer him?" Henry, usually under control, lost his temper and shouted at her, "Why didn't I answer him? Why didn't I? I didn't answer him because the son of a bitch is not listening to anything I say." It is reported that Illana's face reddened and that she apologized to Henry's adversary for her husband's behavior.

20

Even after Henry moves in with Patricia, Illana continues to pretend to the children that she and Henry are together as before. "Why are you doing it?" my wife says to her when she comes to visit with the three children, who range in age from six months to six years. "If I were you, I'd tell him to fuck off." Illana, who rarely smiles, smiles at that. "I would if I felt that way," she says. "I'm not angry at Henry. I want him to be happy and if he's happy this way, then that's the way it has to be." When Illana is gone my wife says to me: "One of these days she's going to realize how angry she really is. And then...."

21

A call from Henry this morning at work. He wants us, he says, to be the first of his friends to meet Patricia. An appointment is made for dinner at a Chinese restaurant called Hunan Feast. My wife says, when she hears of the arrangement, that she won't go, that it is a disloyalty to Illana even to meet Patricia. I mention that Henry is also a friend and that there is no reason why we have to take sides. "I can't forgive him," she says, "He may be a friend of yours, but he's no friend of mine."

Patricia seems as nervous to meet us as we are to meet her, and the experience reminds me of the blind dates of my adolescence. None of us seems able to strike the right note. "What do you think?" Henry whispers out of earshot of the women. "I think she's... (I search for the word) fine," I say generously. My answer seems to disappoint him. "Is that all?" he asks.

22

"What do you think of her?" my wife asks when we're in bed that night, the first either of us has risked the subject. "She's different from what I imagined," I hear myself saying.

"I don't know what you mean by that." A note of irritation in her tone.

"Does that mean you don't like her?" I ask.

"It's not a question of liking or disliking her. She's nothing. She's a blank. Didn't you see that?"

My silence offers denial.

"My God, Joshua, I've never seen anyone with less personality. She's pathetic."

"Well, what do you think she has for Henry?"

"I haven't the faintest idea. What do you think?"

"Well, she's not unattractive," I say.

"Not unattractive? She's the most ordinary looking woman I've ever seen in my life."

23

Henry is on one of his periodic diets; we go to a health food restaurant for lunch and have a couple of shredded carrot sandwiches. Our conversation is correspondingly low on calories. "Patsy liked you and Genevieve," he says a few times, rephrasing the remark so as not to seem to repeat himself. "She felt the two of you accepted her." "She seemed extremely nice," I say. "Very . . . " The word eludes me. "Unconstrained," he says. "Unconstrained," I repeat. "In that way, she's the opposite of Illana," he says. "Do you think you'll stay with her?" I ask. He becomes thoughtful, which is a form of reprimand with Henry, an indication that you've overstepped yourself. Then he says with a forgiving smile: "We take every day as it comes." It goes like that until later in the meal when Henry says, "Illana and I still love each other. The situation hasn't changed that."

"Then you are thinking of going back to her?"

"It's impossible," he says, smiling enigmatically. "We're both happier this way."

"Both of you?" My incredulousness seems to escape notice.

Henry eats his yogurt and nuts with a beautific smile.

"Is it sex?" I ask, expecting no answer.

"Never been so good," he says.

24

"It's not sex," says my wife. We are still trying to understand our friend Henry. "Or sex is merely an excuse for something else."

"If Henry says their sex is good, why should you doubt him?"

"Henry," says Genevieve, "is trying something out. He wants to see how far he can go, how outrageous he can be, before Illana will say 'no more.'"

"That leaves out the implication of Patsy altogether," I say.

"Patsy doesn't count. Don't you see that?"

"If you ask Henry, Patsy is the only one who counts."

Our conflicting views of the reality abrade against one another, strain the limits of our friendship.

"Why are we fighting over Henry and Illana?" my wife asks.

The continuing argument becomes its own answer.

25

Henry and Patricia have been living together for six months. Henry visits with the children on weekends and sometimes comes over in the evenings to put them to bed. Illana, although she sees other men, appears to work at it as if a recommended though pointless exercise, remains in her heart faithful to the Arrangement. How do I know this? Illana tells us or tells Genevieve, which comes to the same thing. Genevieve becomes increasingly impatient with Illana's stance, though talks to her almost every day on the phone, gauging her emotional temperature from the evidence of the unspoken. "She has no idea how angry she really is," says Genevieve. "Her calm is a form of self-oblivion. Meanwhile she won't allow herself to get interested in any of the men she sees. I can't stand it."

26

My wife says, à propos of my arm around her, "You're behaving like Henry."

"What does that mean?"

"Henry and Patsy, as you know, behave like teenagers in public, but they have an excuse. They're new to each other."

Her rebuke turns into a fight. I recall my arm and take refuge in another room.

She follows after a moment. "Don't you see what you're doing?" she asks. "You're jealous that Henry has another woman."

"Maybe I am," I say.

27

I overhear Genevieve complain to Illana on the phone about me, her way I think of criticizing Henry indirectly. All of our men are unreliable, says her tone. And what have I done? Whatever it is, she refuses to forgive me. "I am not Henry," I say to her.

"You wish you were," she says.

I call Henry from work, but he is not available for lunch that day, which is too bad. He is precisely the person I need to talk to in my present mood. An odd coincidence: I run into Illana at lunch; she is with another man, I am with another woman. We hail each other across the restaurant. At first I didn't recognize her—how absolutely smashing she looks!—was staring at her in admiration. "We'll have to talk some time," I say to her. She says, "Yes, yes."

28

Have I drifted from the subject of this investigation? The subject itself drifts. To tell someone's story is to identify, to some extent, with the inner life of that person. In explaining Henry, I explain myself; in explaining myself, I explain Henry. Although not influenced by Henry's behavior—I am convinced that he is not my example—I have just split with my wife of ten years. My situation differs from Henry's in certain definitive ways. I haven't (at the time, at *this* time) fallen in love with anyone else. Genevieve and I weren't getting along, were fighting too much, were making each other unhappy. I realize this sounds evasive, but the disrepair of our marriage is too immediate for me to see it with any clarifying distance. It is easier, if not altogether more edifying, to talk about Henry and Illana. Henry continues to live joyfully, passionately, with Patsy, who is neither more nor less beautiful than his wife and who, despite apparent differences, resembles her more than not. Illana continues to make do and to accept her husband's manifest disaffection with public and private grace. I envy them both. My situation is neither pleasurable in itself nor might it engender the admiration of others.

29

Tonight I have dinner with Illana and the two older children, sitting at the table with them in their makeshift living/dining room as I had times before in significantly different circumstances. Illana prefers, she says (the evening's arrangement is her idea), to eat with the children like a family. After dinner, I help her put them to bed, a chore of some complication. "How do you manage by yourself?" I ask. "Henry usually comes to help," she says. "But since you were coming I told him there was no need for him to bother." I indicate some surprise that she had mentioned it to Henry. "We have no secrets from each other," she says with that seriousness characteristic of them both.

"What now?" she asks.

The question is not meant to be answered. We sit on the sofa, holding hands, talking about nothing. At one point, she says—we have just kissed somewhat awkwardly—"Joshua, do you think of me as a cold person?" I reserve answer, kissing her again as if that urgent gesture (is it really as urgent as it seems?) were a response to her question. And yet what I think one moment ceases to be true the next. She is passionate yet remote as if her passion were a private wellspring separate from her day to day nature.

30

I return to my hotel room at four in the morning and have barely dropped off when the phone rings. "I want you back," the voice says. It is odd that I am unable to identify or rather confuse the identity of that voice. I finesse my confusion. "At this moment?" I ask. "As soon as you can," says the voice. (I will know in a minute who it is, I think. Keep her talking and she will reveal herself.) "Why do you want me back?" "Oh, God! Do you have to ask? If you don't come to me, I'll come to you." She hangs up abruptly though soundlessly, fitting the phone like a piece of a puzzle into the base. Three hours later (all time is an estimate here), a knock on the door wakes me from an erotic dream. "Who's there?" I ask the nurse in my dream. The knock repeats, replays itself. I put on a bathrobe and stagger to the door, bumping invisible furniture en route. "Do you mind my coming to your room?" she asks, stepping in, locking the door behind her. Perhaps she says nothing at all and the voice I quote is out of that interrupted dream. There is no time for questions and explanations; there is barely even time to kiss. Coupling is impersonal and urgent like some natural disaster. "Who's with the children?" I ask later. "Never mind," she says. "The children are well looked after."

31

Henry seems unusually jaunty when we meet after work at O'Neill's for a drink. I am not eager to talk to him, would have avoided this meeting if I hadn't felt obliged to face him. It takes him two drinks to get to what's on his mind. "I don't know that I like what's going on between you and Illana," he says casually and then again with added weight as if he hadn't heard himself the first time. "I've always liked Illana," I say. He nods. "She's a terrific person, and I don't want to see her hurt." Although expecting something like this—Henry is one of the most consciously moral people I know—I can think of nothing useful to say. "Are you in love with her?" he asks. "Henry, come on," I say. His face clenches and for a moment, just for a moment, he is so infuriated he can barely keep himself together. "I feel very close to Illana," he says softly. "I appreciate that," I say. His glass overturns and the bartender comes over to mop the counter. "It's all right," he says. "I'm not angry with you." The conversation seems to repeat itself. "I don't understand what you're asking," I hear myself say perhaps for the third time. "I don't want to see Illana hurt, that's all." Henry says once again.

"Are you asking me to stop seeing her?"

"I don't think I have the right to ask you that," he says.

32

Illana seems to call at least once a day, which is all right, though sometimes I wish it were Genevieve, who never calls. One night at her place, she says, "I really want a husband, not a lover."

"You have both," I say.

"I have neither," she says. "Joshua, I'm opposed to disorder."

"I'm not sure it's over with Genevieve," I say.

Illana laughs. "She says it's over. We talk about you on the phone."

That night after the children are in bed and we have made love with our customary hunger, rushing through the act as if it might be taken from us if we waited, I have an odd perception. "You would take Henry back, wouldn't you, if he was ready to come back?"

She thinks about it and thinks about it. "I would," she says finally, "but afterward I'd be sorry."

JERRY BUMPUS

The Dirigible

This gray winter morning descends like the huge lead-coated balloon I had one summer when I was a boy. I called it my dirigible. As I pulled it along with clothesline, it didn't bump and bob like nice ordinary balloons but smoothly cruised, profoundly preoccupied, and as I lowered it under the back porch and nosed it through the kitchen door when I brought it home from the carnival, my folks were stunned.

When they got their breath they managed a comment on how uniquely I had spent my money. But I saw more in their faces. For the first time they let slip their disapproval of something at the center of me. Or that was the first time I had seen the slip. In a glance I saw it all. I wouldn't be surprised by later, fuller revelations of their wariness of that person who had started off as their boy and relentlessly turned into something different from themselves and anyone they had ever known. What I saw on their faces wasn't fear, though it was going in that direction. It was a mixture of suspicion, fundamental doubt, and dread—not the sort which comes from incomprehension but from recognition of something old and familiar.

Stunned myself, I blamed the dirigible for what was happening while we stood there in its shadow. They blamed it too, probably, then tried to convince themselves this was merely another case of young Sonny going too far. But this time he had outdone himself, having worked up from turning the place into a leprosarium the summer half the dogs in town had mange, to luring a 40-pound snapping turtle into the house and claiming it had chased him home, to deeper commitments such as harboring blue racers and even young water moccasins in the bib of his overalls. Now this great awful gray-black steel thing, this floating petrified fish, this ghost whale thing...

After the carnival left town the helium, or whatever magic had held the dirigible aloft, began leaking out. It shrank somewhat, becoming steadily denser. One morning I woke to find it on the floor, with pathetic nobility resting what I felt was its head on the limp clothesline. I tried sneaking the dirigible out but the rumbling as I rolled it through the house woke my family. I felt them watching from the kitchen window as I worked at the far corner of the garden. I miscalculated on the hole; the dirigible was bigger than anything I had ever buried, and I was running out of steam. Maybe by a long stretch of imagination and tolerance my folks would think the big jutting nose was ornamental. Also it could serve as a common marker for the birds, snakes, possums, raccoons, cats, dogs and everything else crowded into that other garden which lay beyond theirs. If my folks bought that, would they also go along with my notion that the same spirit which had levitated the dirigible might lift beans, tomatoes and onions out of their garden, for hadn't the Pilgrims learned similar magic from the Indians who religiously stuck fish in the ground when planting corn?

GEORGE CHAMBERS

March 11

My wife asked me to write a story. The buzzer on the alarm clock had just gone off and she reached out of the covers to stop it. We were folded together, quite cozy. New light on the white plaster walls. Outside we could hear a cardinal singing, the duck-like honk of the nuthatch also. We listened. At 6:15 she tapped my shoulder.

"Write a story today," she said.

"What about?" I asked.

"Oh," she said, "about, about a husband and wife."

"Is that all?"

"Yes."

"How long a story?"

"Seven, ahh eight pages," she said and began to slip out of the bed. I put my hand on her bottom to guide her out, to assist.

"Don't shove like that," she said.

I corrected her, I told her I was helping. She left the bedroom and returned shortly, wearing her bathrobe, the big furry brown one that makes her look so huge, so bearlike.

"I put on water for your coffee," she said. "Will you get up?"

I shoved my body around, took advantage of the whole bed. The light was, how shall I say it?, *expanding* the room. *Husband and wife* I heard. Outside a titmouse was at it, belting out his song. What else have I been trying to do, for some months now, but to write a story? But each attempt succeeds less, no matter what confirmation the "world" provides. These

39

days I can hardly get a page into a story before I feel, what is it, loss?, yes, *loss:* and also, *lie.* So I come back to records, statistics, weather reports. There, there. *Here.* It is a lovely day a-dawning. It is cold, bright and cold. But you can see the warmth in that light, in the zip and tumble of the birds outside. I was wondering if the raccoon we saw before we went to bed last night came back later and ate the sourdough bread my wife put out for him in the aluminum pan.

I got out of bed and dressed. I went into the bathroom to use the toilet. My wife was in the tub, her pink body sunk in Mediterranean blue. The black kitten sat on the edge of the tub, scrutinizing the operation, bemused by the fact of water: how it is there and then not there. I walked into the kitchen and poured the boiling water into the cup, *instant* coffee. My wife had let the dogs out and they were at the back door, wiggling in the cold, hungry. I let them in and fed them. I took a sip of coffee. I thought about the cedar waxwings I saw yesterday and wondered if I would seem them again today. My wife told me about them, how they flock about and how sometimes they will take a berry and pass it among them back and forth until one decides to eat it. But story, *story,* I heard. What do I have to tell, what truth, what experience? What I know is my distrust for what I have done, what story I have attempted. I think the reason is some radical distrust of whatever materials I bring to the story. *Write a story.*

One afternoon when Betty got home from work she told Bob that she was getting worried, that if she had just one more whisky she might, well, just *crack,* she said. And there I would stop, not trusting that invention you see. *Betty and Bob.* You see.

A better story would be very close to some record of the day. For example, I was in town on Saturday to return some books and records to the library and to retrieve a pair of binoculars that were being repaired. It was a chilly, windy day and I was feeling very shaky. So I asked my wife to hold my arm as we walked along. Now that seems like important material, to me. Further, I would like to discuss or at least accurately describe the trouble I am having with *space* and *time* lately. It seems relevant to present them. I feel, thinking of space, that I am going to fall into it. Walking along, through the parking lot, I think I may fall. Or why on earth is it 2 o'clock? What earthly reason is there for it being that time? But these, you see, are hardly the materials that make a story.

So I took my coffee (that is also a problem, the possessive pronouns... I find I am correcting myself a lot lately, crossing out the possessive pronouns: is it my coffee my wife my dog my house my car my life? No, it seems inaccurate to say so.) and sat down in a chair to read a story that a friend had sent me, a *story* story about fifth grade kids at a parochial school rehearsing their sins before Saturday confession. It was a lovely story, but a story. I loved it but I didn't trust it. My wife leaned in and kissed me goodbye. I was worried that I didn't take the pipe out of my mouth as our lips met. I thought, as she leaned out, that I should have taken the pipe out, that a kiss should never be casual.

I did love the story, however. I went to the typewriter and wrote of my enthusiasm to my friend. Did I *love* the story? Perhaps I lied there. I am trying not to lie these days. I used to sign my letters with that word but lately I have stopped that. Now when I end a letter I just sign my name. No, that's not true. I just wrote my brother and I used that word.

I wrote my friend and I read here and there in several books, and then I did some exercises to the *Phil Donahue* show on the television. It concerned the problem of fat on American women. When it was over at 10 o'clock I got up and began this story. I rolled the paper in the typewriter and typed my name upper right. That somehow signified an intent, that what I was about was a story. Beneath it to the left I typed: MARCH 11, which is the date today. Now it is 10:40. I am on page four of my story. I just opened a package of gum and now I am chewing all five pieces. So far this story is accurate to the experience of this day, more or less. I have left out a fast breakfast of cottage cheese and grapefruit. I have left out certain private matters which have crossed my mind, a few worries I have which I shall leave unrecorded. At least for now. I may circle back to them. While I was watching the Donahue show I saw the silhouette (I stopped to check the spelling of that in the dictionary) of a cedar waxwing. I found the binoculars and trained it on the bird. Sure enough: a cedar waxwing, warming itself in the rays of the morning light.

I'm going to stop for a while now. I want to read this over and I want to check the seed trays on the back porch. I'll be right back. It's 10:44.

There is plenty of seed in the feeders, nothing outside with which I am unfamiliar: a crowcall deep in the woods, chickadees here and there, squalling. Way up, the vapor trail of a jet. I take my binoculars to it and they reveal a four-engine bomber. I hear a train horn in the valley below. I stare into the blank woods. It is bright and cold. Then I came inside (yes I noticed the shift of the tense above) and read this story so far. It is dull and largely accurate. Rising from the chair to resume this typing it occurs to me that what I have written, for all its presumed truth-telling, is no more interesting and no more trustworthy than the greatest of fish stories. Perhaps I think it is even less so, in some way I as yet do not understand.

Husband and wife. (Switch on the FM Radio—a divertimento by Mozart.) (The cat, not the kitten, is howling in the kitchen. I feed her.) What I would like to record is something about us, *this* husband, *this* wife. (Ooppps! A great ladder-backed woodpecker is backing down the hackberry toward the feeder! He's at it now, a very cautious bird. Gone.) I'd like to record the precise quality of our happiness, the exact nature of what we share and what we don't share. I'd like to present some of our more outstanding arguments. I would like to discuss *her:* her capacity for joy, her way with this world. Last night, for example. When the raccoon strolled by the patio glass door and stopped to look in on us as we watched the television. How it stared at the kitten, and how frozen the kitten was to see so large, so awesome a being, a masked bandit, two feet from her nose! I would like a reader to understand the absolute joy of my wife watching that raccoon eat the sugar-coated baked chicken she had set out for him, the lovely exhalations of breath that came from her as she exclaimed its precise movements. How its paws carefully turned each piece of chicken about, how slowly it chewed, how it looked up into our faces from time to time. Her joy: the best, very best thing ever to happen has happened, that animal feeding on the patio, searching finally through the pan of sourdough bread for another piece of chicken. (I stopped to light a pipe. The one-legged chickadee is balancing on the edge of the window-feeder, checking the seed with its keen eyes. There better be some sunflower seed there or I'll catch hell, there will be hell to pay.) (I took the cat out to her chain on the patio.) Her joy, the absolute joy, the superior joy. She could watch that animal forever, she could play with her kitten forever.

It is now 11:22. I am going to walk a letter to Mastercharge to the mailbox. It is a letter of complaint of longstanding, concerning a mis-billing.

What I perceive now is an urge to lie, to paint this up a bit, to provide some allure, to hint at some *dark theme* to keep you attendant. (Clapping on the radio, the divertimento is concluded.) To move perhaps beyond the peculiar adornment of the story and into the dark stones of crushingly bitter truths that foundate this life. To move into some more naked form, something *faster*. (More clapping.) I asked my wife this morning something. I forgot to tell you. After the alarm sounded I heard a patriotic song and had some of its words on my tongue. I forget it now except that its lines were very busy, very clotted. Oh yes, here it is:

> He hath trampled out the vineyards where the grapes of wrath are stored.
> He hath loosed his faithful lightning with his terrible swift sword.

Yes. She, my wife, remembered some of the second verse and spoke it for me. It was then that I assisted her from the bed. I used that word, *assisted,* to provide some pleasure for my readers, to indicate in that way precisely the nature of my action.

Here I am already on page seven. I think I'll stop this now and hope that my wife will read it over after lunch, if she has the time. Perhaps she will suggest where it might go next, what germs lie here that could be fecundated. Now I shall rest a bit. I type standing up and after a while my feet go to sleep and my shoulders get sore. *The* shoulders, I should say.

So far, the wife likes it. She read it after her lunch.

"I do like it, it's a good story," she said.

"I wonder what will happen next," I said.

"You'll probably be drunk by the time I get home," she said.

I held the kitten up to the window so she could see the birds. She watched intently, sighed a few times.

"See ya later," she said.

"Bye," I said.

It is now precisely 1 P.M. I am going to take a break now and walk around the cornfield with my two dogs Tookie and Charlie. We'll be back a bit after 2 P.M. I'll make a cup of coffee and continue with this. The first thing I'll do is tell you about the mail I received today. For now, then. (May I suggest that you also take a little break, a walk, a bit of coffee perhaps, before you return to these words?)

2:30. Some walk. We were much impeded, as are all spring offensives, by heavy muddd. We returned. Tookie, Charlie, and myself, at 2:15. I heated water for coffee and cleaned my field boots. As we began the walk I considered this story so far, but very soon I was immersed in the walk itself, the path the mud the wood the occasional cry of a bird. It did occur to me that I have less trouble with the space in nature, perhaps less trouble with time then also. It also occurred to me to tell you that what I distrust in most stories is rhyme. Yes. That is, (here we are already on the last page, according to the dictum of my wife!) I distrust the means most of us use to make things cohere, and thereby to lend what is presumably some *significance* to the tale. Any repetition, for example. For example, on the news this noon we heard the story of the Doctor who wrote *The Scarsdale Diet,* how he was shot to death today. Now if I mentioned that in this story a reader might presume that I was connecting that with the theme of the *Phil Donahue* show that I have recorded earlier in this story. You see the relation, no doubt.

Well, here it is, 2:39. I want to tell the truth. I do not wish to repeat the lies of yesterday. I want every word, every gesture, here, to be trustworthy. In the past you may have trusted my stories about the pains of human relationships. But they were lies. I think. I don't hate women, not at all. I love women. Also, I am afraid of women. I have hitherto covered that fact with the face of hatred. Also, it occurred to me that women are often attracted to such men, perhaps sensing their mask. I don't know. But I pretended to hate women as a means of seduction. And, may I say, it largely worked. So, in losing that fear, I lose that theme. Likewise for much else that has constituted my life (I am 48) to date. In the past I could rely on several habits to serve my fictional needs... mostly despicable to be sure, but the very stuff, the absolute mud, of fiction. But that also has dried and fallen off my boots. And so here I am, naked before you on the path, the slippery track, of this wife-begotten story. What I have left is a secret happiness I dare not present to you, a mild persistent longing for the old days of pain and sorrow. What I most fear now is that I am numb, that years of steady happiness have closed my heart. Yes.

Betty told Bob she was afraid she might *crack* if she continued to drink; that whisky was leaching all meaning from her life. Bob was in the kitchen having a drink; it was not his first. He stumbled toward her.

"Poor, poor, Bet," he said, hugging her.

She shoved him back.

"You drunk," she said, registering disgust.

"We'll stop tonight," he said, watching her closely.

She took off her winter coat.

"Make me one," she said. "I'm going to change clothes."

Bob went back to the kitchen where he was peeling potatoes. He finished that job and then prepared a whisky for Betty.

"How many ounces?" he asked, loud.

Hearing no reply, he measured three ounces of whisky into a glass, added three cubes of ice and filled it with water from the tap. His own drink was getting low, so he made himself another, nipping from the bottle as he prepared it. He was beginning to feel good. It was almost 5 o'clock. He was slowing down, into that time. He was hearing good sweet music from far off. He would have liked to dance with his wife but she would reject that. She would be tired and sullen, ready to *crack*. So she would just sip her drink and watch him, *for signs,* he thought.

"Here I am," Betty said, entering the kitchen in her bluest blue jeans, buttoning her bird-of-paradise shirt.

Bob looked at her, again stunned by her loveliness, this lovely, fragile woman, this nymph. Or was he angry with her, did he want to smash her, pick a fight, disturb the coolness of her waters, contribute to her *crack?*

"Where is it?" Betty asked.

Bob pointed to the counter where her drink was sweating.

Here I have not been faithful to the noon hour. I ate a ham sandwich with potato soup and a glass of water. When my wife came in she cooked bacon for a bacon and peanut butter sandwich. She drink milk. The kitten jumped on the table to watch her eat. She gave the kitten a few sips of milk from her glass. My wife told me about the girl at work whose production she had evaluated. She told the girl that as a result of a review of her record it was clear that she was not producing for the company. The girl broke down, in tears. This angered my wife. She suggested that the girl go home. The girl said she was pregnant, that she was exhausted all the time, that she had ridden to work with others and thus could not leave work. My wife told her that she would find her a ride home. It angers my wife that people are so unprofessional. When she left for work she said something like Well here I go back to another weepy again. Those were not her words, but that was her scorn. (I might say here, in defense of my wife against those who detect some coldness in her, that my sweet wife is all tenderness, all tears. But that they are flowing inside. Last summer, for example, when we were burying our beloved cat Jack who had been run down by a car on the highway, we were placing stones on his battered body in the grave I had dug for him in the back yard, heavy stones so that some scavenging beast would not, smelling him, dig his body up, and with each stone my hot tears spurted out, I was just loose with grief, but my wife was not crying outside, no, she was just plain white. She keeps her grief to herself.)

As she ate, I read the mail. Just one piece of any importance. A letter from my dear brother, in some trouble with his body. Some temporary good news. A letter from an insurance company. A circular from a store announcing *Hardware Week*.

Then my wife had to rush back to work. She did read the story, as I have reported. She smiled, she liked it. I asked her what was going to happen next in the tale and she said I'd probably be drunk by the time she returned. Then I stopped writing and went for a muddy walk.

Husband and wife. How about a pair of woodpeckers at the suet cage? In the waning light, hacking away? It is now 3:44. I am very tired now, my feet feel swollen. The Mozart Hafner Symphony is on the radio. There's a *phony* in "symphony." All the animals in this house are snoozing: the cats upstairs on our bed, the dogs under their favorite chairs in the living room

Betty took the slippery glass and raised it to her mouth.

"Whose turn to cook?" she asked.

Bob stepped toward her. He pointed at his nose with his index finger.

"Yours," he said, "but as you can see, as any god-damned fool can see, I have started it."

Betty turned back and wandered off into the living room where she switched on the light and began to read her seed catalogs. Bob was thinking of the thundering, crashing last movements of Beethoven. If only he had a huge stereo to blast the ice out of his life. He took up one of the potatoes he had peeled and carried it to the door of the living room

"Hey," he said, to get her attention. Betty did not look up. Their black kitten had crawled into her lap. Bob tossed the potato in a high arc toward her. He should have fast-balled it, he thought, as the potato missed its mark and bumped to a stop on the rug. Bob looked at his wet hand. What he needed was not another drink. He retracted his steps to the kitchen to find the bottle.

A husband/wife story, she said. That is to be my project for today. Another thing I don't trust in stories, I have mentioned the way, the trick, of most stories, the rhyming to convey the illusion of coherence (when you know as well as I that nothing coheres), is the sex-theme. It, I take it, is yet another means to suggest value and truth in a story. But this is not so. What you will do, if you are honest, is realize that at the moment of sex in the story you forget the story itself otherwise. You are caught by the pure utilitarian pornography of it. It arouses you, specifically. That is why I can no longer write sex messages in my stories. So I am less. I am left with fewer possibilities to make a true story beyond records, statistics. But how long will you stand for me merely reporting the time, the weather, the conditions? It is very dull. More interesting would perhaps be for me to explore my problems with those two dimensions I mentioned before, sometime this morning. (It's almost 4 o'clock. I'll probably make myself a drink at 4 o'clock.) *Space.* I think enclosed space is the problem. Or man-made space. Parking lots, for example. Grocery stores. I feel out of focus in space, too large. Waiting in the check-out line I will wonder what I am doing in that line. I will feel as if I don't belong. In the parking lot, walking along with a grocery bag full of food, I will think I might fall, that I might drop it. *Time.* I don't see how it can pass, how it can be later. How now it is almost 4 o'clock and yet this morning it was 6 o'clock. When I get back to the house with the grocery bag I will feel almost something akin to *fear* at the passage of time, fear that time is apparent to me, so *present,* and that I don't understand it. (The cat is howling to be let out. I let her out.)

The bottle was empty. Bob went to the liquor cabinet and took out a bottle of Yukon Jack, the spirit that got many a man through a lonely night. He carried it into the kitchen, cracked the seal, unscrewed the cap, and took a sip. It was very thick, sweet. He poured some over the ice cubes in his glass. He looked out the window, the waning light of the day, the dark fields spotted here and there with snow. As he sipped he cut the potatoes and put them in boiling water on the stove. The radio was playing music. He went into the dining room and shut it off. His wife liked silence. She wanted it quiet. The stillness of disaster, the quiet that precedes all great disasters. The kitten strolled toward him, casually reached up his leg and used it as a scratching post. When she finished he opened the refrigerator and studied its contents of left-overs. Mashed potatoes and what else? Something to attend the loneliness of men in their huts on long winter nights. Meatloaf, baked chicken, fish sticks? The water boiled up again and he turned the gas down and covered the pot.

It is just after 4 o'clock now. I'm going to stop the record and make myself a whisky. When I return I'd like to discuss marriage with you. I would like to discuss freedom and joy. And a certain persistent need to lie. Also, I'll try to think of something for us to eat tonight. My wife will be tired. I'll think of something simple.

Well, I am back. I must say I am tired of being bound to report to you the mere passage of time. What sense does it make to tell you that it is *later,* that the day is on the wane, that the lovely light on the fields is long, muted, that birds are preparing for night?

About husband and wife? Well, I can say here that I don't feel quite alive unless she is with me. That if she is gone my dominant sense is that of *waiting.* That increases my time-confusion. I am sure. I like my wife in the house. Even though I may not be otherwise with her, I do prefer her to be here. I want to tell the story of daily life, the nothing-specialness which is after all the life experience of most of us most of the time. A story about the silent meals, the slow passage of the hours. The sound of quiet, the chewing, the little peeps of the birds as they feed. The practical discussions of daily life, the preparation of shopping lists. The dominant daily questions: what shall we eat tonight, did you get the film, where is the broom? Bob took out the meatloaf and shut the refrigerator door. He put it in an aluminum tray and turned the oven dial to 400 degrees. Perhaps when my wife comes home she will read this so far and suggest where it might go next, what gesture it might make, what turn. I myself am feeling a need for some surprise, of writing something I can't quite know, a modest little probe into something wonderful. Some wonderful acknowledgment that will seem to arise naturally out of the materials here recorded. But what that might be I cannot imagine. I see life continue, going on its muddy track of days without special meaning, without great significance or change or understanding. I wonder if I would trust something other than the predictable repetition of ordinary events. I would resist. I could not accept. I want to inhabit fully the memory of my life and I want that to be the story. The full inhabitation of the moment that my wife is capable of; that complete entry into the skin of the raccoon as it chews her baked chicken. In that dimension there would be no space, no time.

I am 48, as I said. Ahead of me, the time is infinite, x number of years. I would like to live those years yet to be. What I am trying to do is prepare myself for those years. To cast off the useless past of habit and memory. To be done with judgment, with comparison, with loss. With lie. And to find or discover or invent the means to make a trustworthy coherence of this experience, experience which now rages in its particularity. Bob looked at his watch. He decided that he would be able to serve the meatloaf and potatoes in 45 minutes, just before 6 o'clock. There would be time to offer Betty another drink. If she is going to crack it might just as well come now although it won't. He wished that she would come into the kitchen. He wished that she would hug him, tell him that everything was going to be fine. He placed the rubber stopper in the sink drain and let the hot water run. He would need to do a few dishes before supper. Plates, silverware, wine glasses. He poured liquid soap into the rising water. There is no end to record-keeping. It is not the answer. The answer is to become the bird, to lift off the trunk of the hackberry on great wings and swoop into the dark woods and sit on a stone, to inhabit being, *to come inside*. Record-keeping is lies. Like weather forecasts. How many years have I listened to weather reports and what has been the difference? Statistics are a form of *prevention*.

The whisky is good. I have before me one big drink of 101 proof bottled-in-bond *Wild Turkey*. As the time of my wife's predicted return grows shorter the time passes more slowly, the sense of waiting increases almost *painfully*. She will be here in less than 30 minutes. The dogs will hear her car before I do and rush to the door wiggling. Then I will hear the garage door opening.

I need, you see, to find the faith to continue. I am, as you can tell, at some defined *end*. I am not *through* yet, but the end is where I am now. At least I hope so. What I fear is more years of the same. What I fear is that my life such as it is is simply *over*, that I am not at the *end*, that I am not in transit *through*, that some *toward* is not before me. But I will have the care to monitor this, to proceed? I don't think I can....

The whisky is very good, the sun is bending itself out. I'll have to think of something for supper, perhaps meatloaf. Or perhaps I could make a quick tuna casserole. How big the feet of the junco are. They look like bamboo rakes. Which is how they use them, they literally *rake* the ground with their feet until they spot something edible. I'll hear the automatic garage door grind open and my wife's car will enter it. Then she will walk around the side of the house and enter through the sliding glass door in the living room. The dogs will greet her, the kitten will stroll in also. I will maintain my position in the kitchen. As the day continues I lose some of the faith and hope with which I arise each morning. I decline with the light. *Wild Turkey,* not quite sure why. I am not a wild turkey. If I were to name a whisky it would be *Sundown*. Well, in a marriage like ours, it is the wife who makes things cohere. My mode is downward, destructive. She deflects that drift somehow... keeps it off course, I think one could say. This isn't much of a story so far. Although my wife liked it to page 10 or so, I think she may be disappointed by the turns it is so obviously not taking. I think she might like to bring the couple together, to have them play with each other perhaps. Well, in any case she will read it, and she will probably find something *good* to say. When she heard the sink filling with water Betty came into the kitchen, the kitten patrolling behind her. She carried a catalog called "Roses '80." Bob watched her carefully as she approached.

"Lookie here," she said, holding the catalog up to Bob's face.

"What?" he said.

Betty opened the catalog.

"It smells," Bob said.

"They scented it," Betty said. "Lookie."

"At what?" Bob asked. "I see roses."

"Read the names," Betty directed.

"Love," Bob read. "Honor and cherish."

Betty looked at Bob, awaiting something.

"Well?" she asked.

"Well *what?*" said Bob.

"Well give me another drink if you don't know," she said. The black kitten curled itself between Betty's legs, looked up at her. Bob put down his dishrag. As he prepared her drink he ran through the left-overs and asked her what she thought she wanted.

"Which do you want?" Betty asked.

"Oh I don't care," Bob said, "meatloaf I guess."

"I mean roses, *roses,*" Betty underlined, her tone angrier than Bob's mistake.

"Why don't you just get them all," Bob said quietly. "It doesn't matter."

He handed Betty another drink and told her to go back to the living room, that he would decide supper and serve it in there so they could watch the television.

"I know which rose you want, Roberto," she said, sipping her whisky.

"What's that?" he asked.

"Guess," she said.

"Oh, I don't know. I'd say buy all three, they all look nice."

"Roberto, you are not listening, did you *hear* me?

This *through* I hope I am in, oh some months now. Sometimes I feel a glimmer of change, of a new coherence. But as the day wears on I lose the confidence of this time. I don't know. The dogs are barking and wiggling, my wife is entering the driveway, in a few seconds I will hear the garage door. She will come in, she will say *I'm home* and the life of the husband and wife will resume, their story will pick up speed. Close to this end of the story I want to deliver some truths, some instruction. It has been an ordinary day, a late winter March in the Midwest. Nothing special has happened, no more or less than occurs on most days. A simple day. I suspect that the form of this piece may suggest a conclusion to you and I must say that I had thought of that also—after the fact, however. And so, risking your displeasure, I will not suddenly write it. My name is not Bob nor is my wife's name Betty. It could not be so, it would be a lie of old magnitude, a form which I no longer permit. The dogs are at the sliding door. It is sliding open.

"Hi, I'm home," says my wife.

"Hi," I say, and walk to greet her.

She looks at me. "You finish it?" she asks.

"More or less," I say and help her off with her coat.

MOIRA CRONE

Crocheting

I am crocheting a blue wool hat for my mother because she is dying. Her head is a gray balloon: Her eyes swim at the top of her face like two small fish. Her skin is hard from the tugging and swelling caused by the drugs she takes which are meant to reduce the mass of knotted veins around her tumors.

Crocheting is a system of knots made with one string and one needle, over and over, invented by fishing net knotters' wives who wanted to make nets for their tables and one-needle lace for the ends of their collars and curtains, for the hems of their children. In Brittany the fishermen drag scallops and fishes and mussels up in white nets. On the high hill overlooking the sea, a child huddles under a shawl next to his mother who is looking westward at the Atlantic and hoping that the wind will go back up into the sky.

This hat is sky blue, and so is the scarf already finished. It is rounded like a stole instead of flat as something woven because I failed to count the stitches. One extra or two too few and a scarf meant to be straight becomes round and gathered, somehow irregular. If you split yarn with the needle even once, however, it will be impossible to unravel back to your mistake.

I went to see her Tuesday. The thin doctor at the door waved his hand and said it was fine for us to go to the gift shop downstairs on the G floor of Oncology. Mother wanted to buy a card to thank people for seeing her.

It is a famous and enormous hospital. Outside, behind the

terraced plaza for the Cancer Wing is a heliport. There is a brick wall around it, but I imagine it is a phosphorescent target, a cross in a circle, painted on tar. I was afraid of holding her elbow, of holding her anywhere. Gerald told me he saw on her chart that she would be brittle now, and later, more so.

When we walked into the shop, several people stared at her pinkish cowl-necked robe, at her bare, bald, marked head.

She is decorated with purple marks like the designs on the painted bodies of the Blue Druids and Picts as they have been imagined in watercolors. She noticed this in the mirror and said, "See, I told you I was a pagan." The lines are meant to show the x-ray therapists where, exactly, to irradiate her. There are borders, axes, and faded circles.

Her skull is very large, hard, difficult to kiss. Her cheeks are taut as leather. But the rest of her body is slack and insubstantial. It is in the process of wizening. She shuffled into the elevator next to me. She leaned toward me to tell me she was happy to see me, which she was. She doesn't see me often. I am afraid to see her.

I learned to crochet when I was nine. My French grandmother, her mother, now dead of aneurysms and Pall Malls, taught me as she had learned it from her grandfather, who was a man who could make wine from greens, liquor from berries, who could make and mend his own socks. My grandmother taught me to hold the needles the wrong way—parallel for knitting, and upside-down for crochet. I have never been able to learn the proper way, and to thus understand the elaborate photographs and diagrams which explain new stitches in the pattern books. I've never learned anything much beyond chain, double and treble. Popcorn and featherstitching, possible with a single hook, have always been impossible for me to understand. And my grandmother never told me to count. She said to answer all the stitches I had in the following row, and not to make any new ones, unless you are adding them to make a hat, which is a spiral. "I go by the rhythm," she told me. "... You feel awry if you drop a stitch."

Sometimes I cannot feel it.

In the wool shops, I am a left-handed child. "Who taught you to hold a needle like that? Where do you hold the yarn for tension?" I use my thumb. "Valerie, look. Come look at this!" the clerk shouts to the needlework teacher in the back room. I leave.

I am crocheting a blue wool hat for my mother because she is dying of cancer in the bone and the spine and the base of the skull. The hat should be soft on her scalp which itches because her hair is a fine stubble, and all new every few weeks. It grows in between the radiation treatments. The doctor said three days ago that she was lucky. She wouldn't have to drink the chemotherapy doses any longer. They could inject them directly into the spine now. They will use a spongy implant called a reservoir, which they sewed into the top of her brain last week. That dispelled all the marijuana and leukemia stories I might have told her before I gave her a joint. She doesn't need any. She has an appetite, and no nausea, but she also has this steely pain I have no idea about. She seems to have less and less daylight in her. I keep thinking of trying to do something to take her and pull all this away from her, but I am afraid that if I touch her she will break.

She has one single long window that reminds me of the narrow doctor who left healthy people to do further training here as an oncologist. All his patients behind the open doors on her corridor have grayish skin with a blue glaze, and the same oceanic eyes. They are all suspended, hoping to be let go. The window looks out on the concrete shelves that will one day be another wing of the hospital. Next to it, there is a bulletin board, filled with notes from all of us: thank-you notes, get-well notes, printed pictures of bouquets, pictures of candles and Mary. One of my grandmother's sisters used to buy our family novenas for Christmas. Mother would take a crinkly ribbon, in the old days, punch a hole above the Mary on the novena card, string it through and hang it on the tree. She told me it made her nervous to know a group of nuns in Minnesota were rising nine mornings in a row to pray for her name. But lately, she does not seem to laugh about it. She even told me there was a priest who talked to her. I would buy her a novena if I knew who was selling them.

My grandmother was interested in heaven. On the night she died, my mother sat with her. Grandmother said she was already in heaven as she passed in and out of consciousness, and in and out of breath. She had double pneumonia on top of three aneurysms already in her chest. "Heaven is beautiful," she reported to Gloria, my mother, whose head is now a silverish balloon, whose eyes float like two sea twins, whose body is shrinking under her odd, out-of-style pink robe. Grandmother even greeted her long-dead brother Phillippe, someone she had never really liked in life. He was walking over toward her across a green statueless park. "I like heaven," she told my mother, who believes ultimately that when she leaves she leaves sans every-thing, so she was standing next to me in the gift shop staring at the gold chains and the bad prints of the hospital as if she meant to memorize every object, as if she wanted to know how every trinket came into being, to understand how every shell on a chain in the glass case below us came up out of the ocean in a net.

Grandmother's dying was a supernatural event. I remember being in her house shortly afterwards and trying to find her. She seemed to be there so much I decided she had amplified, and dispersed. She had atomized, had turned into everything else, even the air and the water in the kettle. My sister brought a five-day old infant to the funeral. The old ladies at the parlor said something like that always happens, that a baby is born in a family when someone dies. Grandmother was not really in the box, but released, I imagined. The funeral over her body was slightly irrelevant, for someone else. My sister and I smiled at one another, and laughed, and played hearts the day after the funeral. We tickled the baby who cried and coughed at night like a monkey. My sister, who refused to nurse, complained that her breasts gave her pain.

But right after the burial, there were distant members of the family and neighbors in a line to tell me that they all "loved me very much," and I was drunk with taking their hands and knotting myself up in their arms. And then I was holding my mother awkwardly around the neck. My watch got caught in the crocheted shawl she wore over her head because she was once a Catholic. I think she pried me away.

Mother doesn't watch television in the room when she is alone. Neither does she crochet, which is something that skips a generation. When every stitch is filled in, there is no pattern at all, only a monotony: the incestual danger of too many repetitions. Novenas are interesting to me, quaint. Lourdes water is appealing, like my grandmother's upside down method of working.

When my mother dies, it will not be a supernatural event, because she is in that room, and in that body, which they are poisoning daily into something else, and I am afraid that she will die inside it as she is. Her head will continue to swell and her spine may break, and her bones will become more brittle, and then, after morphine elixers and what they call extraordinary measures at this famous hospital, they will allow her to.

Right now I am crocheting a hat for her head in case she lives through the winter. They have allowed her to go home until she has healed enough to stand more treatments. This winter she should be warm. The stitch is three trebles in a row, skip a beat, three more, which is called the scallop stitch. Little hands or fans move in a spiral more or less outward from the top of her head where her soul, according to legend, will flutter out for heaven, a place she never particularly liked. They have allowed her to go home, and this winter she should be warm. The stitch is three trebles in a row, skip a beat, three more, all into the same spot, skip a beat, chain, three more, which is called the scallop stitch. Little hands or fans move in a spiral outward from the top of her head where her soul, according to legend, will flutter out for heaven, a place she never particularly liked. Little hands or fans move in a spiral outward from the top of her head, where her soul, according to legend, will flutter out for heaven, a place she never looked forward to.

Gerald didn't say he read this, but I think that before she dies her skull will soften like a baby's and she will need a crocheted cap to hold in her ideas, to remind her that her name is Gloria, and that I am her daughter, really.

I am afraid to touch her head when I go back. It is swollen, it is a silver balloon. Her eyes float above the center like two sea twins. Above them are the gentian violet targets.

Grandmother left my mother novenas in perpetuity, like a scratched record repeating over and over into infinity mother of grace.

On Tuesday, after a while, she shuffled over to the card counter to read everything on display: "To Dad on your 25th Anniversary;" "To a Beloved Mother-in-Law, Get Well;" "To Grandmother, Our Sympathy;" "Congratulations on your Bundle of Joy." Mother counted the syllables or the verses as she read them to me, unconsciously, with her mouth, knowing when they felt wrong. That sort of rightness is in her like the regularity of the stitches, made of a single waltzed string. One two three. Every row must be the same number of stitches if the fabric is to stay flat.

But in a spiral hat, the added stitches do not matter. In fact, you have to add them, more and more, in order to allow the hat to grow larger. If you don't the hat becomes a tightened mass as impossible to unravel as her tumors. You have to cut the yarn and start over again if you don't continually expand from the star-like caesura at the top of the head where the soul comes and goes according to.

Now the hat is finished. I'm trying to tie it off. It is lopsided. She will say oh how nice, when I give it to her tomorrow. She will tug it over her scalp and her watery eyes will narrow. I will hand her a mirror. She will tell me it is lopsided. Tugging the edge over her left ear, she will undo the finishing knot. While I try to think about who she is, that she is my mother, really, she will ravel this spiral backward to the top of her head. She will smile. On the hospital bed between us will be a wad of crinkled sky blue yarn. I will promise her I can crochet it again. When she leans over to hug me, I will pause under her thin arms. Then I will pry her away. Prying her away is what I have to do.

RAYMOND FEDERMAN

Report from the World Federation of Displaced Writers

we had never known our old man to be that violent, on the contrary, more like him to talk or double-talk his way out of a fight, either in French or in English, or in both simultaneously, except once, in 1993, when he was seventy-five years old, imagine that, our old man getting into a fight at seventy-five

yes I remember it was in Sofia Bulgaria, Moinous exclaimed, not that long ago, when he kicked a guy in the ass, a critic, and then punched him in the mouth

it was during a literary conference, a huge international conference on the future of literature, that's right in Sofia, Namredef confirmed, The World Federation of Displaced Writers, W.F.D.W., we were there too of course

all the literati in the world were present, some already dead, others half-dead, others on their way out, they had gathered urgently in the Dimitrov Great Hall of the People to discuss the critical situation of contemporary literature at a crucial moment in history when literature was seriously and painfully questioning its raison d'être, when the very act of writing was being challenged and displaced from all sides by technological substitutions and all sorts of creepy artificial languages and computerized intelligence, as the 20th century drew close to an end, dwindled away into scientific technocracy and pseudomystical fantasy

the critic in question, I mean the guy who got kicked in the ass and punched in the mouth, was some pitiful entremetteur of literature, for every cliff there is always someone to jump off, Moinous cut in, a pushy pimpled juvenile academic critic in his early twenties, an embryonic mind, from Johns Hopkins University, at least that's what the name tag on his lapel said, a typical file-card pmla scholar who stood up in the middle of an animated argument about the present and future morality of the novel, that stubborn moribund genre which was still, at that time, refusing to die

John Gardner and Dennis Pudd-Pahl were tackling each other, moralizing on the one side and demoralizing on the other, when that pushy asshole of a critic jumped right in to complain, in twisted xylophagouscacademic terms, that fiction today has become totally unreadable, that fiction has lost touch with reality, imagine, as if that dead horse, that carcass of reality was still something to be concerned with, because, he went on, too many writers are indulging in egocentry logomachy

he was obviously referring to our old man's work and to the little speech our old man had made earlier, quite eloquently, in defense and illustration of what he called the leapfrog technique in digressive fiction, yes definitely referring to him and to some of his contemporaries even though he did not mention names, that little shitpot, such as Ronnie Schlunick, Clarion Vapor, Stove Klotz, Warner Abolish, Dave Plush, Morbid Caillou, Ludovic February, Phillipeau Soleil, Tudor Les-Oies, Oswald Bartender, Bill Gasoil, Johnny Vulture, and others of that generation with whom our old man had been associated for years as a daring disruptive subversive experimentalist, all of

them were present of course in the Great Hall of the People, and
who were still that day at the center of the lively controversy
about the validity and superiority of postfuture fiction over
neoantediluvian fiction, that endless quarrel of the postancients
and the suprapostmoderns

that dumbass critic was complaining, whining rather, that all
these so-called sursurfictioneers are masturbating their futile
experiments without any regard for communication and exis-
tential gestalt, wallowing instead in self-conscious solipsism,
destructuring and desyntaxing language for the sake of playful-
ness and dislogotraction, oh he had some vocabulary that puny
criiitic, he paused a moment to admire his little pun, and
consequently, he went on, these superegoisticnarcissists are
deserting their moral responsibility toward Man, with a capital
letter he emphasized, and Society, also with a capital letter, can
you believe that, one still argues on such a pitiful basis, in 1993,
doesn't that little fizzle of a critic understand that these avant-
garde writers neither think a kick because they feel a kick nor
feel a kick because they think a kick

but he went on, that mentally retarded paraplegic parasite of
mediocrity with his squeaking effeminate voice which kept
rising as he spoke, saying that the concern of most of these elitist
collectivists today is only with language, language and nothing
else, but a theory of fiction as mere language doing its tricks is an
outlandish notion, I'm quoting him verbatim, Namredef pointed out, and he continued, he was endless that critic, explaining
that reading fiction should not merely be an act of looking at
words distributed on the pages, but rather should be like falling
into a dream, and that after reading a few pages of a novel the
language should simply disappear, what an idiot, language
disappear, yep vanish, just like that, pssitt muscade et voilà,
what a cretin, and only images should unfold pleasurably in the
mind of the reader, unbelievable, like a private television show,
like mental cinema

Roland Barthes was sitting a couple of seats away from us and I
heard him mumble, how stubborn these illusionists are to still
want to peddle leur cinéma intérieur en 1993 as the primary
function of the novel, but what about l'émotion, pourquoi
serait-elle antipathique à la jouissance, c'est un trouble, une
lisiére d'évanouissement, quelque chose de pervers, sous des
dehors bien-pensants, c'est même, peut-être, la plus retorse des
pertes, car elle contredit la règle générale, qui veut donner à la
jouissance une figure fixe, forte, violente, crue, quelque chose de
nécessairement musclé, tendu, phallique

at this point our old man stood up, he was sitting directly behind
that constipated critic from Johns Hopkins whose name of
course shall not be revealed here, and turning to Barthes he said,
t'as raison coco colle lui ton phallus dans le cul, and as he said
this he kicked the critic in the ass, and I mean hard and right on
target, you pompous pederastic punk, he said letting his lips
explode scornfully into the alliterations, don't you understand
that a concern for the dignity of decrepitude of language is, after
all, a concern for the dignity of decrepitude of man, for a writer
to disdain to do anything more questionable with his art than
explore relentlessly the nature of his own medium, in this case
words in extemporaneous arrangements, the question of human
dignity can not present itself in any other terms than those of the
dignity of human language

Half of the audience applauded with dignified enthusiasm while
the other half booed and hissed nervously, it was indeed a very
mixed literary crowd representing many tendencies and movements, from all extremes, avant-gardists, breakthrough fic-
tioneers, surexperimentalists, paracritics, social neoreligious-
realists, antipostsymbolists, literary prehistorians, superpastir-
realists, and even a few aposteriorinaturalists

the pushy critic meanwhile turned toward the old man fuming
with rage and still rubbing his ass shamefully, he tried to grab the

old man by the neck, and that's when the old man punched him in the mouth, a perfect solid right uppercut to the jaw

immediately the crowd split into two camps, the postancients with their critics on one side and the postpostmoderns with their paracritics on the other, and everybody started punching, scuffling in the aisles, throwing books at each other, pamphlets, dictionaries, even unpublished manuscripts, pens and pencils, portable typewriters, scriptodictos, erasers, anything they could get their hands on, they were spitting at each other, pulling each other's hair and beards, scratching each other's faces with overgrown nails

it is well known that writers are noted for being dirty fighters, as when Charles Perrault and Nicolas Boileau scratched each other's eyes out during the famous Querelle des Anciens et des Modernes in 1693, amazing how the world of littérateurs vibrates in a twofold manner every two or three hundred years, or better yet when Norman Mailer gave Gore Vidal one of his resounding knee-in-the-crotch publicly at a fancy literary cocktail party in 1977, what a scandal that was, our old man was there that day, standing only a few feet away from Mailer and Vidal when it happened, and he even heard what Mailer said, My dear Vidal there are those who kick balls and those who get kicked in the balls, I'm sure you know in which category you belong, and when Gore Vidal tried to scratch Mailer's face, the latter shoved his knee up Vidal's testicles who folded at the waist and shrieked, Oh you animal, you big brute, it was quite a scandal indeed, amazing how history repeats itself

meanwhile here in Sofia Bulgaria we were in the middle of another historic brawl, what a scene, the battle was raging, Moinous and I were watching from a corner of the conference room standing on top of a table, trying to duck the blows and the flying objects, the misguided objets d'art, Moinous said as he caught a copy of The Divine Comedy in full flight, we had lost sight of the old man in the commotion, but finally caught a glimpse of him buried under an angry pack of neoclassic gothic novelists, he was flat on his back and these burly fellows were pounding at him with their fists, but it was impossible for us to go to the help of our old friend, all avenues of approach were blocked, so we remained on our observation table, keeping track of the skirmishes, recording individual and collective victories

finally someone managed to crawl to a microphone which had toppled over on the floor and screamed into it, in Polish I think it was, or perhaps in Slovanic, the official language of the conference, Hey you idiots, stop that, we didn't come here to have a literary riot, especially now when half of the planet is still starving for knowledge, obviously the speaker was an erudite social realist, but it was useless, and now the sirens and whistles of the Bulgarian militia were screeching in the corridors of the Great Hall of the People as the battle raged on until a raucous authoritative voice came over the loud-speakers in the ceiling

Achtung, Achtung, it was the voice of Günter Grass who was then President of W.F.D.W., Bitte meine Damen und Herren, I must say the women participants were quite active and rather belligerent in this confrontation, using their innate feminine agility to overcome their more loutish male assailants, at one point Moinous and I watched Joyce Carol Oates flip Gabriel Garcia Marquez over her back in a neat judo move while next to her Margaret Atwood was twisting Alain Robbe-Grillet's arm behind his back

Bitte meine Damen und Herren, the voice of Günter Grass insisted, beruhigen Sie sich, lassen Sie uns mit Würde, besonders jetz wo die ganze Welt uns beobachtet, besonders wenn die Bletchtrommel der Opposition heult wie die Hundejahresoldaten der Vernunft muss standhaft bleiben un nich umfallen, nich Katze and Maus spielen, ja, muss nich flappen, Bitte kehren Sie zu ihren Stühlen zurück und lassen Sie uns in Ruhe fortsetzen, and these powerfully rational words worked like magic, instantly everyone stopped fighting, there was an embarrassed moment of silence while the audience regained its composure

then Harold Pinter, who had just been awarded the Nobel Prize for literature, for 1993, and well he deserves it, approached the microphone on the main platform, he stood there for a full minute staring at the audience while shaking his head in a gesture of reprimand

someone behind us said in a Japanese whisper, Amenokado hitotsu hirakete mae ni ari utsukushiki kana yama ni tatsu niji, I turned around, Ssssh, I said, Oh so sorry, my name is Yosano Hiroshi, I am a poet, who is that speaking now, can you tell me, so sorry, That's Pinter, Harold Pinter, the famous British playwright, I informed the oriental poet, Ah so, there before our sight one of the gates of heaven is swung wide and how beautifully stands the bright rainbow on the mountain brow, Can you please be quiet, I said, and skip the poetry, Oh yes yes, ah so

Pinter began to talk, pointing to the old man while marking each word with deliberate Miltonian emphasis, I do not know this gentleman personally, or perhaps yes we did meet once, a long time ago, but that's not important, I have read his books, I have read and reread them, and let me tell you something, the farther he goes the more good it does me, I don't want philosophies, tracts, dogmas, creeds, ways out, truths, answers, nothing from the bargain basement, he is the most courageous, remorseless writer going and the more he grinds my nose in the shit the more I am grateful to him, the audience stirred as all heads turned toward the old man, he's not fucking me about, he's not leading me up any garden, Right on that's the way to go man, someone shouted from the back of the conference room, Ah shut the fuck up you jerk, someone else shouted back, Pinter banged his fist forcefully on the podium and continued, he's not slipping me any wink, he's not flogging me a remedy or a path or a revelation

or a basinful of breadcrumbs, he's not selling me anything I
don't want to buy, he doesn't give a bollock whether I buy or not,
he hasn't got his hand over his heart, well, Ladies and
Gentlemen, I'll buy his goods, hook, line and sinker, because he
leaves no stone unturned and no maggot lonely, he brings forth a
body of beauty, his work is beau-ti-ful, he paused and stared
haughtily at the young critic who had been the cause of the
disturbance, the room grew restless, Pinter leaned forward over
the podium, beau-ti-ful, my dear Sir, he repeated detaching each
syllable, even if it is un-read-able

Samuel Beckett who had been sitting quietly in a remote corner
of the great hall stood up and started applauding, all eyes turned
to him in deep reverence, honni soit qui symboles y voit, he said
in a soft tone of voice and sat down

the old man was deeply moved, visibly moved, he had difficulties
holding back the tears of appreciation, and we did too, it was the
first time, as far as we know, in the fifty years or more that he had
been banging on a typewriter, working uncompromisingly in the
lonely semi-darkness of unrecognition, that someone, no not
just someone but a world-renowned writer whom he greatly
admired and respected had praised his work in public, he stood
up, blew his nose in a large handkerchief, walked over to the
platform tipping his head slightly as he walked past Samuel
Beckett, and shook Harold Pinter's hand with marked emotion,
Pinter embraced him while half of the audience applauded its
warm approbation and the other half whistled and hissed its
vicious objection, and so it goes with literature, always split
down the middle

it was in 1993, now some people might say that such a situation is
not very encouraging, but one must reply that it is not meant to
encourage those who say that, after all literature is an endan-
gered species

B.H. FRIEDMAN

Whispers
(the first three)

his: #1

Can you hear me?

The New York I love is so cool you may not recognize her. Cooler than the neon at Times Square. Cooler than the drinks at Yankee Stadium. Cooler than the snow in Harlem. It's cool near the top.

I love what critics hate: executive dining rooms of Wall Street banks, big legal offices with rows of CCH reports, the patterns made by teleregisters, and the way necktie stripes move up to the left among men who move to the right. The towers should be connected by bridges. I go down only to refuel—i.e., when not eating at some cloudy club. Down there, I like those filling stations in the mid-forties—Christ Cella, Pietro's, the Palm, places where they cut meat the thickness of lumber—and the French ones farther north where fish swim in sauce. . . . I like them because the food is good and cheaper than the places that cost money. New York is almost free, if you love your work. (Once I saw a guy ask a cab driver for a receipt.)

The skyline's free. I like leaving the city and returning to it by air. The city planners haven't been able to organize the air. I like the top of the G. E. building, as visible from the garden behind our brownstone house as are the chandeliers by Louis

69

Comfort Tiffany in the windows of Second Avenue antique shops. I wish Comfort were my middle name.

I'm too well dressed to go into Third Avenue bars; my clothes are always picking fights with people. (Are my lapels as narrow as piping?) I miss the protective shadows of the el.

The guys are right who look in garbage cans, if they don't have to. They're painters or poets or businessmen. I like everything disposable. Cigarettes, whiskey, newspapers, soap, candy bars, razor blades—those are the businesses to be in. Imagine going to bed each night with the knowledge that you have packaged people's desires, that you have given them that sense of reality only waste can give. I like art before it goes into museums. I like a city that can throw away the Ritz without batting an eye (and then sell its elevator cabs to Texas oilmen to convert into ranch-style bars). I like what's in parentheses, too, more than seeing those same cabs sold to Hollywood as lampbases. If life is a choice between lampbases and bars, I choose bars because they remind me of parentheses. If life is a choice. . . .

I like the papers I see on businessmen's desks: Dun & Bradstreet reports ("Credit is Man's Confidence in Man"), Proudfoot, Dodge, Standard and Poor's, Moody's. Moody I like best of all. I wish Moody were my last name. I picture him as he must have been: a beard. The others all sound as though they knew exactly what they were doing. I like letterheads, trademarks, logotypes. I like statements of income and expense— outcome: black ink. I like black ink. I like analyses of projected earnings: inventories; contracts; licenses; permits; legal documents of all kinds, especially those in pale blue binders. Getting and spending we lay waste our money. I like the printed literature that comes from trade associations. I don't forget it wasn't always printed. I don't forget the tender New York girls who took it down in Pitman or Gregg. Take me down, gently, gently, as you would a word.

I like the sad world of the wastepaper basket. I like the cleaning ladies who give office buildings that arbitrarily illuminated look at night. Seagram is wrong. Uniform elegance is wrong. Waste can't be that well organized. Oh, that blue light at the top of the G. E. building—more than arbitrary, a surprise, a displaced star. I wish it hung in my home. Again I wish Comfort were my middle name, and Moody my last. I wish I had a first name instead of initials.

What else goes on at night besides the lights? The music. You've got to be crazy to pass a law forbidding people to blow their horns. I hate low quiet cities. I like it up high where the hum bounces between Rockefeller Center and Wall Street. I like, too, those sterling phoenixes of the boom, the Empire State and Chrysler buildings. (I want to think the latter was named for a violinist who hit high notes: a monumental misspelling.) I like thin air. I make exceptions sometimes, plunge downstairs into smoke, and usually regret it. Hell went underground in the 'fifties (like everyone was digging like). I prefer places where you can walk straight in: the Half Note, say, if you can get a cab to go to Hudson Street. I like Hudson. I like his river. The wild ones with the Indian names all belong to Thomas Wolfe. This one belongs to us. A tame tender river with nothing but a destination. It's just kind of there to say hello to, like Santa Claus outside of Macy's at Christmas. The East River's tame and tender too. It's just kind of there to say hello to, like Santa Claus outside of Bloomingdale's at Christmas. To the distant sound of bells and horns, these rivers embrace us.

New York has two seasons now, according to the engineers. There's that foggy time during the summer that makes me want to try haiku:

    Moon rain
    air-conditions
    New York streets

Or:

    New York
    moon rain
    from air-conditioners

Or:

    Air-conditioners

moon rain
New York
(No matter how I turn these phrases—typically, towards the
sun—they will not fatten into traditional haiku: I need a briefer
form.)

And there's that steamy time in winter, when verse forms
become still more difficult (begging for still more missing
syllables), and you can't get tickets to anything, and the stores
(even the little ones upstairs) are crowded. Smoking a cigar after
lunch, I watch other executives ice-skating; they wear pin-
striped suits and scarves and gloves. New York is a Japanese
Egyptian etcetera kind of place. All the different newspapers
and magazines at Hotalings. All the different kinds of cars in
showrooms. When are the Russians going to build a good sports
car? I want to drive a fast car to the moon. I want to touch the
real moon rain.

I like invisible voices, frequency-modulated voices. I like
the idea that people who sleep during the day can get the
commercials at night.

There's nothing on Broadway except a few good movies
that will reach your neighborhood playhouse. (My neighborhood playhouse is my bed; my living room is my bedroom; the
TV's so close I can touch it.) There's not much off Broadway
either. The best plays are being made in bed—or never get
produced. I hate the whole theater-concert-prison situation. I
want to drink and smoke and move around. The best thing
about theater is the intermission. I like the furs and cigarette
holders. I like that particular draft which enters lobbies in the
West Forties. I like the dash to the nearest bar. I like the Rolls
with the blue lamp up on top.

I like the hearses that even the cabbies respect. I hope I leave
town tying up traffic, on my way to suburbs so full of cemeteries
they can bury everybody horizontally even though the efficiency
experts recommend vertically.

Efficiency experts! Experts of all kinds! Business is a world of delights I cannot afford in the other world, the world of home. This is my home, my recaptured childhood, where chairs swivel and roll around on little wheels, where I have two telephones on my desk, where the drawers slide out on runners (never too far), where the bar in the executive conference room has an executive refrigerator with an executive ice tray in which there's *always* enough executive ice, etc. I have a secretary who frees me for business and from bills, personal income tax forms, wife presents, dealings with garage mechanics, watch repairment, G.E. (in the other home everything breaks). Just a phone call for shirts or underwear or socks: always the same. She can buy my anonymity from haberdashers as others buy their identity. My identity is my anonymity. I don't exist away from my office, except in other people's offices. I adore this girl who understands the subtleties of a *Who's Who* questionnaire, who understands a thousand subtleties I can't understand:

"Put Mr. A. on. Mr. B. is waiting."

I'm Mr. B.—I'm not waiting.

I'm not waiting, but I'm awed. O my secretary, my lovely machine, you are the subject of my book as I am the subject of yours, that stenographic pad you hold on your knee. I depend on your racing efficient fingers, as you depend on my voice, as a mirror depends on the transient image it holds . . . Take a letter: *Dear* . . .

There are messengers waiting to be shot in any direction. And there's a supply closet—toy closet, I almost said—full of rubberbands and clips and rulers and staples and machines for writing (the French call them) and machines for adding and machines for dictating and machines for duplicating—luxuries, like nonsmudge carbon paper. At home, what have I to compare with these? What have I to fill the time? A wife, children, a house. Nothing. At home I have myself. Evenings, holidays, weekends I must manufacture the irritations that are mine, free, at the office. At home there's always the possibility that the decision may be important. At business the important thing is to decide.

I have decided, like a certain kind of artist (the artist as speculative businessman), to bet on the future. Contrary to popular belief (my secretary's phrase—I adore her, I adore her), New York doesn't exist in the present. It doesn't exist. It is becoming. It is the future. It is aims, plans, preconceptions, projects, means. It is my city, the city of tomorrow's sale. I'll find myself here. There's no time now, but I have forever. (I say this, looking straight ahead, across the street, into the windows of another office. I'm afraid to look down).

The cool nerveless city planners look down. They don't see us, but they, too, see the future—in statistics, traffic and population trends...We're nothing. We're the six or seven zeros. We're what they buzz *their* secretaries for, if and when they want us.

Money talks quietly, like me. It's all zeros. Duels now are fought with zeros. The best tables are bought with zeros. The best seats are bought with zeros. Money whispers. Bills no longer crackle in the hands of a headwaiter or a cop. Power used to be noisy. Not now. Now typewriters are silent. Now carpets are thick. Now acoustical tile (simulating travertine) soaks up sound everywhere. And, even in the general offices, vinyl has replaced asphalt; it's quieter, and easier on the feet of clerks who wear sponge-rubber soles so thick one hardly hears them take their coffee breaks. For them, the day is all soft, silent foods, a mush of doughnuts and danish and coffee, mid-morning and mid-afternoon. At lunch they have hamburgers and ice cream, while I chew glass. They're not yet rich enough to chew.

Zeros! And less than zeros: minus quantities. Deductions, Everything's deductible. I'm deductible. Cocteau, I think it was, remarked, that for the poet $2 + 2 = 5$. For the corporation $2 + 2 = 3$. There seem to be twelve men sitting around the conference table. There are only eleven; one gets lost, ground up among the cigar butts. Everyone has a hand on the wheel of the steering committee. It can't move. Sub-sub-sub-sub a committee down to one, and there's hope. Two minds are worse than one. The corporation is always equal to less than the sum of its parts, and those parts are always equal to less than the sum of their parts. What's good for General Motors (or Electric or Telephone) may be lousy for me. I'm better than my corporate identity. I'm better than my public image. I'm better than the exact fraction I represent of my club, staff, nation, bureau, organization... I'm better in indirect proportion to the number of people who shape me in a given situation. I'm better anonymous. I'm better as nothing. I'm better as zero than minus one.

It's quiet. The whisper you hear is air rushing through sheet-metal ducts, hissing its snake-song, forever: 72° F., 50% relative humidity. The air is filtered. The seasons are filtered. The engineers are wrong. There's *one* season. If nature's quarterly dividend is dead, her semi-annual dividend is dying... A perfect day is a state of mind, a day in which a deal is made, *the day* in *the season.*

So no "summer" reading for me. What do I read, away from the office? It doesn't matter much. Anything that will fit in my pocket. Anything that will replace the ringing of the office phone. At LaGuardia I pick up Roger Shattuck's *The Banquet Years,* a reprint, of course; I'm always a few years behind. My secretary reads the current books for me (just as she sees the new movies, and I watch the old ones on TV). I read about yesterday. Doing that makes New York possible. Thesis: tomorrow. Antithesis: yesterday. Synthesis: now, an illusion. *The Banquet Years:* about the birth of the avant garde before the avant garde went into business. Hell, three big banquets in thirty years (for Rousseau, Apollinaire, and Saint-Pol-Roux)! I'm invited to three a week at grand ballrooms, one grander than the next. Was fun half as much fun before it became a business? Shattuck says, "The most notable artistic figures of the Banquet Years practiced external non-conformity in order to attain a conformity within the individual." I practice external conformity in order to attain a non-conformity within myself. If tension builds, I turn it into words. Better than letting it become ulcers or cancer. Cancer: the big *C,* not to be confused with the small *c's* in cardiac, or that other little one plunged like a hook into the center of ulcer.

Everything works. Nothing is wasted. Would it have made any difference if I had read something else? All I wanted was an irritant to substitute for the phone, the air-conditioning . . . Odd, the shock sometimes when, precisely at six, the air-conditioning stops. Like any businessman, it's at times like these (evenings, weekends) I find my theme. A journal entry:

It is Sunday. My wife and children have gone to the country. I am left with silence. The silence is my leisure. I don't know what to do with it. I listen. I hear it, the silence, rushing by like air, like the air in air-conditioning ducts. There is no balance to the silence, no calm, no poise—only pressure. This silence, this luxury, this leisure begs insistently to be enjoyed—and destroyed. Finally, I scream. For a few seconds, during the scream, it is quiet, and then the noise begins again.

Appreciate whispers. Two cars collide at an intersection. It's a beautiful sound, but what does it mean?

The sixties so far have been my season in heaven. Will the late sixties be greater yet? The seventies? Up, up into the highest cholesterol. Up, up into the highest brow. Fat will be fashionable. Baldness will be fashionable. The moon will continue to be fashionable. There'll be souped-up elevators in office buildings. There'll be souped-up office buildings in outer space. All soups will be cool and chic: gazpacho, vichyssoise, infinity. Everyone will have his bowl of infinity. There'll be second helpings of infinity. Just tell the waiter, quietly, you want *more.* The coolness of it all, the endless whispers of it all send endless shivers up my endless spine. Up, up to the ears. I can hardly hear me.

his: #2

The words are more tired now. I'm to go on vacation.

Each year or so I do that—that's done to me. Each year my efficiency at the office reaches a peak which embarrasses everyone. They send me away to slow me down. I have, after all, become so efficient—I have concentrated so hard on my work—

that I hardly have time to appreciate the office environment: its pure hard air-conditioned fluorescent seasonless beauty. They say I need a rest.

I face my vacation bravely, as I would the bore of a gun. What's a month's death, if they will let me return? A month, thirty days, twenty-four hours a day, every day, traveling with my wife and without secretary, executive lunches, clubs, lawyers, accountants...without reports of their golf scores, their bridge hands—their lusts, in short. I turn the sabbatical cheek.

The other possibility doesn't exist: to send them away, to stay in New York, which I love. New York, the monkey on my back. A month's exile, a month's withdrawal...I have only a few weeks in which to make up my mind, in which to select my prison.

At our elevator landing, distinguishable because it is decorated with photographs of our product, I touch DOWN. the plastic mechanism, responding to the heat of my index finger, blushes red. A moment later there's a *musique concrète* ping, and the doors of an elevator spring open...Down, down, down...I race across the terrazzo in the lobby, defying its slipperiness. I spin through a revolving door. I hail a cab. I say where I'm going (not ultimately, but now). I overtip. I am absolutely, existentially adjusted to my urban environment. (That's one of the things that makes me so efficient at the office.)

At home (away from the office), I tell my wife the bad news: we've got to go to Europe—or somewhere. We brace ourselves with drinks. I take down the 24th volume of the *Encyclopaedia Britannica,* the one marked "Atlas and Index." We look at a map of Europe. Every place appears the same—not the same as every other place, but the same as every place looked last year— very abstract, very.

France is green. Spain is a sort of bluish-gray. Portugal is yellow. Italy is yellow, like Portugal. Ireland is green, like France. Great Britain is pink, like Switzerland. Iceland is yellow, more yellow, seemingly, than Portugal or Italy, surrounded as it (Iceland) is, by the blueness of the Atlantic. Iceland is a cool scene. The only place that approaches it is Sweden.

Sweden is not completely surrounded by water, but almost. It wears the Baltic Sea like a stole...

Iceland is tempting. Odd thing: there is no *Baedeker* for Iceland—and no *Guide Michelin*. We look everywhere, on every shelf, above, below, and around the gap left by that 24th volume of the encyclopaedia.

All this is a charade. We know exactly where we're going. After New York, we like Spain best, blue-gray Spain. That's where we spent our last vacation. There we found our prison-away-from-prison: a country of strong schizoid (humanoid) contrasts: a country like New York is a city...

The canapés are served, and the world divides into those who continue to take that blue-gray cheese-spread they love, and the others, who keep looking, hoping that perhaps the green, perhaps the yellow....

The world divides.... The wife of a retired business associate once wailed, "We went on a round-the-world cruise last year, so we don't know where to go this year." There are voices everywhere, some louder than others.... Perhaps this lady remembers too much. Perhaps she remembers a bad time, a time less comfortable than at home.... But then she should whisper.

And what, really, do I remember of our last trip? It, too, was a tourist experience compared with the day-to-day reality of the blue fluorescent light, the crisp conditioned air, the clicking of business machines, the muffled roar of the flushometer in the executive john.... These, these are more real than the sky, the air, the trees, the wine in Spain; more real, too, than castanets and guitars.... All I can do—now, over martinis—is pray silently for a safe return.

his: #3

There are the short trips too, weekends which lean heavily on sporty props: skis, skates, boats, beachballs, air-mattresses, surfboards, guns, tennis racquets, golfclubs.... In any season on a Friday afternoon we can stand on the corner and watch the cars, heavy with equipment, crawl towards a tunnel or a bridge.

Or sometimes we are in one of them, a sports model befitting our activity, and we crawl along with the rest. Like children, we crawl towards some land or sea of play.

In Europe the cathedrals and museums are an excuse for shopping. Here the weekend games are an excuse for drinking. The props change—and the costumes—but the alcohol is constant; every place is a place to drink.

It takes a full weekend to unwind, to get into the spirit of play—and death, what the newspapers call "the weekend toll": a product not only of cars, but sun, campfires, back-swings, rough seas, thin ice . . . the entire uncontrolled non-office environment.

Yes, by then, after a weekend, the stomach and nerves have unwound, gone slack in alcohol, and we are ready again to face the highways.

THOMAS GLYNN

The World's Most Amazing Prophet, a.k.a. Wallace Mumford Amazon Polleau

Dear Christian Friend! This letter may come as a surprise to you but it is a blessing in DISGUISE and straight from Heaven so be prepared for the Big Hit. I am on my way back to your home town after everybody talking about me down South and leaving a trail of Bigger Hits than thought possible only through the blessed services of yours truly, the World's Greatest Prophet. But keep this under your hat as some people get greedy and others promise but don't deliver YOU DON'T HAVE TO WORRY ABOUT THAT WITH ME. Peoples everywhere is talking about the trail of hits I left, in Quincy, Elmira, Natchez, and don't forget New Orleans where I left them with the scores left and right only they didn't go blabbing it about but kept it to themselves and sent me plenty of tips which is all I ask plus the general donation.

You can ask your friends about me. I'm the ones they all talking about anyway, the World's Greatest Prophet, Wallace Mumford Amazon Polleau, you probably heard all the talk but now I'm telling you straight. What they say is true. I got the straight pipeline in and you know that for a fact. Folks of all races and economic persuasions come and I don't care if you're white black or green, once you get the MONEY BLESSING the hits will come through the roof. They may come in through the door or you may be walking down the street and run into a Big Hit or maybe even a Double Hit and that's a straight-on fried fact my friend.

Say you come on Wednesday. Well now, I put it on you and if you don't go blabbing your big mouth you can look for the hits to start on Friday. They call me the Mystic Man who CAN, and I don't fool around, I give you the double guarantee and that will really set you straight. If you have money problems and NEED quick action FAST no time for fooling around then come on down to the service but get there early and rent a chair and cushion because believe you me you won't be the only one no sir plenty like yourself will be there so come early and sit right up front where you can CASH in on the big Hits.

I have branch offices all over in South Carolina and Georgia and Ohio and what I say is so as in Mobile where I give my followers Psalms 27:8 and you could hardly stand up for all the hits that come.

I am a man of God and don't fool around and if you want fast action and the guaranteed Double Hits may God paralyze me stone cold in the extremities right in the market if that isn't so and you know it is. Now if you want the SUPER Big Hits, you know, the ones folks been talking about up and down the coast and you probably heard about it from your neighbors then you come down two hours early and bring a little extra cash with you and you can CASH IN yes you better believe and not be like them doubting Thomases who go around with no money all the time complaining when people get some and cash in on the big hits. I know you are not like that and that is why a trusted friend told me to write to you he said you were having a little money problem and I know about that having fixed folks up quick you don't have to WORRY! You can get every dime back and then some. There's lots more where that came from and I know and you will too just by looking at me because on stage you watch what I say and do and watch what I wear.

You will see teeth full of diamonds and fingers full of gold and that's just a start friends. I've got so much I can't wear it all I can't even drive it all and you know if I didn't deliver on all these hits I wouldn't have all the riches I do. No sir. It is one of those signs and you won't find a preacher in this whole wide earth even under God's own green skies richer than I am and THAT'S BECAUSE I DELIVER THE HITS.

I tore up Natchez and people is still counting the money and that's only the big bills the smaller ones they just put in shopping bags and put it behind the TV.

I have the thing for you that is going to fall dead straight on Friday and you can bring a friend if he or she don't blab and got the $25 to get in and you can hit for as much cash money as you want on Friday and then some. I am always crowded whenever I come to town so come early and get one or several of my blessed Seals that will make you hold money once you get the Hit and it cures too.

I am going to upset your town again so don't forget.

Now there are many Prophets who would ask you for a whole bunch of money why they make you keep running back and forth to the mattress they want so much and then THEY DOn't DELiver! Yes, friend, you heard me right. But I only ask that you come prepared with the cash and then after you make your hit you can send some of it and that way you make sure you've got the Double Blessing for the next Hit. Yes friend, if you want to keep the scores coming you send me something from the last one and I'll do the right thing by you when I talk in the pipeline.

Now I'm not like a lot of preachers who don't back up what they say but I swear on a stack of bibles why you can come and put your hand on them youself fair and square.

Now you can ask youself why I can do this and why can't nobody else or you can come and make a donation and already begin to cash in. That's right. You can bother your wooly head about all kinds of negative questions like can he really do it how come I can't do it by myself can't anyone else do it. Now I am an honest man. So I say you go right ahead and ask all the questions you want. Don't bother me none. You can keep asking the questions too long after your neighbor has made the hit, then the Big it, then the Double Hit, then the SUPER GUARANTEED DOUBLE BIG HIT and he's walking around with so much cash money he don't know where to put it while you going on beans again and he's got so many steaks he can't eat them all he takes a bite only from each one and throws the rest away. So you can ask all the questions you want my friend it don't bother me no mind at all. Just tell a friend who wants to make a hit instead of asking a lot of questions and then you'll be doing him a favor and you too since you'd rather ask questions than make a hit or even a Big Hit.

Now people want to come up close and touch me thinking that will get them the money blessing more and have the Big Hits and the Double Big Hits rolling in that much faster and if you want to too, especially any sisters among you, amen, you can see me after in the dressing room and bring some extra cash with you above the donation since I have expenses which you can understand. I would urge you this if you want to get youself straight in a hurry.

Now if by some chance you aint a Christian friend but Jewish or Muslim or even something else, don't hesitate to come because I got lines into them all. Now I left them really wrecked in Mobile and lots of those counting the green were Folks Of Other Persuasions and that's OK BY ME TOO only don't forget the donation. Of course I got to charge more because my expenses is more and I can't be fairer than that can I?

Now maybe you're wondering just what happens at this service just what do he do at this money blessing? Does he jump up and down or do some special dance or got some Haitai oils that put the fix in REAL GOOD or something of a similar persuasion. Well friends, I can only say, come down and see for youself. Then when you get the hit on Friday, or the Double Hit, you won't worry about what I do on Wednesday you will have stone cold forgotten what I DID since you hold the long green in you hands.

Now if you say you can't walk then I want you to roll on down since I know you can always use the money blessing and I can set you straight for the big score too. Roll right down the aisle, and if you can't move at all just tuck the money in your shirt pocket ushers will be around to collect don't worry I will work for YOU TOO. Same rate for Hits applies to you and that's about as fair as they come.

Now perhaps you are wondering how the World's Most Amazing Prophet lives and I can tell you folks, don't. It's true I have several wives AND AM ALWAYS LOOKING FOR MORE and if you think you qualify my organization gives examinations every Tuesday night in your area only don't expect anything extra in fact it will cost you because of expenses etcetera and I will personally have to conduct the examination to see if you qualify being the world's most amazing etcetera I must keep the standards up and all I ask you to do is sign a form and then of course there is the examination.

Now if you are already married you might still qualify only don't go blabbing it to your husband because then I got to disqualify you and you might even have the anti-hit put on you and that would BE HORRIBLE, wouldn't it? Not scoring for the rest of you natural born days and lying around all day without the hit and of course not the Big Hit or the Double either. So keep it to yourself friends.

Now if you have trouble coming up with the donation please don't come by. I am a fair man and an honest man and I don't Fool God so don't expect to get in on credit or something else and I can't be any fairer than that since I got my expenses too. No checks either, just cash, though on occasion I will take an especially fine gold piece or good cut diamonds though the market is down a little lately. Pawn tickets, stamps, all that other crap you can leave at home because that won't get you in either.

Now I believe in fast action and QUICK results so if you get the Big Super Guaranteed Double Hit and the Hits come faster than you can hold onto them why just give me a call and I'll hold the stash for you and for a slight fee put my special money blessing on that so the gates don't clog up and you get more of that flow and Open Other Flows Too.

Everywhere I go people flood the halls and come running out doors and they want to see me and get a piece of that Hit too and that's only natural and the way it should be since God made money he meant for us to have some and the more we have the better. Friends, let me give you some straight advice and you better pay attention since this is the World's Most Amazing Prophet talking. Let me set you straight on one thing. Wallace Mumford Amazon Polleau will not let you down and how do I know that? All you got to do is look at me. I'm rich as hell and that's a fact and that's how you tell a preacher who does it to you straight and one who twists and turns and promises but only delivers a hill of beans. As my old followers can tell you I got blocks of garages full of big cars, the kind you thought they didn't make anymore. Yes and I got houses all over, more than I can sleep in, furs and gold and lots of cash. I'm partial to cash. I don't care what any of them fancy bankers say they're always trying to take it away from you but cash is the best friend you got better than pappy or mammy yes sir. When you cold and hungry a friend aint gonna do it but cash is. Oh yes sir!

May I say this friends. I don't care what your game is. I don't care if numbers tickles your fancy or you go to the bones or hit the cards or even mess a little with the Mamas. What's your business is your business and I'm a man of the cloth fully licensed and my blessings have got the straight Hit to them and it don't make any difference what you mess with since that isn't my concern and what I know about is getting you dead STRAIGHT for the Hit.

I line you up and then I roll it out and you sit back and watch it all roll in and if that aint the God's Honest Truth may the waters of Israel smote the temples of Jericho down this Instant!

Now may I say this friends. Some so-called preachers and prophet folk tell you they cure the lame and heal the sick and they promise that and swear on cartons of bibles and so on. Now friends, let me tell you this straight. My super double GUAR-ANTEED Hit blessing is so strong that sometimes it spills over and does other things that other folks claim. Now if you are in a wheel chair or got a cane and are looking for something more than a hit or else someone is reading this to you on account you can't... COME BY RIGHT AWAY. Yes. For a little extra consideration I can do WONDERS only please no funny money we got little machines that can pick it out right away so don't think you can fool me and come by with the real cash, you know what I mean, the stuff you've been saving for times like this when you need the real thing and don't be stingy and I won't neither. I am only fair and have expenses and must make them up and etcetera so dig a little deeper and whatever you've got in cash come by and bring that and sell to the pawnman and come by here with the extra cash and you won't be DISAPPOINTED. I trade in satisfaction and that's what I deliver only you must bring cash, except if like I said you got some gold or good stones, none of that cheap stuff, and don't think you can flash by any of that cheap stuff on me as I got a full staff of expert appraisers who worked in the best jewelry stores before. And They Know Their Business so bring by the real stuff and leave that other stuff for the pawnman.

Say if you're a businessman or a corporate executive I can set you straight on the Double Track and guarantee you bona fide Hits whether its stock option takeovers or merger acquisitions and the only thing I ask is my special business donation plus extra considerations such as percentages of preferred stock and negotiable stocks/bonds recognized on the NYSE and in select cases the ASE.

Likewise marketing executives looking to increase share of market in Neilsen A markets and new product design engineers. You all need the Super Guaranteed DOUBLE HIT and for the appropriate up-front fee plus franchise costs you can cut yourself in on this lucrative and booming business. Special inflated rates available for International Oil Cartels.

If any of you good friends out there are cleaning ladies I have special deals for cleaning ladies since my dear old mother was and still is the very same.

Now, I hope there are some of you that are reading this God Given message with a skeptical eye. Yes friends, I delight in talking to you skeptics out there and those of you with little faith. Time and time again I have had my old followers tell me of the blessings they have received and as they count up their bank account I see a special light in their eyes because they were among the biggest skeptics. I know that may sound hard to believe but I love to give the money blessing to those of little faith and skeptical also AS LONG AS THEY COME UP WITH THE DONATION, CASH ONLY, EXCEPT IN SPEC-IFIED INSTANCES. Yes, it is you unbelievers I am talking to now, you who think I don't set you dead double straight to hit the big ones at the track or candy store or wherever you go to make you hits. You see I am fair and square and the Lord couldn't ask for squarer and fairer than me and that's why He lets me deal the Hits and the Double Hits without discrimination or regard to race, class, or social standing, including unbelievers and skeptics I treat them all the same as long as they come up with the donation and He appreciates that.

Now I always find out what the thing is going to do and then I set you up so it will fall dead straight for the Hit. Now what the thing is going to do can change and in fact is always changing and some folks think that once they see a little part of it that's the way it's going to be but friends that's not the way it's going to be because what the thing is going to do changes and you got to set youself dead right with the man who sees where those changes go and that's only a prophet and the onlyiest one around who can do that is me, Wallace Amazing Polleau.

Some folks call me Wallace Amazon, specially the women folk, and some folks call me Wallace Greenboy, account of the hits, but all folks call me Amazing and the World's Most Amazing and you can leave it at that.

Along with a straight hit I can also bring about a roundabout hit if you aren't in too much of a hurry and if the Money Problem is at your door rather than on your back. When the roundabout hit will score I don't know exactly but soon enough you better believe.

Some folks like to follow me around closely thinking if they watch what I do they learn the secret of the Hits but friends, let me warn you now, THAT IS DANGEROUS. After you make your donation and come to the service and the service is over go straight home and go to bed otherwise you may lose the Hit and especially if you try to follow me around except under special circumstances as mentioned before with Mamas or whatever or if you want to go to the money blessing services in different cities that's OK TOO but after the service we split and don't follow me it could be dangerous I am well protected and the people around me do not deal lightly with the curious and besides you could lose the Hit like I said. I am as upright as you'll find and expect those around me to be the same and you too and if you fool around with me you won't get a second chance and I can testimony to that.

Suppose you're lonely or just lonesome or don't have no friends or suppose you need love life that being a natural condition like the money condition I can set you dead up straight for that. Love is my speciality along with money and I can give you the love blessing too and you wouldn't expect anything less from the world's most amazing etcetera.

You'll find my temple convenient to get to. Bus train or subway and of course car plenty of parking and inside whatever you need or want for the services we'll take care of that too and at very competitive prices. Sodas and candy are available, no liquor of course.

Now some folks have asked me about group rates and I frown on that. When the Hit comes it is never stingy as anyone can testify so why should you be stingy as it will only cut down on the Hit and if you have a money problem like bills or you need the operation or maybe someone is in trouble and all it takes is a little money and that's all it ever takes or you have a son or daughter and want to get them something nice which is only fair or say none of these. You play fair and square with me and no cut rates and I'll set you straight up for the Hit. What could be fairer than that? Say you want to discount your Hit or take a smaller hit than what you could get, many times smaller, then I'll consider a reduction in the donation but since I don't think you want to do that and in fact I would consider you a damn fool if you did and I don't deal with damn fools I don't give no discounts or reduced nothings. What could be fairer than that? Everybody who knows me says I am as straight as they come and you can't get any straighter than that.

People have asked me about giving more than the donation and I don't frown on that it being a sign of faith and there's nothing like a better foundation under your Hit is there?

You'll see all kinds of folks sitting next to you at the service for the money blessing, poor folks, rich folks. Does that surprise you well it shouldn't since it was my money blessing made them that way in the first place and now that they got they don't want to lose and why should they and would you of course not so you'll see all kinds at my services. That is why my services aint just for white folk or black folk or any kind of inbetween folk but for everyone and as for me, why I got only one color. Green. That's right, green, the same kind color that goes on the bills you aint got now and if you think that's funny you won't when your friends start counting up their Hits the next day.

Now what do you do after you Hit? Folks ask me that. They come on bended knee, sometimes crawl that way for miles they are so grateful. I don't blame them. Well, I ask for a tip and then I make sure they come back again to another service. There are some simple forms they fill out depending on the size of the Hit and that only covers business expenses and etcetera since I'm sure you understand the size of the operation I've got here my overhead is tremendous and my operations and communications and so on you understand. If you want to keep the Hits coming you come back to me and you'd be a fool if you didn't and like I said I don't deal with fools so you come back and we work out a deal and everyone is satisfied. I'm fair and square and you won't find any moreso. Especially when it comes to the money blessing but like I say the love blessing is one sweet Hit too.

I broke up Natchez, Mobile wasn't the same when I left it, and I spread the Holy Terror in Alabama so you get down here early before all the cushions is rented out and the undertaker fans is gone and thats the New Era Ballroom and you know where that is only get there early sharp doors open at seven you get there at six and get there early because crowds come for the Hits.

Yes sir.

Lots of prophets would charge buckets of money for what I do and they can't even do what I do and thats a stone cold dead fact yes sir.

Now, suppose you lying in bed and can't move a petrified bone in your body. Suppose you can't get out to the New Era Ballroom? Is Wallace Amazing Polleau going to leave you there? On my word he isn't. All he asks is that you take twenty dollars and fold them up nice and neat and then wrap some paper around them so the greedy folks in the Post Office don't know you sending money through the mails and rip it open and keep the stash for themselves and then ever so gently put it in the envelope and make sure its sealed nice and tight and mail it off to me, Wallace Most Amazing Polleau, General Delivery Sandeau Mississippi, and when I get those crisp greens in my hands, only not too crisp account of I get suspicious when they feel too crisp, then I start working on the money blessing for you and you soon get in the mail A STRAIGHT DEAD HIT SURE THING, enclose one dollar fifty extra for postage and handling. Aint nothing fairer than that under or over God's green earth and may pigs fly if that aint so. Yes sir!

Is there anyone too young or too old for the World's Greatest Prophet? No sir. Anyone too sick or too lame? Too evil or too unlucky? Too rich or too poor? No and no and no again. I want you all out there. If you can't walk then ride and if you can't ride then crawl and if you can't crawl roll or fall or get someone to push you here but YOU COME you hear! Thas right.

Doors open six and ice water is only 25¢ a glass.

MARIANNE HAUSER

The Seersucker Suit

Those were the halcyon days forever gone when I shared my little room with R on x street. Yes, I am forced to take cover behind initials. Since the remarkable events which I am about to reveal, I have been swamped by poisonous letters and callers, most of them silent and anonymous all. Only yesterday a member of the sacred police, disguised from head to foot in white, appeared to shake me down or break me up. I shan't answer the doorbell again, except by prearranged signal.

Two rings short and three rings long: R used that signal whenever he had lost his key which was always. For love spells loss, and we were lovers, snugly installed in my room where stove and bathtub shared the floor with us and our bed. The TV had exploded during a cooking program. But more of that in time. Our meals were casual. The mattress was ample, and our days and nights were filled with the wail of those river boats which seem forever to depart and never arrive. —Life is an endless chain of departures, my father, a gay dog, would say to my mother whenever, nattily dressed in his seersucker suit, he'd be leaving her for better or worse. So be it. R too has left, to bark up heaven knows whose fire escape.

It was by way of the fire escape that he jumped through the broken window into my life faster than I could breath amen to his manly intrusion. For he was shirtless in his undershorts, and his chest, a wilderness of brown curls, seduced me at a moment's notice. He dropped upon me, panting and wet, having maybe

93

jumped ship, though he never said he was a sailor. He never did say much about himself, past, present or futurewise, and this discretion I honored in him as a man's congenital privilege. How am I to describe his features? Alas, they are a blank like his past. But oh his furry chest remains engraved upon my mind hair for hair. For hours, nay, whole nights and days I would rest with my face in his fur as in an autumnal meadow, a stray hair lying question-marked under my tongue to remind me of life's transientness. I do not know how he amused himself while I would thus graze or dream in his meadow. More likely than not he was watching TV—America the Bountiful, or How to dig your Neighbor's Grave: those, I believe, were his favorite comedies. And it was during one or another that the machine turned itself off with a shotgun blast and a flare in a puff of smoke.

"What the ****!" R hollered into what could have amounted to silence, hadn't it been for the ear-splitting traffic noise. "You mother ****** what did you do to the ******* box!" And he slapped me across the mouth, hard.

But here I must explain that this was an unusual occurence from all four angles. R was a gentleman, respectful of woman-hood, and if he spoke at all, it was with a stammer. Only when he cursed did the stammer vanish and the fur begin to fly. To hear R curse was like hearing the Almighty tear through his own heavens and blow up the stars left and rightly.

"*!?;*!*" He kicked the TV and unwittingly me which was the one time he attacked me, except for that other time when he tried to drown me in the bathtub by accident.

Marriage means give and take. If our union was blessed by neither clergy nor jury, we yet were just like any married couple, only more loving. Still at odd moments I couldn't help wishing we had a child. To fondle at my bosom a little R or I, would surely add cheer to cheer, I liked to think, determined, however, to keep my mouth shut and leave it up to R to push the button. But one mellow summer late in the afternoon, the true blue hour when even the departing ships swing blue, my heart got into my mouth and I spoke.

But let me first present the scene to you: R sitting on the edge of the tub, his gorgeous chest catching the copper glint of the beer can as he raised it to his thirsty lips; and I on the fire escape in the balmiest breeze, longing to graze in his meadow, yet putting off the delicious moment in the knowlege that delay piled on delay is the woof and arf of eroticana.

So there you have us both removed and near. "O R!" I suddenly proposed without hindsight into the blasts of the boats. "If we but had a little R or I, we could call each other father and mother!"

Had he heard me? My heart was hammering inside my mouth to beat all angels. And what with the outside racket—the trucks, the fire engines, the bloody police—conversation, unless conducted from hand to mouth, was well-nigh fruitless. So whether he responded with "Yes baby" or "No baby" I would not know. But he did upon my word hurl the beer can toward the fire escape where a carrier pigeon had just alighted. R loathed all pigeons. But carriers made him see redder, and I've watched him chase them down the waterfront, from Karl's Bar to the Bureau of Federal Interpretation. In short, R aimed for the pigeon, but by default hit me, it being the twilight hour, with the moon not yet up to give him light.

I think it must have been that night that a policeman knocked at the door to say the neighbors complained of the screaming. But they must have heard the ambulance sirens—no fault that could be layed at our steps. And after the policeman had spent a few private minutes with R in the public toilet down the long hallway, he never returned and no charges were pressed or ironed.

As for the little R or I, the matter was dropped, perhaps because of the population explosion. And R was frequently away, at Karl's Bar and other high spots where he put in an honest man's working night. He often came home with a nailed-up crate of victuals or spirits, always by the dozen and of one kind at a time, as he did not seem to trust a mixed diet. And now and then he'd even throw me a genuine bracelet or ringlet which he would let me wear and then would take away again to hock or sell and support us further. For he was a decent breadwinner. He saw to it that we lacked nothing, feeding two mouths with one stone, and often quoting the lilies which did not spin. I realize I am digressing. But digression is needed if the reader desires to understand more than four words or letters.

"Here's a **** to keep your ******* neck warm," R lulled one rosy-fingered dawn as he came staggering home from his work bombed out with fatigue. And he tossed me a fur thing before he dropped onto the connubial bed to sleep off his labor.

We still were deep in the summer. But R had already planned for the winter and how to keep my neck out of the draft. It was a pretty bit of fur he had brought me, a brown soft bundle of curls and swirls. I stroked it tenderly, thinking how it smelled like R, only sweeter. I blew on it, when suddenly I noticed to my delight that it had grown a tail like a small ostrich plume. And scarecely had I pulled at the tail, when—lo and behold—the other end of the fur trick had grown a head with a glossy caramel snout, short, pointed ears and a pair of soulful eyes, one a clear amber, the other a dark brown.

Now, it is not uncommon for the weaker sex to wear a whole batch of dead foxes around the neck, heads, tails and all. But this little creature which had begun to wiggle strangely in my lap, belonged to a different species. This was a dog child, and miracle of miracles, it was alive. It was male. A smooth pink tongue was already responding eagerly to my kiss. What grace my dog child showed, what playful antics as he rolled over and stood on his head and slipped the tip of his tail in his mouth with a wistful smile, anxious for his new mother's approval.

"I wonder if R knows what a blessing he has brought into the house," I marveled aloud into my lover's well-deserved snoring.

"I doubt that he knows anything. He was quite tipsy when he picked me up at Karl's Bar," a tiny voice articulated with precision.

A talking dog. One does come across them occasionally, yes, in jokes. But this was not a joke. This was too much, at least according to my rationed light. "What's your name?" I ventured faintly to test my own eardrums.

"The name is Karl," that same fine, fluty voice instructed me, and this time there could be no doubt that my gift dog had spoken, as I was looking him straight in the mouth.

"Oh Karl! My son! Fruit of my never-womb!" And all but swooning in maternal joy, I sank onto the bed, with Karl's fuzzy head at my bosom. But R, awakening late, with many starry exclamations to find the sun about to go down again, saw only my fuzzy head. And giving it a lusty smack for fun, he cried: "What's for eats, you ******* slut! Why aren't you off your ***!"

"Tut tut—such language in mixed company," Karl admonished in his cultivated voice. Who can blame R for giving me a sounder smack in the belief that I had talked back at him. As for Karl, he had hopped out of bed, and was daintily relieving himself on the fire escape.

"Sweet sweetheart! We are the parents of a dog child! A speaking pup!" My head was swimming through my ecstasy full speed. Still R would not acknowledge our son's presence, but stood in his underdrawers in what is called a brown study, although he wasn't nearly as brown as Karl.

"He prefers to ignore me. He has no mind to face reality," said Karl. Since his retreat to the fire escape, he had gained in length and height, which may have been due to the healthy air that blows from the sea up the river. In splendid form he dived into the tub and proceeded to make his toilette amid empty beer cans, while chanting the nostalgic refrain of a ballad—in fluent French. Cross my heart.

"Shut up. I'm thinking," R grumbled as he paced glumly, head down, to search for an article he never had owned. For the first time I studied his torso with a degree of detachment. His fur, luxuriant though it was, could not compare with Karl's in thickness or gloss. Nor would his poise match Karl's, I decided, unsurprised that our son had grown almost to R's height, and was standing on his hindlegs like any youngster. Surely, R could not remain forever blind to our gifted dog child, I thought, wisely buttoning up, however, as I knelt to gather my lover's clothes from the floor. He started to dress harum-scarum, one trousers leg up, shirt inside out, and no belt or tie to hold him together. But our Karl was already gotten up in perfect if outmoded fashion, having donned a narrow-waisted seersucker suit, a starched shirt with a high collar, a black cravat, and a pair of taffy-colored, pointed shoes. A marvel he was to behold, this upstanding young dog or canine youth whose brush was waving proudly behind him through a slit in the tight pantaloons. But R would not so much as shake Karl's paw. To the father, the son was air.

"I've got to cut." (This from R)

"Cut whom or what?" (This from Karl)

R: "Cut. Split. Take a powder, idiot!"

Karl: "If a pinch of flea powder would help. . ."

R: "*******"

Karl: "That phrase is not in my repertoire, sir."

R: "Your what? Drop it. Drop dead."

He stared at me. He swung around, and slamming the door, he disappeared from our cosy home. But from the corridor he yelled: "I need some bread, fast. You better get hold of some bread, bitch, or you'll be a dead bitch." Then his stars subsided and his footsteps faded into another land.

Karl, a conventional youth, took bread for bread, and was already running to fetch some. But I, more mundane, knew all too well that bread was money, and that I must find it to pull my lover out of whatever trouble he might be facing, jail, hail or bail.

However, money didn't grow on trees, and besides, there was none in sight. What was I to do. So I sat brooding, mooning and munching the dry heel of bread which Karl had brought me with a winning "bon appétit!"

"What a pity I can't earn my bread and your butter," he said, nibbling at his own heel as he stretched out at my feet. "However," he went on (and here his amber eye gazed up to me with adoration, while the dark eye remained modestly low) "I lack training. I never enrolled at the Dog Problem Center. And the Obedience School kicked me out because of my refusal to snarl, or jump a minor, or bite the major." He sighed and moistly buried his tongue in my hand. "Dear me. Life has become too dear. And nowadays, without a higher education, a third degree or diploma in one of the sciences. . ."

Oh, fateful words! Why had they passed his lips? No sooner had my ear got wise to science, than my brain went clicketiclick and my heart was swept under the rug by figures and facts. A talking dog was money in the bank, I reasoned out cold. A talking dog wouldn't have to go begging, but was sure to attract men of science who would pay a tidy sum to hear and accept what R had rejected.

Down on my knees! I swear by all that's whole to dog or man that never, not even during those seconds of frosted reason, did I mean to sacrifice Karl on the recessive altar of human progress. I simply intended to get my hands on some ready cash, so as to keep the family together and secure a normal childhood for our son.

That, graceful reader, was my honest plan. And if I fastened a leash to his high collar, it was to guard against the dog catchers who ply their ill trade at night. For night had fallen low and dark. With Karl on the leash, I clambered down the fire escape and onto a bus, the driver looking the other way as I mentioned our destiny which was the nearest university campus. There a Professor Y, notorious light in the green fields of remedial science, would have a friendly chat with Karl, and first rights on his story for history at a price.

"A brief, informal chat with the professor, and your father will be back to embrace you," I said to my son who wagged his tail in genial anticipation. He was a happy dog, and glad for the leash which he viewed as an added cord of affection between mother and child. But once we had reached the benighted campus, I let him run free, so he might frolic among the coeducational lovers who were desporting themselves in the moonglazed grass. A bitch with mangy fur and dangling tits was cruising near a rose bush, and Karl, sniffing her piss, went down on all fours and declared his amorous intentions in French by reciting La Fontaine, his L'Avantage de la Science—of all fables. This scared the bitch away into the shadows, but brought to light Professor Y who had been crouching behind the bush in quest of statistics on campus love at first sight.

"What goes loose!" the big man thundered in conflicting accents. "Why are you not in class!" he thundered, evidently taking us for the student body. "A demerit for each, and three days in the dog house flat on water. No bread."

And here he stooped to hide behind the blooming bush again for further research. But fate had layed her snares for me, wherefore I begged him to lend us a minute of his invalid time. And before he could cut me off, I stated my mission, while Karl had stopped his campus capers, and was shyly pressing close to me.

"My dog, Professor Y," said I, "may look like any well-dressed dog to you. But he is more. For he can speak like a man, and his name is Karl."

"Every dog has his days, some bad, some worse, as they say in Dubrovnik," Y sneered, his spectacles catching the moon before she could warm up behind a cloud. For his manner was so blistering, the roses fell off the bush and the lovers in the grass disbanded. But I held my ground for R, and giving Karl an amiable nudge, I urged him to speak for himself. And it was then that I caught the first shadow of grief upon my son's gentle dog face; the first note of strain or sorrow in his voice as he stated haltingly and with a tremor that he was honored to meet the learned professor.

"My learning is beyond your pall," Y shot back. (And now Karl's ears were twitching nervously, and his tail was clamped between his quivering thighs.) "You disinterrupted my study behind the roses. For what advantage to the Institute? Speak up!"

Again I nudged my son. But he leaned, tongue-tied and ashiver, in a sudden blast of wind. "He is bashful. But he does speak. He speaks the Queen's English in more than one tongue, and you have heard him with your own ears," I implored, though in my troubled heart I began to wonder if Karl mightn't be better off, had he never let out more than a bark.

"I heard you both. Ya, ya, deaf I am not!" Y raged in all the accents of all the nations. "Look here, my good woman," he continued after a sneezing fit and all at once without a traceable accent even from Brooklyn. "I am a research fellow. What I hear with my ears, is of no interest to me or the Institute. Supposing we were to establish the unlikely fact that the vocal cords of a dog can produce sound effects similar to those of a homo (excuse the expression), your pet would have to submit to a series of rigorous tests, too complex for your untutored mind to grasp. Have you ever been tested before?" he demanded of Karl, boxing his ear and pulling him up by the collar.

"Say something! Anything! Recite La Fontaine!" I entreated.

But now my suffering darling could do no more than emit a pathetic bark.

"You see, he is by no means eloquent." Again Y sneezed and blew his nose into a scrap of paper covered with square roots. "Let's get this straight," he informed me brusquely. "I have no patience with science fiction, fables or fairies. However, in view of the fact that a canine computer has just been installed at the Institute, your mutt may come in handy—may, I say. We'll rush you through radiation to salvation or damnation for God and country," he jocosely remarked to Karl who had shed the last shreds of poise—cowering at my feet in the dew-wet grass; panting and shaking and whining in such mortal terror, I found myself cry: "I won't allow it, Charlie! I'll take you home with me now!"

"Don't be a fool," said Y, winking and shoving a bundle of greenbacks into my clutch purse which I had quite unconsciously unzipped. He chucked me under the chin and pinched my haunch to divert attention from his three hooded assistants who had sprung out of thick air and were already wrestling with Karl. For now my son was struggling wildly to save his life; snapping, foaming at the mouth; howling to make my soul bleed, and even taking a bite out of one of the assistants' pants. But before I could rush to my darling's defense, the three had thrown a sack over his head. They had put him into a straight-jacket, and were speeding off with him into the night.

"They're only doing their job." Y patted my hand. "Now you go home and get some rest. You may visit your dog on the campus tomorrow morning, at the Institute on Avenue Y."

My heart is racing through my memory. . . A fog had

swallowed my child and his hooded abductors. Unescorted I returned to my abode of former bliss via the fire escape. No Karl to lick my tear-streaked face. No R to sock it. The fuzz on the unmade bed might have been shed by either son or lover. Down I lay, and there was no call for the dawn to kiss me awake, as I never closed more than one eye, keeping the other open for R's sake. In fact, before sunup, a sailor squeezed through the window and roughly demanded that I hand over the money by order of R. And so anxious was I for my lover's welfare, I obeyed, no questions asked, and even stuffed a bottle into his duffle bag to take to Karl's father.

Knock knock. They are knocking at my door again. But the signal is not R's, and I shall remain holed up and unravel my yarn to the bitter finals. The hour had struck. When I arrived on the campus, autumn had torn yesterday's leaves to shreds, and the last red rose of summer was ashes. No lovers on the lawn that chilly morning. Bleary-eyed with tears and wind, I saw no familiar landmark, except a tombstone. The distant, doleful baying of a hound gave further voice to my profound apprehensions. Repeatedly I asked for directions from passing students, failing instructors too, but received little to go by, some pointing east or west, some down or up as they hurried on to meet their Master's. At last a leather jacket on a motorbike had me jump on the back seat, and soon threw me off it again at the corner of Y— a broad majestic avenue which, flanked by deflowered dogwood or plain-clothes men, was to be the one-way street to my doom. But of that I had no premonition. On the contrary, the sight of the Insitute, a vast and silver-faced basilica whose collapsible dome loomed larger than reason, injected me with instant faith. No harm could come to Karl in this bright temple. Hands folded for happy thanksgiving, I pilgrimaged into a self-propelled revolving door. And I might still be turning around in that door, lulled by piped-in organ music, had not a Charity Sister in white drawn me into the vestibule with one rubber-gloved hand.

"I've come for my Karl," I whispered, still under the holy spell. For the vestibule too had a sanctified air, designed as it was in the shape of a double cross, and inscribed with interdenominational memos: WAR EQUALS PEACE. DO NOT ASK Y.

ETCETERA. It was the etcetera that made me feel vaguely apprehensive again. Besides, sister had grabbed my elbow a bit too roughly for one of her persuasion. So, hearing the old fears knock at my inner door, I inquired if Karl were safe.

"Safe enough," she grunted through a handkerchief, "A damned side safer than the ones who gnaw on the forbidden bone of dissention."

And overconfident by now in her fraudulent habit, she made the crucial slip which exposed her as a member of the male order. "You wait for me here, babe," she mouthed through a stubble of whiskers, "while I retire to the boys' room for two wee minutes and see a man about a dog."

Oh, perfidy! A horrid stench had annulled the sacrosanct odor. Off I sped on my own, driven by a sudden cry of agony which I had instantly recognized as my son's. "Let me go to my mother. . ." This over and over. This louder and ever so loud, repeated by a hundred loudspeakers above a hundred doors, down the aluminum corridor which appeared endless, yet ended unexpectedly in a lecture hall whiter than white.

Aghast, I halted on the dotted line. Karl's martyred cry for his mother was all at once a faint whimper, rising, I saw through my tears, from a tape recorder on a platform where men stood in a learned huddle. "Where are you, Karl?" I meant to shout. But tears and fears choked my throat, and besides Professor Y was already giving a summary of what he chose to call Operation R, the devil knows why.

"Operation R must be chalked off as a failure," he lectured from a TV screen. "For although one specific dog appeared to speak with what we shall term, for lack of a more precise definition, the vox humana, we have no reason to assume that canis familiaris per se is articulate beyond the common bark and related bunk. As for the mutt himself," (and here Y sneezed and pointed upward with his thumb) " I doubt he'd be fit, at this low point in the peace game, to play informer behind enemy bars, or for that matter inside the bars of our own water frontier. So I suggest we shelve the doggish prattle, and return to research more constructive and explosive. Let sleeping dogs lie."

This seemed to be an old academic joke, since everybody laughed before Y had finished.

"Attention!" Y snapped. "You are required to forget what you have learned. Operation R has been labeled 'top dog secretion'. There must be no leakage. Thank you. The class is dismissed."

Whereupon he clapped his hands to applaud his own lecture, and switched off the recorder as well as himself on TV.

And now as the screen darkened and the hall cleared of the last human hum and haw, my eyes beheld—But wait! All I beheld at first was Karl's seersucker suit hung up on a hook from the ceiling in so lifelike a manner, I thought for a fraction of unspeakable shame that they had hanged and beheaded my son. But in less than a drumbeat I saw the stretcher, and on it Karl, a moveless form; his four legs trussed with twine; his noble head ignobly wired to electrodes; and his tail shaped into a question mark, unanswerable and eternal. His dark eye was shut. But the amber eye was open—fixed in a glassy stare on a heaven he never might be allowed to enter, as he had not been baptized or circumsized, or penalized by any rites or wrongs, save those of the Institute.

"You may claim the carcass, though not without the proper clearance by our institutionalized staff," a woman's voice rasped over the microphone.

Spare me the painful account of the countless steps I was forced to take; of the papers I swore at; of the oaths they made me sign with an x for an R in Karl's name, before I was free to claim his mortal remains. Now autumn was winter. Many bridges did I cross in the blinding snow, with the coffin on my shoulder to take home for my lost love to mourn. Passing Karl's Bar, I thought that I heard my lover's starry incantations ring in the howling blizzard. But when I peered through the ice-flowered door, I found the bar deserted and closed by the law. So I processioned in still deeper grief down x street, up the snow-packed fire escape and into my room. The room was cold and empty—empty as was the coffin which contained, I saw as I tremblingly raised the lid, not Karl's body, only his seersucker suit, folded into a small bundle.

Farewell then, father and son. I have no tears left to wash your path clean of my sorrow. Let the forces ring, rap, pound, badger and bully. The truth is out. But I'll remain inside, forever, if need be. Someone has stolen our bed. Good night. I shall sleep in the tub. Karl's folded suit will be my pillow.

FANNY HOWE

The Ruth Tractate

So the mother-in-law went home, and Ruth, her daughter-in-law, with her; they returned from the Country of Endless Woe, round the D--d Sea, until they came near the City of Early Light. Spring was beginning. The mother-in-law had there a relative through marriage, a rich farmer, and his name was The Nice Man. And Ruth said to her mother-in-law, "Let me go in to The Nice Man's field and sow lettuce—there where I might find security, for us, from him."

And later I said to Ruth, "When you left the Country of Endless Woe—your country—did you know you were leaving home for good?"

No one leaves twice. Even revolving doors or garden gates can't repeat an occasion. Winter's over and light across this latitude is fuller. Skies become visible near five. Clouds always break up before the loss of the sun, reveal Nihil and the Nile. These events are repeated. But no one leaves twice.

"Has it been easy?"

Exile's evil, sees outside people, then turns inside, sighing. Nostalgia's a river you can't build a dam in.

"What was it like in those days?"

In the days of the prophets it was dirty to admit—still is—the sexual frenzy of the cosmos. The same clamping went on then, and now, throwing the shyest into an ecstasy. But the air was more swollen than it is today. More full, and sensual. An endless spring, with pulses of humiliating heat. And when the mystics passed by, like fragrance of cinnamon, the air was charged, just as the pink of their lips was the sign of a secret insight, which the Big Nothing gave to them, beat and swallow. Frenzy was something they knew, like some occasions we do too, but with lovers.

"Why didn't you choose that frenzy, instead of a marriage bed?"

Loving a person's flesh is easy to be wholehearted about, like sniffing a rose's plush little petals.

"And wine from green grapes is beautiful to taste, but all pleasures of the flesh can be replaced. So why indulge them?"

Nothing good can be replaced, and certain mistakes will never kick up the traces. All actions, especially sexual, are indelible. At least these facts are measurable.

"But do you honestly believe a woman can love a man?"

If she has his child, she can, and if she is his child, she can. But if she's like, say, a concubine, and the two are equal at all times, there's no tragedy between them. See, the tragedy's the hard part. The heart of the Heart.

"Didn't you ever wonder about the meaning of life?"

When I was really young, depending on my mood, I moved from one school of thought to another. It took a while to figure out I was closer to the truth when I was nearly an infant, and there was no sex or name attached to the one tone I heard around the cosmos. To hear it again would be like trying to bring back a day from childhood. Impossible.

"You can still continue to question, though, can't you?"

I grew deaf from questions and interpretations. Gods as human types carried to an extreme don't interest me. After all, they're not very nice. They devour whatever they desire. The tastier you are, the closer you are to being eaten by them.

"What do you mean by tasty?"

Good. . . .Tasty's measure is how close you are—in act and thought—to someone under seven. Sacrifice, superstition—even they fail in the worst way.

"So what's the point of a life for you?"

To build a just society. I never felt at home at home. I wanted to feel at home in the larger landscape. To do so, I had to think in terms of materials, and improvement.

"Very functional. What did you bring with you?"

One summer garment, one clean linen wrap, and one half-worn. My best dress. An old dog. And a vial of perfume.

"And was your journey hard?"

Solitude has always been my best friend. And so has my mother-in-law. So only the land was alien—speckled with scrub and sand, ups and downs, like emotions. These geologic wonders come in dreams, too, you know, as trapezoid and rhombus. A shape, in sleep, tells a story. I saw animals the color of sand and reptiles the shapes of plants. To pick your way through a landscape so fraught with a sense of weight and danger is to know what to fear and who.

"Who should you fear, and what?"

I'll tell you. Other people are more cruel for jewels, say, or sex, than lions are for blood. It's like a woman finds a man to hide her, from other men, and a trip through an alien place is just a way to learn how wild the world and the souls in it are, always uncovered.

"Did you travel with the idea of finding a man to protect and marry you?"

I guessed someday I might be given, again, a real love situation. And then someone might give me, say, a son—an other, not my own gender. That transaction is, to me, unnatural. A miracle of a Miracle.

"That sexual exchange is strange. But how did you have so much hope?"

Many of my appointments have turned into disappointments, but I think in the future tense. In the past I used to wish I could meet a man with whom I'd study sacred texts, and this way demolish the sexual difference, and attraction, between us. But now, no.

"What changed you?"

When I lost my husband, I became helpless. I would do nothing for myself, but fed myself on suppositions. No supper, without cooperation from others, and it came. I opened my doors only to those with offerings as useful as bread and wine. And they came. Mostly women, of course, strange figures moving from door to wall, kindly donating time and energy to the cause of my well-being. In the end, I was so overjoyed that they were better than me, I went into the streets and became devoted to humanity, in the most physical sense.

"Some people say that the bodies of women contain the holy spirit. Babies have to pass through us to get it. Do you believe that?"

A baby has its portion of paradise it offers to you, as a mother. Where did that spark originate—with one or the other, child or mother? I don't know.

"I can't answer that one either. Tell me, then, what made you follow your mother-in-law, as if she were your own flesh and blood?"

Nothing but love, which is a kind of gravity.

"This I can understand. But people are always fascinated by that aspect of your life. I happen to be more interested in other aspects. For instance, the question of intermarriage?"

Oh, when I crossed over race and culture to marry her son, neither of us were conscious of its social meaning, which was the sin of ignorance. We were on my turf then. But by the time I loved his mother, I couldn't cross back, consciously, because it would have been the sin of a Sin. This is the irony of action.

"In what way?"

Every action is the end result of character. Force terminates the life of the forcer. It's the victim who acquires knowledge.

"Do you think of yourself as a victim?"

No. Because I chose to be obedient, and passive, in order to learn. It's the only way. The most important thing is to be ready.

"So you went and picked lettuce."

There's no decadence in lettuce, but it takes decades to discover how much wine to drink without becoming idle.

"True. What do you think of marriage, now that you know?"

Marriage, like papyrus sealed in jars of clay, has a secret purpose in society. Without it, no pity's possible between people of the opposite sex.

"Pity?"

That's where charity begins. Pity is physical, hot as fecal stuff and as fertile.

"You can pity without marriage."

Maybe, but you can't have children. And without them, what's what? No one else is so reassuring. They comment on everything in sight. To have one you have to merge with some man. And to love a man is a very hard thing, as I've said. You have to make him womanly somehow.

"But how?"

Resist temptation. That is, never allow a lurid fantasy to enter your head and fall upon the body of your husband. This way, he'll be your friend, both day and night. Temptation isn't the action, but the form of attraction.

"Wouldn't you get bored?"

No, because it's such hard work. You have to learn how to love the taste of one man in order to make sons, and a man must have an appetite equal to yours, in order to give you daughters. This is laborious.

"It must be. If a man offered me out to a life as a drudge, I'm sure I'd begrudge him the new demands he'd make, as if there's no justice but only judges. Why not remain solitary?"

Men are like judges all day, it's true, but at night they give up their power to you.

"Who needs it? With solitude you don't have to deal with these things."

True. But don't let the contagion of cowardice affect all your limbs or you'll think you're different from everyone, as they stand in line beside you. You'll see them as signs of Signs, not human like you.

"Haven't you ever tried solitude?"

Yes. I used to live out a day for the dream it made at the end, and always had a good time under. But then I decided if I was a person pursuing happiness, for myself and others, I'd better build a happy house and move in.

"Don't you think you could have been happy alone?"

Historically speaking, 'where there's a will, there's a way' has been true for men only. For many oppressed people, and women, 'where there's a way, there's a will' has been the rule. To find a way is the primary urge for weaker beings, as it is for donkeys. Out of the way comes the will. And the way is often given by a man in the form of economic security.

"But what does it lead to?"

The cell of a home life and its hundred credos and rituals, both vertical and horizontal, is the only area of comfort equal to that of devotion to the divine un-time. Home is the victory of the common person over time. The balance is held by keeping materialism and mysticism at equal arm's length.

"You can do it more efficiently in solitude, and also give yourself more freely to others who need help and attention."

The graceful groans of a garden gate, when someone you love is coming home, make the salad toss.

"A settled home is history's abyss."

The perfect salad is made of spring lettuce, avocado, sprouts, an oil and vinegar combination, including spices, in which the amount of salt is crucial.

"Salt stands for affliction. When I put salt on my salad, I know I'm spicing my time with affliction."

Being afflicted is superior to causing affliction, because action's the end of character.

"Affliction's end is often just a sigh of a Sigh. You have to live alone to know what this means. . . . Tell me, anyway, what happened in the end."

I went down onto the floor, and did everything my mother-in-law told me to do. And when The Nice Man had eaten and drunk until his heart was high and cheerful, he went and lay down at the end of the heap of lettuce I picked. I moved over softly, and uncovered his feet, and lay there. But it wasn't until we were married that he came into me and gave me conception. And out of that occasion, I bore a son.

HAROLD JAFFE

Pelican

> "The Pelican is greatly devoted to its young
> and, finding them in the nest killed by snakes,
> tears at its breast, bathing them with its blood
> to bring them back to life."
>
> —Leonardo da Vinci
> (Quoted in J.L. Borges'
> *The Book of Imaginary Beings*)

We did it for about a year and a half, okay? The real stuff, I
mean. Before that we like did it with another pair two, three
times. The same pair, people we knew. And it was pretty good.
We—Burt and me—had went a little flat and getting it on with
this pair it helped us. We got our edge back. But then after a
while we went flat again.

"Flat?"

Yeah. I mean we balled and stuff, just there wasn't much zip
to it. Burt and I been married almost nine years and we couldn't
like uncover anything new about each other. Each other's body.
So we talked about maybe getting into swinging to like see how
it was. Either that or separating for a while.

"Why didn't you just separate for a while?"

It's a hassle. We have a joint saving's account and stocks.

Plus life insurance. We have a real good insurance policy but it depends on us living in the same household. And there are the kids. Besides, we still kind of loved each other, okay? So we sent away for this swinger's magazine that has photos and phone numbers and stuff. We went through it real careful making a check next to the ads that appealed to us. We were a little nervous about it, but it was a turn-on too. Just going through the ads got us feeling real sexy and we got it on like right there, on the carpet. Few days later we sent replies to two of the ads from Central Jersey near where we live.

"What sort of replies?"

What sort? Photos. Not nude photos—we didn't have any nude photos of ourselves then. Photos, details about our age, jobs, family, what we liked to do in sex. Like I'm bi but Burt isn't. We wrote that. Anyways, one of the parties responded and the other didn't. This isn't unusual. We found out later that half or more of the swingers you wrote to didn't respond for one reason or another. But the party that did respond were interested. They were about our age, pretty nice people, and the woman—her name was Joan—was real sexy, petite and delicate, very graceful. Which needless to say turned my husband on. Joan's husband—I think his name was Stan—wasn't all that much, kinda overweight, not at all like his photo. But he was friendly and he was hung nice and when we got down to it he knew how to get it on.

"What was the sequence that first time? How did you get into it—do you remember?"

Yeah—I do. Lot of other times are jumbled together in my memory even though some of them were real sexy. But this one, being it was the first, I remember all of it. The etiquette is when you respond to a published ad, you have first choice about where to meet. And we wanted to do it at our place thinking it would be easier there. Joan and Stan—no, his name was Stew, short for Stewart—they didn't mind. So we sent the kids to Burt's mother on the shore for the weekend, and Joan and Stew came by around ten o'clock on a Friday night. What was the sequence? We talked, drank some of this strong sweet liquer called Chartreuse, which they had brought over. It's supposed to be a kind of turn-on, I guess. We shared a joint too. Things were moving kind of slow, we were still all dressed, and to tell you the truth I was feeling a little like the whole thing was a mistake and not at all turned-on, when Stew suggested Burt take his wife into our bedroom. Burt went for the idea and so did Joan. While they were in the bedroom Stew and I did a little bit, not much. Touched each other, talked. Then after a while we went into the bedroom where Joan and Burt were into it pretty good. We took our clothes off and joined in.

"And you saw this couple—Joan and Stew—again?"

We saw them once more about a month later. Also at our place. It was okay. Not super. Burt really was turned on by Joan, like I said. And I didn't blame him, I liked her too. But Stew, in spite of being a good technician, didn't do it for me. Besides, we were into a few other things by then which were pretty interesting. There were other pairs, and there was this single, an olive-skinned girl from Trinidad. Her name was Lakshmi, real pretty, bi and turned on by just about anything. Lakshmi was perfect for us because we were still a little unsure of ourselves and our technique.

"What do you mean turned on by anything? Like what, for instance?"

Well, for instance Greek. Lakshmi had a great ass, and she dug enemas, she dug being butt-fucked. We swung with Lakshmi maybe six, seven times, and it was only like the last few times that we found out she was into bondage, rubber, the whole S&M scene. The next-to-last time we saw her she came with a guy, young, maybe gay. All he wanted was Lakshmi to whip his ass and Lakshmi—in rubber and six-inch spike-heels—really did it to him. We all got off on it. I'll tell you what: if we had had a big male dog Lakshmi would have made it with him. She was a regular sex machine.

"You and Burt never made it with an individual male?"

Never. I kinda wanted to try it. Lots of male singles advertised in the magazine, and sometimes we'd meet a guy at at party or something that turned me on. But Burt couldn't handle it. Like I said before, he isn't bi, so he wouldn't be able to do much besides share me with another guy, which he didn't really want to do. I never made a big deal over it. The pair scene was good, the occasional female single thing was good, and me and Burt were in a real nice groove together. Until that first thing happened.

"When was that?"

About five, six months after we got into it. It was going good pretty much. Not that we didn't have some clinkers, and there were a couple of times when the other people thought us, or one of us, were clinkers too. But then we were pretty heavy into it, two and three times a week a lot of times, and also we were doing larger scenes, two, three other pairs and more.

"What's a clinker?"

Rejection. That's your commonest clinker. I've seen like real beautiful chicks and guys rejected, okay? I mean everybody has their own head, that's the way it is. Another clinker is banging your own drum, forcing your own shit on someone that doesn't want it. Which is what happened to me. We were with two other pairs in Danbury, Connecticut—we weren't sticking only to Jersey anymore. One of the pairs was okay but I saw right off that the other pair was weird. The woman was like stoned on Quaaludes or something, she was kinda nodding out. The guy—he was a stocky aggressive dude with long dirty hair, like a biker. And he had eyes only for me. My instinct told me to like cut out, but Burt sort of liked the woman from the other pair, and the guy from this pair was kind of sexy. So we stayed and we got into it, all of us except the biker's woman who was sort of laying there. Well, the biker started really coming on. I don't mind rough, but not his kind of rough. Right off he took hold of my head and forced me down on him, like he thought he was down on the docks with a queer or something. Then he tried to butt-fuck me, and when I pulled away he slapped me around. We were in a big wide room and Burt was busy in another part of it. But when I started to scream Burt and the guy from the other pair came over and tried to pull the prick away from me. But then he went really crazy and attacked Burt, hitting him in the face with his fists, trying to kill him it seemed like. This went on for like a long time, the dude had pinned Burt to the floor and was beating the life out of him. It was weird because while he was slamming Burt he was silent, not making a sound. The rest of us were screaming, trying to separate them, but this mother was too strong, too fucking crazy. Finally he just stopped, got up, put on his pants, grabbed his nodding bitch, and left.

"When did this happen?"

What's this? December? It was in the summer. The summer before this last one. Burt's nose was broke and both of his eyes were badly bruised. But worse than that, he was really messed up inside. Getting beat up bad like that under those circumstances got him real down on himself. He didn't want to see people anymore, started saying these super moral things about how bad it is to make it with other people and stuff. He wasn't even making it with me, his wife. I didn't push him because I knew it was a terrible thing, the whole thing that happened was terrible. It just wasn't good for him to be so down on himself, so guilty. But no matter how supportive I tried to be, it hurt us. It hurt our relationship, and we were even talking again of separating for a while. We were both real down, I can tell you, and the kids naturally were picking up on it too. And then we heard from Rory and Roy.

"They wrote?"

No, phoned. If they had wrote we wouldn't have answered. Not the way we were feeling. They had seen our ad in a back issue of the magazine and Rory phoned. It must've been a couple of months after that other thing had happened and things between Burt and I were at an all-time low. He usually slept in the day-bed in the living room. Sometimes he didn't come home at nights, and a few times I didn't either. The kids were grumpy. The only reason we didn't actually split up was what I mentioned before. Anyways, it was a weekday night, Burt was helping Carol, our youngest, with her homework, and I was doing my nails in the bathroom. The phone rang and Burt answered it. From the bathroom I could hear him talking and listening and then talking again, and something in his voice told me it was an unusual phone call, a good call. I sort of heard his voice change from grumpy and depressed to interested and charming, like his old self. I was wondering what the hell was going down when he called me: "Baby, I'd like you to talk with someone." He sure hadn't called me baby in a long time. I got on the phone while Burt picked up the extension in our bedroom. Soon as I heard Rory talk for a little bit, I understood how she had gotten to Burt.

"What was it? Something in her voice?"

Something in *her*. Her voice, her way of holding herself, everything she did, really, showed what she was. I found this out later when we got to know Rory. But then, listening and talking with her on the phone, there was something sincere and open about her. Burt and I both felt friendly, at home with her, right off. We must've been on the phone forty-five minutes and I can't tell you now what we talked about—besides getting together, that is. She and her husband wanted Burt and I to get together with them. We said that we had kinda stopped swinging, and Rory suggested that we talk about it together and let her know. Not only did Burt and I talk about it, we made love for the first time in a long time and it was great. We saw Rory and Roy for the first time the following Saturday at their place. A real cute place on the Jersey shore. Rory answered the door and she looked pretty much the way I expected. Real attractive, tall and slender, with long wavy auburn hair, in her early thirties. Another thing I noticed which didn't surprise me when I thought about it was her scent. Instead of perfume or cologne, she smelled of talc, a real fresh, clean scent. She led us inside to the living room where three other people were sitting and talking, a pair about our age and a man who looked to be in his forties in a wheelchair. That was Roy. I remember that Burt and I looked at each other, wondering.

"How did Roy respond to you?"

He smiled and held out his left hand. He had a very sweet smile. He used his left to shake hands because the right side was where most of the damage was. He explained this to us in a very direct, quiet sort of way, while we were all sitting there having a drink. The other pair—Mack and Joanne—already knew the story. Roy had survived a plane crash about fifteen years ago, but his spinal cord had been damaged and he was a quadraplegic. In his case that meant his right side, legs and arms, was paralyzed. In the past I had always been kind of turned off— scared, I guess—by wheelchairs, but I didn't feel that way about Roy. Still Burt and I were surprised when Rory sat on his lap and they started necking. After a bit Rory got up and suggested we go into the sun-room, a lovely glassed-in room with plants and pretty rugs and cushions. Rory helped Roy undress and laid him on one of the rugs on his back. He had a pretty nice body, a little soft maybe, but nice skin. He didn't at all look paralyzed. He was hung okay too, about average. He had a nice broad chest. The crazy thing of it was that while I was watching how gentle and easy and sensual Rory undressed him and helped him onto the rug, I got turned on. Mack and Joanne were also getting undressed, and so me and Burt did too. In a while we were all laying around kinda touching each other, almost like kids. Everybody was relaxed and gentle and it was a lot of fun. A while later we got into the adult stuff and it was great, natural and sexy and relaxed.

"Roy was able to perform adequately?"

Roy was fine, except that he depended on Rory to get started. The accident had damaged the nerve endings between his penis and his brain—I don't know if I'm explaining this right. Anyways he couldn't get an erection by thinking about it, so

Rory got him hard by first masturbating then sucking him. Then Joanne sat on his cock, and then I did, and let me tell you something—it was good. He was right there, real alive. That's how he felt to me, like somebody half his age but relaxed, gentle. Roy and Rory were bi, and so was Joanne. Mack and Burt held back a little, but after a while they got into it too, everyone was with everyone else and it was great. It was like the best time we had ever had swinging and Burt and I talked about it for a long time afterwards. We didn't know whether it was because we had stayed away for a while, or whether it was the people. For sure they weren't the sexiest people we had been with. They looked good and Rory was beautiful, but it wasn't so much her body that was beautiful as just all of her. Her body was in good shape but she was probably closer to forty than thirty, there were stretch marks on her breasts. But it didn't matter. With Rory the looks thing didn't really matter.

"You saw Rory and Roy again soon after?"

We wanted to see them again real soon, but the thing was they moved around a lot. Mack and Joanne, who we swung with a lot, told us that Rory and Roy had lived in Africa and South America and Hong Kong, I think it was. Like we saw them on Saturday and the following Monday they flew to Mexico, and from there to Guatemala. Mack said he had no idea what Rory and Roy did in these places, except maybe swing. Anyways, we saw them again at their place about three weeks later. Mack and Joanne and a real attractive black pair were there. Sheryl and Joe, the black pair, were having a kind of problem. Joe had hurt his knee real bad and had it operated on and wasn't able anymore to fuck like a cowboy-stud on top of Sheryl, which is the way she liked it. Rory and Roy showed them how good it was, and how varied too, with Joe on his back and Sheryl on top. Like I said, Rory had this simple relaxed way, and she knew when to kid around—she and Roy were always kidding each other. Joe and Sheryl dug the new positions real quick without being uptight, and it was great all around, a long, long session and we didn't have to toke up or snort or anything else to keep it real.

"You said you enjoyed making it with Roy. How was it with Rory?"

Great. I think I said about balling Roy that he was all there. So was Rory. It's hard to describe this feeling, but you must know what I mean. When we—Rory and me—were together, caressing, going down, whatever, there was a sweet, steady kind of feeling about it. In scenes people tend to be like on the move— a taste here, a taste there. Rory wasn't like that. Burt agreed with me too, he loved balling Rory. I think he dug balling her more than he did me.

"And that didn't upset you?"

No. Swinging sex is recreational. It's not the same as loving somebody. People who swing say this a lot, maybe too much, but I think it's true. Let's face it, in the year and a half we were into it, there've been guys I really dug balling, but I haven't loved Burt the less for it.

"How many times did you swing with Rory and Roy altogether?"

Just four times. After that they took off again, this time for India and Nepal—that area. They sure picked far-out places to go to, and it must've been a hassle with Roy handicapped and all. Anyways, they said they'd probably be back in a year or so. And it's been almost a year since they left. They sent us a couple of cards, but with no return address. That's about it. We miss them. Me and Burt both miss them.

"You stopped swinging for good?"

Yeah. I think so. We'll see how we feel when Rory and Roy get back. After they left we did it for a while, but it wasn't the same. Then Carol, our youngest, came down with a real bad infection which the doctor thought was spinal meningitis. She was real sick for a long time and we didn't want to leave her. By the time Carol got better—and it took about five months—we had just kinda lost interest. In swinging, I mean.

"Do you still keep in contact with any of the people you swung with?"

Not really. We talked to Mack and Joanne a couple of times, though what we talked about was Rory and Roy. And believe it or not, that weirdo biker that beat up on Burt actually phoned me a couple of months ago. I told him to leave me alone or I would call the cops. He didn't call back.

"And with you and Burt? How does it go?"

So-so. We're hanging in there.

STEVE KATZ

The Zippo Stories

Look Mayan to Me

The Calumny is not a lie. Sunshine is the blanket of the poor, some say. Not I. I say this Calumny is a tropical fruit that abounds somewhat in a broad band of tropical sunshine. "You know something funny," says Zippo, "about you? Is that you look Mayan to me." "I know I do," I say to her back as she takes a walk. So succulent, this fruit, but dangerous. Deadly, in fact, but for a brief period each year when it tastes lush as the zapote, reliable as an apple. A period of forty-five minutes each year, usually in late August or early September. I ate this fruit too soon and so I am going to die. But first I will go crazy, señor. The fleshes of this fruit is a passion of the tropics. The youth assigned to monitor its ripening begins its vigil in July. In the first week of August crowds crowd under the trees. They discuss the first taste of it, dainty as the essence of ferns, giant ferns that made grandiose the age of dinosaurs. Were we there at the time, señor? Quien sabe? Only the epicarp tastes like this, a golden layer just under the skin, that has an indefatigable crispness, like fresh lotus root. True! But only when the Calumny is picked within the first seven minutes of its brief maturity. Maturity we know as an ephemeral period of safety. You kiss the skin, an ochre velvet dappled with azure, before your incisors pierce that firm layer, a gentle snap through like the moment of release of your lover's resistance. The shade, some say, is the air-conditioning of the poor. Not I, señor. This tree manipulates sunshine to intensify the heat of midday. This tree is known to me in particular by the name of Borges, to whom I now humbly dedicate this account, telling it to you from a bench under a live-oak in the Alameda de Leon in the city of Oaxaca in the nation of Mexico under a rain of fragmented seed-pods on this eleventh day of March in the year nineteen hundred and eighty two. Algunos balloons have escaped into these trees and hang there despicably inedible as the fruit of the Borges, if we accept that as the name of the tree we describe. O where are the children now who once owned those 'globos'? Do they remember those trees that recaptured their balloons? The 'vendedor de globos' chirps by now, whistle in his teeth. Some of his balloons have long legs, to make them resemble the octopus or 'polpo', that looks so white, boils up so delicious served to you in a cradle of lettuce sponged lightly with lime. A child here presses his face into an ice-cream cone as if it were his mother's breast, and gazes into the tree. Could one of those balloons have once been his? Quien sabe? Within the crisper layer of this fruit the mesocarp is another surprise, a flood onto the tongue, so much liquid like brimfuls you would expect to cascade down the chin and lap at the feet in floods, but this isn't liquid, it's like a textured gel, with the taste, those who have experienced both can testify, of the palms of human hands, supreme delicacy in more sophisticated cannibal cultures, sweetened with licorice, as is the custom in many of those places. Don't eat this, however, except during that forty-five minute period that comes usually in August, but sometimes in September; and it can happen at midday, or in the morning, or the evening, though it hasn't yet happened between the hours of 10:30 P.M. and 2 A.M., a blessing in disguise because it means three and a half hours rest each night for the young people assigned to watch the Calumny. Time for them to ask questions like, 'Why are we sent to war?' and 'Who are those shadows that claim to own the world?'. Sometimes one of them makes a mistake, as I did, being a foreigner, and *that* one dies, as I surely will. But first I will go crazy, señor. These deaths come as an affirmation for the living of their own vitalities, of the quantity of life breasting in each of them, while they wait for the fruit to come into its time, their time. Therefore the death is a cause for celebration, my death a Carnival at the foot of the Borges, as if everyone is sitting on this bench, dreaming up this yarn, this cocktail out of its own language, dead myself to everything but the wistfulness of writing this as if speaking to someone, and suddenly in front of your eyes the dark face of a girl child, beautiful as a pure note played behind you on a flute, f-sharp on a panpipe blown by a wind scattering lips, and she says, wistfully, "Chiclets? Chiclets?" Who can say *no* at that moment? Do you think I am crazy, señor? One always wants to speak to someone, to say *yes, yes,* to Zippo, for instance, back from her walk, as if what you say now can be a palpable result, the produce of what you have taken to call your 'work': "¡Hola! Zippo. This Calumny is the fruit of the Borges tree. Taste it. Gorgeous and deadly, but here it is, and worth a bite."

The Attack of the Conceptual Artists

Uncle David opened the door and Bushmill pounced on him. Across the street, behind the hedge, Adelaide Herkimer was buying a baby girl from Narcisso Gutierrez, a native of Bogota, Colombia, in this country illegally, selling drugs and babies. Inside the houses a herd of elephants crossed the Serengeti from one Baobob tree to the next. They crossed in each of the eight houses except in the one at the end of the tree-lined street called Plum. It was a dead end. This last house, a Cape Cod gothic built in 1947, was wired with soft music of the kind called 'mood'. Derek Elliott lay there indoors on the thick pile carpet dressed in eight pairs of bikini underpants. His life-size inflatable doll lay beside him, plugged into a wall socket so its torso and limbs, filled with a fleshlike gel, would heat up. Bushmill tugged on the sleeve of Uncle David's uniform, and pulled him into the living room. He nudged the old conductor into his favorite chair, formed long ago into the concave of his slump. An ad for Arrid flew from a nest in the Baobob. Bushmill fetched pipe and slippers, then lowered the sound by remote. "Uncle David's here." The voice of Sophie Frielich reached the TV from the upstairs bedroom. Uncle David dimly recognized the voice, but didn't expect to hear it coming from the TV. "I hope you understand you have to leave now. Uncle David's here." Adelaide Herkimer carried the baby into the house, through the vestibule and living room, into the kitchen, "Hubba-hubba goo goo," she said to the baby, and lifted the lid of her canning cauldron coming to a boil on her six burner gas range. "Gaaaa," the baby smiled at her. "Gaaaa," responded Adelaide. Derek did forty-three sit-ups to the music, and twelve push-ups on his fingertips. The beautiful doll squirmed on the carpet as its innards got hot. Uncle David's pipe swung listlessly from his tired mouth. Bushmill jumped onto Uncle David's lap, licked his ear, jumped off again. He did that seven times during the evening. Sophie Frielich sang Rossini in the bedroom while someone smashed all the bottles on the bathroom floor. A tigress pounced at Uncle David from the TV console. It pounced in seven houses on Plum Street. In the eighth house Derek held a conversation. "I have achieved a certain position now. I have made my way and it wasn't easy. Of course, I'm handsome, and that helps. Now I have this house." The inflatable doll appeared to be doing a sit-up. Now at least she was hot enough. Only the baby in Adelaide Herkimer's arms sensed that something was not right. But how does a baby express this uneasiness? It hasn't yet learned to speak. It could cry, but to this baby that seemed vain and self-indulgent in the light of everything else that was happening. Bushmill loved it when Uncle David started to snore. He switched off the sound and bounded gleefully round and round the chair where Uncle David sawed his wood. The badges on his uniform were luminous in the subdued light. Sophie Frielich despaired of ever dealing with the complications. Derek Elliott unplugged the doll and lay down on top of it. It was a rented doll. They rolled over and the doll lay on top of him. "You feel heavier tonight," he said. "You know we haven't been the same since the abortion. I feel as if I don't know you any more." The doll cooled slowly. Adelaide Herkimer lifted the lid. Now it was boiling. She dangled the baby over it by the back of its diaper. "Steam," said Adelaide. "Steam. Steam." As if she wanted the baby to learn the word. The baby's eyes flew open. It had never felt something like this before. "I'm sorry," said Derek Elliott, "for the mess I made." Narcisso Gutierrez swung his rented Camaro onto the expressway and headed South. The lights of an American city yellowed the Eastern horizon. He suddenly felt sad. It suddenly felt peculiar to have a feeling. He hadn't expected his life to turn out this way. To pounce or not to pounce was Bushmill's dilemma. Uncle David slept in his own chair. So deep the sleep that he didn't hear the footsteps of the _____ approaching the map of El Salvador on the console from the rear.

Please read the instructions carefully before you fill in the blank, then tear off along the perforations.

Looped in Oaxaca

The time to leave was here and gone. Another cup of Mezcal, señor; in fact, bring us a jug. The borders of Oaxaca have been closed and we stay here forever, alas. We were almost away. Drink up, Zippo, my love. Tomorrow, suddenly, is not another day. For instance, that shawl you bought yesterday, you weren't going to wear it till you got home; well, put it on. And those old pants, mine, so sexy and baggy on you, that you wore for a joke here in the mornings, we thought we'd toss them to make room in our pack for yet another gorgeous sarape, that luckily we haven't paid for. Now they're your private pants. That sarape money will have to last, if bucks is still money in Oaxaca. Let's relax and drink another 'copa'. The exits are sealed, and it's too late to stop. This is politics. How do you feel? I feel peculiarly politically motivated. Seven days have passed since we first heard, and seven jugs of Mezcal. That's enough, I say, no more of this. Ahimé, Zippo, too late. 'More of this' is all we get. More tortillas. More salsa. More frijoles. More marimba, bimba. Gringos forever, Zippo. More and more molé. Have another copa. And señor, you are my best friends in the world and I love the whole world and the world is my great friend, amigos. Now let's fight. Quick, Zippo, immediately start to draw something in your new sketchbooks, particularly Oaxaca, particularly that Oaxaca you knew before you ever saw this Oaxaca. Oaxaca in your mind as you remember it when we were still free of what we know now that the borders are closed. What else is worth doing now? This here is a little copa of Mezcal. Show what it was before it closed on us. I will write a caption for your illustrations as best I can, and in that way maybe we can get some rescue, bug out of this place, but not before we finish this jug, baby. Such a sweet trap, this. So relaxing. And God bless you, next jug of Mezcal. You drink this down to the worm. Did you draw the worm? How about a tree in your Oaxaca? Live oak? Palm tree? Jacaranda in bloom? Is the señora there carrying her wicker tray of watermelon wedges on her head? Do the stone-masons work all night long to finish the Zocalo? Jojoba bush perhaps. Does this policeman stand under the tree in a bead of sunlight? Standing in a blue uniform without shoes? Did you put some noisy trucks into it? Do the tabacaleros march into your picture? Are they on strike today? When do the cops break them up? Does the waiter have a glass eye, the one who brings you something else, until you figure out that you order something else if you want to get what you want? Will you put seven different flowers in it? Is this the orchid family? Is this your family, panicking in the states? Does that horn honk under your colored pencils? Does that machine on the Zocalo quit when the militant speeches of the campesinos begin? Does justice enter your picture, with honest wages? Does this drawing rectify for the campesino the devaluation of the peso? Is the gringo threatened? Can we run down a street that fills seven pages? Ahimé, Zippo, who can draw it fast enough, write it quick enough to escape as I thought we could before they actually closed Oaxaca around us. This is where art ends and life begins, or vice versa. Cripes, Zippo, draw some food, quick, I'm starving. Some frijoles and blandas at the train station. Did you get the train station in yet? Do your trains run on time? One train each evening? One train to Mexico? One jet to the world?

Taking the Cave Man Seriously

So there they are, in that well known zone, and all of them are floating on lines."

"You talk like hockey."

"It's no gone, man. It's someone's life."

"Sounds just as primitive."

"Listen to me, man. I'm talking magenta. I'm talking from day before dowdy to suddenly electric blue eyeshadow."

A white limo pulls up in front of the club and three men step out. The most elegant is a woman dressed like a man. Her name is Myrtle, a name she hates. She hates her parents who named her Myrtle, and thinks it must have been out of spite because they wanted a boy. Though she is dressed now as a man she nonetheless insists they all call her Myrtle. Him Myrtle. She likes Him as a name. Horace admonishes them not to register revulsion or astonishment once they get inside. Horace is a name one can resent as well, though he never thinks about it. That's his name.

"How big?"

"I'm talkin' great big. I mean the woman fills the whole entrance. I'm talkin' ample."

"Now you're getting real descriptive."

"Really. But you should get the whole picture, man. Him too, moving like a mink, banging away. All of them floating on lines."

They press the bell and wait. Claude gazes at Myrtle. He has difficulty seeing her as a man, though she is all spit and polish. He can't call her Him, because he sees her only as the woman he loves. Thus can love penetrate the most wilful disguise. Him is the woman he continually undresses with his eyes. Horace explains that once they get inside they will see people in bizarre situations, ordinary people doing things strange. It is incumbent on them, Horace admonishes, to be nonchalant, keep their cools, to avoid a twitch.

"Flabbiness, I mean gross. At one point she rolls out her tongue and licks all the interior; I mean, grundgy. I mean this is your average contented homemaker on the rampage."

"Why should I be interested in this? I watch a lot of sports. I'm not that kind of person. I use my time with absolute precision."

"A big fat tub of warts slides across the floor on her tongue. You'll change your mind. I've seen it before."

"I think you hate women. You always have to remember your mother is a woman. Why can't you talk about ordinary people?"

"My mother is not an ordinary person. These people are. It's the men too. No one is exempt from the little secret stuff closeted away here and there. That's why this is so great here, and when all of them are banging on lines, floating in that well known zone..."

"What well known zone? Sometimes you talk like a millionaire."

"Sometimes I feel like a millionaire, buster."

They ring again and once more. The wait makes Him (Myrtle) even more nervous about passing. Only Horace of the three of course has come here before. Claude came along of course just to be with Myrtle (Him). Him (Myrtle) is on the verge of suggesting they forget it and leave, when the security window opens and she is hit by a puff of air that smells of something oozing up for milleniums to reach the surface of the earth. A face with the complexion of a smashed goldfish appears in the square aperture.

"Well I have to admit that once I met a person, a woman like that, who did something like that. A nice woman, of superior intelligence. I liked her."

"I'll bet you did."

"Her first boy-friend was the worst. Before they did anything he liked to burn garbage in front of the TV. And she was right there too. Right in that zone."

"Which zone?"

"You know. Same zone. Banging on lines. Floating. But then she married a guy who applied his computer knowledge to making pasta. Now he rivals Ronzoni."

The door opens for Horace, Him (Myrtle), and Claude. Horace steps over the threshold. Myrtle (Him) and Claude hesitate. They have never smelled an interior so absolutely musty, and for one insecure moment Him (Myrtle) takes Claude's hand and squeezes it. When she lets go she feels a bang of courage and steps over the threshold into the well known zone. Following Myrtle (Him), Claude floats on a line of inexplicable joy.

NORMAN LAVERS

Rumors

> I observed, that though we are satisfied that [Bishop Berkeley's] doctrine is not true, it is impossible to refute it. I never shall forget the alacrity with which Johnson answered, striking his foot with mighty force against a large stone, till it rebounded from it, 'I refute it *thus.*'

The asylum, I believe, is located near the old Hearst Castle. The story we hear is that when the Hearsts lived there they kept herds of African animals in their parks, but now, we are told, only a few zebras remain for the tourists, the others having died or been given to zoos. But the hyenas escaped at some early time—this is the rumor—and now live in wild bands in the foothills.

My window faces inland, but when the wind is right, there is a sound which I am certain is the crashing of the sea mixed with the high yelps of gulls, and a smell which I fancy is the iodine smell of the seaweed.

There is no need to conjecture about the hyenas. They are outside my window every night with their quiet woo-wooing, and the dull irregular throbbing of their feet. By day the bone-white mounds of feces catch the light, and are visible from any distance, if you know what you are looking for. Far from being cowardly scavengers as fabled, the latest studies—I have read them all—tell us they are formidable hunters with awesome jaws, fine teamwork, and the ability to look into a milling game herd and spot the single animal with a flaw. Then they are able to run forty miles an hour until that animal can no longer keep up with the herd and begins to flag. At once one has seized the doomed beast by the tail. When it balks, others come around and grasp it by the face, holding it out straight while the alpha animal, perhaps an old female with stretched gut and swinging nipples, begins ripping the entrails out through the anus. Shock mercifully deadens all pain, we like to think. The animal has been partially eaten by the time it stumbles and falls.

My ground-floor window has a heavy steel grating over it, bolted to the frame from the inside, and I have a special wrench which is for keeping the bolts tight. In this respect we are not prisoners, or rather, we are incarcerated voluntarily, for the same wrench could be used to remove the grill, and it would be an easy matter to step outside—to the hyenas. Evidently it is what many do after a while, when they can no longer endure staying inside. I am a long way from that point myself, and keep the bolts as tight as I can. Just from ground tremors, or flexion of the building, they loosen up slightly overnight, so it is a matter of constant checking.

At first if the hyenas caught the least glimpse of me in the window, they would melt away like ghosts, even in the brightest moonlight. Later they became nonchalant, realizing I was no threat, and led their doggy lives right before me, and I began studying them avidly. They are constantly vocal, quietly whining and wooing, adding, when they want, loud cackles, chuckles, and falsetto growls. The greeting ceremonies are particularly remarkable. The dominant males stand still with impressively long erections, which the others take turns sucking. My theory is—probably this is a subjective projection—that when an older dominant animal begins to think about the power of those jaws that are around his penis, he stops being able to have erections, and at that point loses dominance.

By day I tend to my correspondence. At the moment I have three letters to answer. This from my wife:

> Dearest Husband, The wolves [to her they seem like wolves] howled outside my window all night last night. At

two I heard a loud scrabbling at my grate, and when I looked, one had pried open a corner and had his paw and part of his muzzle in the room. I admit I was quite frightened, but I got up and shouted, and he withdrew, though I could see him sitting on he ground outside, watching me. My fingers were trembling, but I managed to get the nut or screw thing back in and tightened it. I went around the grating tightening all of them. I had forgotten to check for several nights, and some of them were almost falling off. I know you will say this is foolish, but you simply can't expect me to devote my whole life to such trivia. It really begins to seem less and less important whether they get in or not.

This from my son:

Hi Dad, Well, the same thing has happened again, and I suppose you will just have to go ahead and be mad at me all over again, though I don't know what good that will do. The fact is the money you sent me to register for this semester is all spent, and I haven't registered yet. Yes, I've been up to some bad things, seriously bad this time. Dad, your little boy has gone and went and tried some heroin. I mean it, the whole trip, needle and all. What was it like? It made me remember once when I was little and I woke up to find that I had started wetting the bed. I thought to myself, well, I've done it now, so I might just as well go and do a good job of it. If you want to, you can send me more money for school, but I can't guarantee I'll use it for that. I have a strong feeling that if I take another shot of heroin I might just let go and decide that's what I want to do from now on.

This from my daughter:

Dear Father, I am not writing you this last letter because I feel I "owe" it to you. I don't feel I owe you anything. Then why am I writing? I suppose I just don't like loose ends of relationships left over. So this: from this moment I renounce you as my father, and see no point in either of us ever trying to get in touch with the other again. I have never approved of the things you did to Mom, or to Steve and me. When I was young, you frightened me. Now you only embarrass me. So goodbye, and thank God it is ended at last.

In the past letters like these gave me great pain and disquiet. That was back when I believed I had a family, and that the members of that family wrote these letters. But the best guess now is that one of the staff here writes them as a kind of therapy, to take my mind off the hyenas. Obviously that completely changes my reponse to them. Now I see them first of all as positive acts of kindness and concern, objects designed with care and intelligence to have a beneficial effect, by getting me outside of myself and my own narrow worries. And secondly, I can enjoy them as art, as little poems. More than that, for they involve me in their creation. I must put myself in their tinseled world, worry about their predicaments, and frame answers that will be of some aid to them. It is more like a group novel that we are writing together. I have to believe in them (in a way) as I am answering them, but at one and the same time keep an aesthetic overview, designing, let's say, "probable" answers for them in something recognizably and consistently like "my" voice.

"Novel" and "poem" are a bit high-flown. Unfortunately whoever writes the letters, well-meaning as he intends to be, is a bit repetitive, and the influences on him are less those of high art than they are of soap opera. But perhaps he is adjusting his level to what he believes my level is. Anyway, I enjoy it, so what does it matter. I envy him his job. I would love to be the one who invents the family and their problems from day to day.

How shall I answer the letters? My own answers have not been such as to push the ghost writer to great heights. I too have been repetitive and predictable. I suppose I have been afraid that if I really stepped out of character, it might end the game, he might not know how to answer, or worse, might feel I was showing my boredom and disgust, when the very opposite would be the case, when really what I want is some sign of *him*. I decide on an experiment, and answer the letters in this uncharacteristic way:

> Dearest Wife, I have been accorded a peek behind the scenes, and have been let into a discovery that I would not have believed in any other way than testing it with my own senses: the "wolves" as you call them do not in fact exist. It is part of the stage managing here. They are trained dogs, utterly friendly and harmless, tail-wagging softies. The rumors were given us to deprive us of our freedom, or desire to escape, to make us believe we were better off where we were, no matter how cruelly and monotonously constrained. I have been going out at night for lovely romps, and one night simply will not return.

> Dear Son, I have gone through the scientific literature on heroin and what I find is that it does no systemic damage at all, and as long as a steady supply is available to an addict, he need suffer no bad effects, and can live a completely normal life. The only dangers are the social ones of arranging to put your hands on the immense amounts of money necessary to obtain heroin illegally, and secondly the health dangers attendant on getting impure heroin, or of infecting yourself with a dirty needle. But it is common, for instance, for doctors to accidentally become addicted, and go on supplying themselves at cost, and continue their careers without any problem. My aunt Harriet's son-in-law is a doctor, and I have arranged for him to supply you with heroin at cost (very nominal, about $1.50 for a normal dosage), and for you to go to his office to have it professionally administered. I am sending more money, and see no reason why you can't enroll in classes, and continue your heroin habit on the side. It's better for you, and probably cheaper, than a cigarette habit would be.

> Dear Daughter, Let me set you free from any lingering guilt you may have for "renouncing" me, as you put it. The truth is when I married your mother, she was already three

months pregnant with you by some other man whose identity I never knew. I knew about this in advance, let me hasten to say. There was no attempt on your mother's part to fob you off on me. I wanted to marry her, so I accepted the situation. I have not minded paying for your food, lodging, education, and so on, but never considered you my daughter, nor, you see, need you worry about considering me your father.

These letters gave me so much pleasure, the pleasure in composing them, and the pleasure of anticipating The Writer's surprise, perhaps delight, at them, that I slept soundly for the first night since I can remember, and for that reason did not once hear any of the goings on outside my window.

But I received no replies to the letters. This was a worry. Perhaps he recognized that I was on to him, and then, perhaps by their rules, his letters would no longer be considered therapeutic, so he would devote his time to writing to other inmates, where his labors would do some good.

It was the chance I had taken, and now great voids of time opened up to me. I dozed during the day, having sweaty dreams, and at night, wide awake, sat before the grating. During this season a white dripping fog came in before sunset, and did not lift till late in the morning of the next day. I strained my ears, and heard the quiet woo-wooing, the throbbing feet, the human-sounding screams of the prey animal at the moment of disembowelment. Once the scream sounded uncannily like the voice of my wife, and I had a moment of terrifying doubt, quickly forgotten, however, when a single hyena emerged from the fog to appear under my window. Though only four or five feet separated us, he did not actually seem to see me. He held his nose up and sniffed noisily, smelling, perhaps tasting in advance, the excrements inside my intestine. I felt my groin contract.

And then, very thoughtfully, he stood on his hind legs and placed his thick white teeth on the slender bars of my grating (had I tightened the bolts?) and pulled back as hard as he could. There was very little give, and after a moment he released his bite, dropped back on his forelegs, and trotted off.

In the morning, I had three letters.

Dearest Husband, You have been an inspiration to me, but only to push me in the direction I knew I would take sooner or later. If the worst should happen, I don't want you to feel the slightest responsibility. Feel responsible only for the happiness I have now. On this night just passed, a night as you may have noticed yourself, of balmy breezes and clear moonlight, I removed the grating from my window, removed the nightgown from my body, and stepped outside. "This is what freedom is," I thought. I was deliciously aware of my body, of the bouncing of my breasts, the breeze riffling the feathers between my legs. I ran a few steps, and of course suddenly they were all around me, running with me. I was frightened only for the first instant. They had broad, intelligent foreheads, which I did not quite dare to stroke. I stood quite still. One came behind me, and got up on his hind legs, and pushed me over onto my hands and knees. I waited with my eyes closed until he touched me with his muzzle. I jumped again slightly, this time not with fear, and he nuzzled and licked me very quietly for a moment, and then they all trotted on. I'm going out again tonight. You were so right, husband, so right.

Hi Dad, I didn't know what to make of your letter. I thought you had finally flipped the old dinghy for sure this time. But for some reason you just stopped me cold turkey. I just stood there. It was so *unexpected*. What's happened is, I've registered for school, I've started classes, and I'm *liking* it. How do I feel? Like when I was a little kid once, I somehow remember standing up and hugging your knees and giving you a big wet smooch!

Dear Father (or whoever?), Well, here I am again, as good as my word usually is. I simply couldn't let your last letter, with its astounding revelation, go uncommented on. Why was I never told this? (If it's true?) Don't you see how it changes everything, explains everything, makes you the decent hero rather than the cold villain? Tells me at a stroke why you never seemed to be enough of a father, and yet were too much father to be something else, something I ate my heart out wishing that you might be. Am I giving away too much already? I want to see you. Is that possible? I would like to rise up on my bestial legs, and lace my fingers behind your neck, and look into your eyes. I have never dared look into your eyes, did you know? Perhaps you know why now.

I was thrilled reading these letters, which proved to me once and for all, not only that they were all written by the same person, but that that person wished me to know it. The repetition in each letter of words to the effect of rising up, or anyway getting up, or somehow standing on the hind legs, was the conclusive proof I had been waiting for. The mathematical odds against this almost identical wording occurring in each letter by chance was too remote to be worth considering. Nor could so canny a writer have done it through inadvertence, but can only have meant it as a message to me. Ideally, we might have stretched our growing awareness of each other over a series of increasingly transparent letters, but in sudden recklessness, I decided to shorten the process, to write directly to him at once, because time was running out for me.

For as a counterpoint to my exertions I noted these changes: from the dense fogs at night, water stood on the bars of my grating during the day, and pockets of rust were burrowing under the black paint to the vulnerable metal below. Little showed on the surface, a few orange blisters, but I knew long mushroom filaments of rust-root were traveling beneath the paint. And this evening, when I gave my bolts an extra turn, one crossed a certain threshold of tightness, and suddenly was loose again, threads stripped, and the remaining three bolts must hold against the leverage of that corner, against an evolutionary history of increasing sophistication in discovering flaws.

Dearest Wife, I see no reason for further subterfuges between us. Let us throw off all disguises and meet each other frankly.

Dear Son, I see no reason for further subterfuges between us. Let us throw off all disguises and meet each other frankly.

Dear Daughter, I see no reason for further subterfuges between us. Let us throw off all disguises and meet each other frankly.

The fat, as they say, was in the fire. This was the most exciting part of my life though perhaps so close to the end. But an end that would be a beginning? This is what I felt myself so near to discovering.

For two nights, the hyenas gathered in unprecedented numbers in the field outside my window, as if for some hyaenid convocation. Rival bands growled and snickered at each other, and there were sudden, brief screeching tug-of-wars at boundaries, followed by careful marking of ground with feces and urine. Then:

Dearest Husband, I am coming to you nakedly. Watch for me outside your window. Won't we have a good romp in the moonlight!

Hi Dad, Well, you've done it again. You're pretty sharp after all. How did you find out? I didn't care so much about others finding it out, but for some reason I especially didn't want you to know. I know you won't believe this, but I always wanted to do something that would make you proud of me—and now *this*. Anyway, you'll be relieved to know I'm not a practicing fag. I've stayed way back in the closet. So no one but you will ever know. I've withdrawn from school. Got most of my tuition refunded, using it all for the old silver needle, which, you'll have to admit, is at least better than the other thing that I might have done.

The third letter, sealed, my name on the outside, was enclosed in a police department report describing my daughter's death by defenestration.

Dear Father, Your last letter has filled me with more joy than you can know. Or perhaps you can know? Perhaps you are feeling it yourself? That is my hope. I address you as "father" with a wonderful sense of wickedness now, now that I know you are not, that the unholiest of desires I have so long hidden is no longer unholy. Do not expect an awkward and ignorant virgin, "Father," who will not know how to delight you. I have done everything ("no reason for further subterfuges" you wrote), because everything has seemed so much less than what I really wanted, so that the worst thing I could do only, in a funny way, brought me closer to that worst thing I could not do, brought me closer to you. Now I only want our bodies to merge. I want to be engulfed by you, to take you into my sex, into my mouth, into my

The typescript breaks off, and there follows a pencil scrawl, which wavers and then drops at a sloping angle towards the bottom corner of the page: "I was always the thorough one, wasn't I, always had to know everything to the last drop. I stopped in mid sentence, and went down to the courthouse and looked at the marriage records, the date of your marriage to Mom, fully a year and a half before I was born."

The fog presses like a white emptiness against the sweating bars of my grate. The hyenas are especially vocal, and must be gathered in the largest numbers ever, to judge by the sound. I am humming and whistling to myself, occasionally singing out loud snatches of old songs I had forgotten. The woo-wooing reaches a brief crescendo, I hear a scuffle, and in the midst of it my wife's voice saying my name, then a choked scream of sudden terror. Oh, it is uncanny how convincing it is! I could touch it, I could put my hand on that voice. But I have seen through to the other side. The truth at last. It lay there for many nights waiting for me to discover it. The three letters with their nearly identical expressions of the idea of standing up that I had thought so convincing a proof of an *other*. Had I not, before receiving them, formulated an astoundingly similar phrase, in describing the hyena getting up on its hind legs to try its teeth in my grill? I am not good at math, but I believe in it. If the odds against that idea occurring in three separate letters at the same time was remote, how staggeringly remote is the chance that it was an idea I had just had on my own tongue? There is only a single conclusion possible: that no other or others wrote those letters, that I created them myself, just as I have created this room, this grating, the wet droplets of fog I imagine that I feel against my face.

And last, and most liberatingly: just as I created the gross ungainly trotting creatures outside my window. As final proof of which, I now remove the bolts from my grate, and step laughing out amongst them, prepared to kick the first one I cross with all my strength, convinced now in my heart that my foot will pass through it as through the thinnest gossamer of deception.

MARK LEYNER

Ode to Autumn

the human bomb is ticking
the handsome blond robotic bomb with the gorgeous pecs and
    the cleft in his chin and the cute mustache is purring: tick
    tock tick tock tick tock
he puts a pinch of smokeless tobacco between his cheek and gum
    and watches a monarch butterfly mince gingerly across the
    hot hood of his idling chevy malibu
and little lovely winged electric razors hover about his head,
    gently kissing it until he is bald—and he dreams of john
    audubon and his lovely watercolor hummingbirds and his
    lovely watercolor chrysanthemums—though, unbeknownst
    to the human bomb, the ceramic cranium developed for him
    by japanese high tech ceramics engineers to protect his brain
    is beginning to crack, so that really his watercolor dream of
    john audubon is not a dream at all but an aberrant pattern
    of electrical discharge generated by moisture seeping through
    the fissures in his glazed skull
and unbeknownst to the human bomb, he's been tampered with
    by terrorists who've rigged his detonator to his prostate
    gland, so the instant he ejaculates—boom!

it is autumn
and i am remembering autumn nights long ago when we
    watched those early episodes in which the handsome human
    bomb was motionlessly posed in the men's department at

macy's in a van heusen cream colored button-down, pierre
cardin pindot lambswool tie, a nut brown ralph lauren
shetland wool sweater, stanley blacker corduroy sportcoat,
and bass weejun tassel front brown leather slip-ons regu-
larly $68 now on sale for $54.40
you were just a flag twirler at pocahontas high in mahwah
it was homecoming night when i met you
i remember you giggling shyly at the seniors bobbing for veal
      medallions in a metal basin of marsala sauce
you smelled of lilacs
though soon the air was churned into a gamy froth by members
      of the fencing team dueling with skewers of shish kebab
that night we learned that ecstasy means the collapse of time
past present future perceived in a single instant
you were watching the trajectory of your own words as they left
      your mouth
words which disappeared into the horizon
words which, due to the curvature of space, returned many years
      later like murmuring boomerangs to your ear
you looked like an italian starlet—jet-black hair in a thick braid
      down your back, sloe-eyes set deeply above high cheek
      bones, olive complexion, full sensuous lips, the strap of
      your nightgown fallen languorously off your shoulder,
      mascara smeared, your eyelids heavy with drowsiness, your
      hair now spread across the pillow like a trellis of vines, your
      voice low and husky, your breath still redolent of anisette
and tonight as we watch television on the porch
your buckteeth seem shellacked in the cadmium light of the
      harvest moon

look at the screen
that's me with the amulets and anaconda pelts and the saucer-
      size lip plug distending my mouth
that's me crouched in the back seat of the human bomb's chevy
      malibu with his chubby friend ulrike grunebaum
though, without the proper software, ulrike grunebaum is like
      mrs. potato head—without eyes, ears, nose, or mouth,

without id or libido, without creed or lineage—a featureless and vacant globe of flesh

but with the proper software, she is ulrike grunebaum the chillingly eloquent marxist ideologue and machiavellian technocrat in a gray three-piece suit and red necktie ruthlessly purging the upper echelons of her ruling politburo

with the proper software, she is ulrike grunebaum executive curator of the jimi hendrix museum in baden-baden

and with the proper software—with a twist of the joystick—she is ulrike grunebaum, the hamburg erotic film queen whose screen credits include "smell me tomorrow," "the edible fixation," "we'll be nude at noon," and "the odyssey of gomer"

we're taste-testing four varieties of lebanese halvah: druse, phalangist, sunni, and shiite

the flecks of shrapnel in the phalangist halvah give it an unusually nutty flavor

we're doing our cellulite exercises; we're doing the nine or ten beautifully firming things you can do for your derriere

they're showing the video we made together for mtv in which i play the naughty pse&g man who's been discovered by ulrike rummaging through her laundry hamper sniffing her brassieres and ulrike wraps her prehensile eyelashes around my delicate reed of a penis and slowly and erotically strangles it until its head is the brilliant red of autumn sumac leaves

when i put my ear against ulrike's temple, i can glean her thoughts—because her thoughts are transmitted in the morse code of her pulsing arteries

the human bomb throws his hot dog in the bushes

i'm about to say something horrible, something horribly unchristian...and please don't start singing, because no amount of mouthwash can camouflage the foul breath of hymn-singing christians...

this is my horrible statement: there's mustard in the bushes

your eyes follow the squiggle of yellow mustard to an ant who's
about to be squashed beneath a shiny tooled-leather tony
lama cowboy boot and the ant looks directly into the
camera and says in yiddish with english subtitles "i want to
live as much as you do"—and this image traumatizes the
country in the 1980's as much as the image of my head
rolling from the guillotine saying "i'm sorry mommy, i'll be
good" traumatized the country in the 1960's
i am on every channel and that infuriates you
that i have the ability to jump out of the television screen,
burrow into your uterus, and emerge nine months later tan
and rested bugs you very much
you're using the violent vocabulary of the u.s.a., you're violently
chewing your cheeze doodles and flicking the remote
control
a computer programmer and mother of two from bethesda,
maryland puts her fingers through the holes in my head and
bowls me further still from jerusalem . . . yerushalayim, city
of peace, from whose ramparts my stream of urine is like an
arching parabola of diamonds
i'm rolling through roanoke, city of rheumatism and alzheimer's
disease; through memphis, city of ulcerated tongues and
saliva turned bitter and glutinous; through pine bluff,
whose inhabitants store the ashes of their cremated dead in
those white cardboard cartons with thin metal handles
made for chinese take-out food; through shreveport, whose
population lacks the enzyme necessary to break down
spaghetti
i appear on the phil donahue show with other children of parents
who'd had unsuccessful tubal ligations and vasectomies
my path connects every dot in texas

—oh dear, i'm quite lost; kind sir, can you tell me where i am?
—my, you're a peculiar sight young man, you're balding but so
pretty, are you gay?
—no sir, i have a cute girlfriend at home who is waiting for me;
please tell me where i am and lend me a quarter so i can call
home and reassure my sweetheart that i have not been slain

–i am ordinarily the very soul of munificence, young friend, but today you find me rather strapped for cash or coin... perhaps in lieu of this phone call you will retire with me to a public lavatory and i will initiate you into the splendors of synchronized swimming

–i repeat with all respect sir that i am not homosexual; who are you, sir, and... who are you?

–i am not an octopus or a hen

–that i can see... nor a crayfish

(later)

–things didn't did they? i mean turn out the way you expected

–no, i was incapable of accepting my mother's death and i frantically embraced fundamentalist judaism because i refused to accept a world in which people were so completely vulnerable and so capriciously arbitrarily victimized, i refused to endorse the purposelessness and the randomness and i rushed into the arms of the paternalistic teleological belief-system of my ancestors, of my parents, the very same judaism i'd so contemptuously eschewed my whole life— but even my newfound jewishness was fugitive

–how tall were you before your mother passed away?

–i was five-seven

–and the day after your mother passed away?

–four-one

–and today?

–today i am eight inches in diameter

–it sounds like you're going to disappear

–no, i'm in a perpetual state of contraction and expansion; now i'm contracting and just as i'm about to become smaller than anything, smaller than even the most infinitesimal sub-atomic particle, i'll begin to expand and i'll expand and expand and expand until there's literally no more room for me in the universe and my head is knocking against the ceiling of the space-time continuum and then i'll start to contract again and so on and so forth

i'm rolling down the pacific coast of south america, but i never make it to tierra del fuego i'm a gutter ball

i was made in hong kong

i have reached a level of unparalleled ugliness—revolting
bloated oily ugliness which has metastasized across every
square inch of my body

sexual relations are impossible—i am hopelessly ugly, hopelessly silly

masturbation is impossible—my penis shrivels at my own touch
and i lack the most minimal powers of poetic imagination
necessary to conjure autoerotic fantasies

my gastrointestinal tract is listed as a must-to-avoid in the
michelin guide for intestinal parasites

wherever i am at the moment is the remotest frontier of the
diaspora

six flags, each depicting a still-frame from the zapruder film,
flutter above dealey plaza

and diffracted shards of sunlight impale the ornamental carp
who cough little bubbles of blood which cluster above the
pond's mosaic floor whose tiles of azure and crimson depict
an exploding head of ideas

as nearby, at james dean memorial hospital, nurses use cold
bottles of milk to cool the perspiring brows of surgeons who
are engraving ideas into the smooth tabula rasa brains of
fetuses

an idea being that which exists at the moment a flyball pauses at
the apex of its flight and bids the sky adieu...

that moment is pregnant

perhaps at that moment, in an s&m bar in plymouth, massachusetts, the 50 ft. woman straddles your face and defecates
17,000 scrabble letters fertilizing the fallow fields of your
imagination...

and a new american style is born

when dawn came it was as if we'd been delivered stillborn from
an assembly line

identically curled in our bed

our arms crooked in perfect symmetry beneath our pillows

we were like twin fossils

two tipsy vertebrates who had crawled into a tar pool in the wee
    hours of the pleistocene and slept through the tumult of
    history
in our mouths the rich creamy taste and texture of raw sea
    urchins, our breath was rank and aquatic
i pushed the hair from her forehead and her face was taut and
    limned in shadow like a death mask

when the forensic pathologists performed their autopsy on you
they cried, those hardened professionals,
because peeling the skin from your head
was like peeling the skin from an onion

the flesh between your breasts
was a thin and pasty dough
which yielded easily to their scalpels

your internal organs seemed as if they'd never been used
still bearing their price tags
like brand new merchandise from a department store

and the forensic pathologists, those hardened professionals,
shook their fists at the photographs of the 10 most wanted men,
one of whom murdered you, and wept

oh amy, what threnody matters
in a world whose software
enables a crossword puzzle, orphaned by your death,
to ask, "who now will do me?"

i am not roller skating through piles of brittle autumn leaves
i am roller skating down the aisles at macy's in narcotic slow
    motion to the music of john philip sousa
i'm skating past every surveillance camera
i'm skating across every closed circuit television screen
salesmen come and go murmuring "jerry lewis est mort . . . jerry
    lewis est mort"
if only i had the software to conjure one macy's salesgirl at the
    end of this endless corridor into whose arms i'd roller skate
    deliriously to the optimistic cornets of john philip sousa
but i don't have the appropriate software
and it would be brainless to continue skating

CLARENCE MAJOR

Tattoo

I am in the loop trying to find one of those little juke-joint tattooing places to have MANTEIV imprinted indelibly on my arm, the left, when I spot a familiar bouncy person sacked in a glossy red expensive silk skirt: Anita! half a block ahead of me, and my first impulse is to run, catch her. I push the tattoo to the back of my mind, I begin to trot: but I am quickly brought to a hesitating pace when I see Anita has stopped, up ahead, and is gaping into a shoestore showcase window. I come within two yards of her. There is something like a courtesan intensity in the dazzle of her eyes, they break the day with excitement, it's high noon. I move closer, I even *smell* her. She smells of sweat, and is throwing off beams, her mind is so loud it ticks the electric currents of her thoughts: "Oh my gooooooooooooodNESS!!! People are going by, refracted; the sun is working optics on daytime neons, the window before Anita is a two-dimensional globe, illuminated with shoes that (I can see from the reflection in her eyes) are so sparkling, so breathtaking, so flesh-like, so resplendent that they might any minute flat up and walk on air, pure light, weightless, shimmerings in eternity! I am only three inches from her. The sexual odor she throws off is humorous, its characteristics I am more than familiar with. I knew the footlights of this odor before I was inducted, I used to simmer in it. I am so aroused by the funky gentility of it that I uncontrollably reach out, my mantle-like tongue scores; I lick her cheek upward, careful to get every bead of sweat. She

155

responds to the craving of some inner voice, just beneath the surface of her mind; her hands, long, brown consuming fangs, scratch desperately at the plate glass. Reflected on the mirror of it I suddenly notice Hilda, going up State Street, driving a new 1966 Cadillac; she has her hair up in pincurls, her face is streaked by the ghostly presence of cold cream, and she is shouting with more intensity than a jet breaking the speed of sound: "By outward show let's not be cheated. An ass should like an ass be treated." I recognized the cheap lines, from Gay's *Fables*. The traffic comes to a complete stop. I try to detect the flicker in Hilda's eye, the one I can see, but I get only her profile; and whose car? She certainly doesn't own a hog! Poor Anita, who has begun to blaze like a meteoric substance, is making the feline scratching and purring sounds of a kitten on glass. "Oh god!" she insists. I open whatever possibility of understanding I have, and watch it go out to her as on a puffy cloud, like the kind hanging over Little Lulu or Henry (in the cartoons of our American spirits). In my cloud. I am affectionately trying to hyphenate into Anita, who, though I begin to shake her arm gently but with persistence, is weeping the largest landmarking tears I believe I will ever witness as she nibbles without restraint at the glass that is keeping her from the beautiful shoes! She works with surgical skill, her teeth are cutting like a glass-cutter. "Baby, these goddamn things ain't where it's at! Baby, *please, please!* control yourself! What about pure progress, what about psychology, knowledge, what about experimental methods, huh, and equality, and ideals, law and naturalism, what about peace, huh, what about optimism, revolution—what about revolution, huh, answer me that, willya, what about the universe, wisdom, words, what about curiosity and democracy, tell me, Anita, what about interaction and interdependence, huh? Huh, Anita, huh?" These words hover almost directly above my head so she'll know I am saying them. But she ain't got hip to my presence yet, and the cars, piled up ten miles South, jammed all the way to the viaduct where 63rd Street crosses State, just because Hilda has spotted us, she is shouting and waving. She has one of those big limp, *"How yawl doin'?"* grins.

I suddenly feel sluggish, realizing that Anita has gotten her arm through the glass, without cutting the substance, without even ruffling the sleeve of her white blouse. She is groaning, hissing, gasping with admiration, as she picks up a pair of fashionable semi-high heel white pumps that reflect the showcase lights, as well as the gentle, natural phosphorescences. Anita murmurs as she lifts the shoes and holds them close to her womb, "Oh god!" Her eyes are shut.

I feel too clouded, I can't speak; Hilda's shouting jumps through the pause in the honking of horns but I do not realize that she is addressing Anita until I see the familiar words, lifted directly from Shakespeare's *Macbeth,* bounce off Anita's solar system, refusing to penetrate it. The words: "A dagger.of the mind, a false creation, / Proceeding from the heat-oppressed brain?" And though I knew she was, in her dally-dally popular-quotations way, trying to warn her old college schoolmate of the danger of lust for clothes, because, before those words even hit the ground, to melt under the glorious energies of Shamash, Ormuzd, Merodach, Tezcatlipoca, Ra or Helios or whatever you call the source of life, the sounds became visible, like sound waves on the wing of a jet the moment it begins to break the sound barrier.

Before this instantaneous transformation can take place, Hilda shoots with flippant confidence the huge cliché from Cervantes: "All that glitters is not gold!" But the vapory quality of it bombards even my mass media condensed sensibilities, as I find myself tugging at Anita's edges, any place I can get a grip. I'm almost climbing up on her like a zealous patriot lusting up the Statue of Liberty. As she's holding up the glossy white shoes, people continue to go by, passersby. Loop walkers, housewife shoppers, looking for the out of season White Sales in all the department stores. Everything WHITE, electric WHITE, is being sold in pairs of seven, seven anything you can think of, seven shoes, three pairs and an extra one for the good luck seven brings, is on a huge LIMITED HURRY HURRY WHITE SALE WHITE SALE LADIES DAY TODAY FREE PARK-ING IN THE LOOP!!! The honking horns! Hilda's at my ear screaming, having left the white Cadillac still blocking traffic: *"Make her listen!"* But Anita's whimpering, as she licks the white-painted leather, murmuring, "Oooooooooh gosh."

Anita kicks off her shoes, Hilda begins to click her tongue, *"Tut tut—"* and she quotes Swift: "She looks as if butter wouldn't melt in her mouth." But I don't get it, at first, until I detect the critical look of one woman *at* another. Anita's wonderland-like solar system continues to protect her from communication as she wallows in the possessive lust for the new footwear she is slipping into, saliva dripping from her mouth. She stands on one bare foot, holding a shoe in each hand; her left leg bent, she forces the tight shoe on, drops her foot, stands on it, repeats the process with the other one, drooling as she steps back in order to see herself reflected in the showcase glass, and I simply stand here dumbfounded, watching also the footlights reflected in her eyes; but when I look at the actual display window I can't see anything theatrical.

People are pouring out of cars, coming toward Hilda. Time and space are being mastered: all this takes place twenty-one times faster than anyone is ready to think. "What's the matter with her, has she let all this whitewash-advertising all this bullshit drive her insane?" snaps Hilda, looking more each minute like the great entertainer Pearl Bailey standing there with that: "Now, ain't dat somethin!!" look on her bulletproof kisser. A man with UPPER-INCOME stamped on the front of his white shirt, unobstructed by his necktie, socks Hilda dead in the money-signs in her eyes. Some of the stars are so phenomenal they crash into me, as they shoot out from the blow. It seems to be done in slow motion, because I can almost count the stars. And he's bitching: "Lady driver! Lady driver! Lady driver!" and right in rhythm to his words Hilda bounces, still on her feet, around and around like a punching bag, in a purple dress. Anita moves a little north on the pavement, just as the shoe salesman comes out, rubber-neck style. His cry, *"How do you know they fit?"* But Anita, always on her ps and qs, seems tickled *chocolate* and privileged to inform him: "Because they fit." And I, like some kind of link in a fragment of conversation, say "If."

Meanwhile forty-two men with the same sign, UPPER-IN-COME attached to them, work in groups of seven, piledriving the weights of their frustrations from urban leisure, down, down, down on the beaten down purple, screeching form of what still looks like Hilda, despite the blood. I am outraged: I charge toward them. I hit an invisible wall, bounce off and fall on the sidewalk at Anita's new shoes, that, like twins, suddenly turn their toe-tips just enough to look me in my morally defeated eyes; seeing my tramp version of manhood, they say to me, "Mother-fucker, we should kick you in yo ass-ss! Git over dah and help that woman!" I feel deep shame, knowing the shoes are correct. "You jus gone lay dah and let dem hunkies strike lightenin' in that sister's head?" Hilda, at my eye level, on the ground, only a few steps away, is calmly trying to pacify my four centuries of guilt, spitting out blood and teeth with her words. "Don't worry—*we shall overcome!* Remember the mighty words of Wendell Phillips: 'Physical bravery is an animal instinct; moral bravery is a much higher and truer courage.'" But it's no consolation. I even see Moke in one of the groups of seven, he's grinding his fist into his palm, impatiently waiting for his group's turn. I leap up, try to penetrate the wall again: but Anita's hand grabs my shoulder. "Listen, nigger, you're my nigger; where you think you're going? You gone pay for this shit, what'd you think you're for, anyway, *huh,* tell me, *huh?* You see this man standing here waiting for his money, give *it* to him. He ain't got all day, the stuff he wants makes the world go 'round." But my attention is split between Hilda's assassination and Anita's demand.

With one last, fleeting glance over my shoulder toward the ritual killing, I see that a young man—it's Frank Engelmeyer!—has a vending cart around his neck, walking among the groups of angry drivers who are purchasing armbands from the runaway boy. Anita has taken out my wallet; meanwhile, I see each group is getting a name, labeling itself. All the names seem to ring a bell but I don't know why, I have a mental block. The armbands are blazing and glowing in the daylight, in natural colors of red, blue, and yellow: names like *Seven Champions,*

Seven Sages of Greece, Seven Bishops, Seven Against Thebes, The Seven Wise Masters, and so on; while police whistles and traditional police voices are blasting up and down State Street; I simply glance once—take it in: all of them have their backs turned to the seven years war against Hilda, on the sidewalk in a pool of mysterious looking blood that's beginning to clot into thousands of groups of corpuscles that jump around in a kind of wardance, chanting.

The shoe-salesman meanwhile seems disgusted, waiting, facing Anita with his hand extended, palm up; trying again to be profound, saying, "It doesn't matter that they are not specifically meant to be *crutches,* but what kind of currency is this?" She, so fascinated by her new shoes, looking down at them, turning this and that way, trying to see them from all angles, hasn't glanced at the money she places in his hand. I slap myself up side the head—Wham! "I forgot to tell you, Anita—" *"Tell me what, nigger?"* she hisses. I scrape my feet and bow a little to her. She shoots these words at me, the ABCs clogging up my resistance. The shoe salesman says, "I think he's trying to tell you—" She chops off his sentence in midair; "Just shut up and let the nigger tell me himself! That's why he's standing here acting like a damn fool now, 'cause you white men are always trying to speak for him!" Now, specifically to me: "What is it, Eli, what'd you do wrong now, that you want me to forgive you for, huh?" Her mouth is twisted to the left side of her face as far as she can turn it. But the disgust, this time, isn't really as gigantic as I've seen it get in her, when I used to "stand her up" back in 1958, '59, '60, when I was a rather optimistic civil-rights minded student at Roosevelt and I wasn't shaping up to her image of what the TV told her a good potential husband ought to be. That mouth would twist, and that head would turn, and she'd growl viciously, speechless with rage.

"It's the money—" the shoe salesman said. He's holding it toward her. I suddenly feel exposed. "DIDN'T I JUST TELL YOU TO KEEP YOU DAMN MOUTH SHUT? Huh, didn't I? *He can talk—*" I take a deep breath. The things of Hilda's resurrected blood, on the warpath, are seeping into the skin pores of the groups of men standing around the remains of her body. They are blood-curdling as they sting each one of these decent, upstanding, smart-looking, proficient assassins, with something instant-acting and deadly!

I'm trying to get my words out as the bodies behind me fall out like tin cans from an overloaded garbage bin going *clang,* each one marked up as a "natural accident" by the score-keeping Cosmic Energy Platoon of the resurrected Blood of the Lamb. I'm really astonished that I can take all of this action in a glimpse. All the more amazing because I never went to Perception school. Just took what came naturally. "Anita, I meant to tell you—" I hesitate, scratch my bushy hair. "I got my own *kinda* money." "*What? What* the fuck are you talking about nigger?" She looks for the first time at the fourteen paper bills she had placed in the bootsniffer's hand. "*What in hell is this?*" she shouts. "*Booker T. Washington!*" Old Booker's gentle face looks up at her from the one dollar bill on top. Where George Washington used to be, Booker calmly occupies the half-oval of the center of the Federal Reserve Note; across the top, just as usual, was THE UNITED STATES OF AMERICA, and to the left of the old mediator, "THIS NOTE IS LEGAL TENDER FOR ALL DEBTS, PUBLIC AND PRIVATE." Anita's eyes stretch! For one iota of a second I think she's going to scream, spit on and tear up the little stack of money in her hand; the next instant, it's clear: she's going through the bills furiously. "Eli, what is this bullshit? Huh? Where'd you get all this shit from, baby, come on, tell me, I'm getting sick! Just look at this crap— George Washington Carver on a two dollar bill! Little Black Sambo—I guess that's who this is, isn't it?—on a five dollar bill. *This is too much!* When I get myself together and start laughing, I know I'll never stop! Now—Who—is—this?" She looks up sharply. I try to duck the bullets of her eyes: but she shoots me, and her words too come like radioactive fallout, hitting me like a volley of doorknobs, squarely in the ears. She's holding the face of the paper note toward me. The white man is in shambles with gutlaughter, losing his, up until now, firmly-maintained cool. He slows up, chokes himself a little, cocking his ear toward me, waiting for the name to drop off my tongue. "It's *Willie,* you know, the guy who used to be in the movies." The shoe salesman is kicking over, choked with laughter, he falls against the wall of the building, holding his gut, the graceless spirits of his amusement leaping up out of him, in the form of lumpy little devils like the clergy used to chase around in the Middle Ages with butterfly nets. Anita is overcome. She is trying to hold back the urge to crack up. But she isn't going to make it. At this very moment I notice a blind white man coming up State from the intersection of Canal, wearing a wooden display-board on his chest, suspended from his neck. The message, obviously printed with the care given to a majestic and precious keepsake:

HEAR YE!   HEAR YE!   HEAR YE!
—Get Your Favorite Tattoo—
TODAY!
Engraved handsomely on any part
of your body! No Hold Barred!
We Will Make Permanent Designs
Of Anything, Person, Or Place
On The Most Secret Parts of
Your Skin!!!
Come to:
JOE'S TATTOO SHOP
& Amusement Center
777 S. State
Open 9 AM til 5 PM.
Suggestions:
1) Those who were born without
mothers, have your own favorite
mother *tatued* on your heart!
2) Those who survived Vietnam,
have the symbol of Patriotism
indelibly stamped on your forehead—
or if you prefer, Joe will
imprint his own original invention

of victory and national pride, the
word "MANTEIV"
Which really means Superman spelled
backwards, on one or both cheeks
of your posterior—
FOR THE LOW LOW PRICE
of just $7 per
etching!

* * * *

WITHOUT DOUBT!!! THE LOWEST BEST
PRICE IN TOWN!! FAST WORK
BY A SKILLED ARTIST
62 Years in
practice.
MONEY BACK GUARANTEE IF NOT
COMPLETELY SATISFIED!!!

* * * * * * *
* * *

PLEASE COME IN TODAY YOU WILL
NEVER REGRET THE MOVE!

!Surprise & Delight Your Friends!
—Endless Possibilities!—
"painless & fast healing, etc."

And as Anita goes insane with the wildest, bloodthirstiest kind
of mad-mad scientist cackle I have ever heard, letting my new
money float from her hand, I suddenly remember why I came
downtown. I wanted to get a souvenir of my military pain, just a
little token of my anti-heroic commitment to what I was doing
over there: just for myself, purely personal classified information. Anita and the shoe salesman are still laughing. I can see
them, reflected in a trick mirror across the street on the side of
the triple-deck Loop parking lot, and she's fat as the Tahitian

whore who propositioned me at the foot of a hill in San Francisco the day before I shipped out for the Far East, in 1961.

I stoop, pick up my empty wallet and bursting through the pack of side-walkers and traffic-gazers, weaving my way through the excitement-seekers, I catch up with the blind man with the advertisement. Several men from the Department of Sanitation are scraping up the last drops of Hilda, as whole squads of ambulances pull up, and speed away in vain, with the stacked-up bodies of all those first-class citizens who died natural American deaths. I touch the old, smelly, white port-reeking fragment of a man who surprises me when he turns, facing me, the whole surface of his face falls forward, a thin slab, dry and neat, like a little door, and it's actually on hinges. In it, on a flat, smooth, white slate-surface, printed neatly in black letters are these words:

WHH   BOP   SH   BAM
WHHBLYOP
WHH   BOP   SH   BAM
WHHBLYOP

And though I was born through these sounds, the character of the message, and the specific location of the scripture is still unknown.

URSULE MOLINARO

Apocalyptic Flirtation

He comes walking toward her from the far end of their street   across the sun-streaked avenue   with that peculiar aquatic shuffle of his: as though his feet were fins, gracefully slicing paved grey water. His motorcycle helmet sits in the crook of one arm. The other arm stretches wide in anticipation of their hug.

She checks his eyes. They're warm & shiny. She opens her arms. He's the most loving man she knows. They have more in common than the plausible couples. (They meditate together.) They're implausible only in the street.

"He must be stupid," two young Blacks tell each other, shaking their earrings as they pass him hugging her.

He hasn't heard them. Or, if he has, he isn't taking it for himself. They don't mean him: they're not into conventional street behavior. They're his brothers, dressed as he is in the uniform of the non-conforming. They've seen his earring.

A gold serpent biting its tail: the symbol of unending life. It was his idea for wedding bands; a surprise present for her on the third anniversary of their living together.

She had hers made into a regular ring, which she wears on her left little finger. She didn't want to have a pin stuck through one of her balance centers: she says.

He says: She was scared of the pain. Her fear of a pin prick is greater than her commitment to their relationship.

To which he is more committed than she is: he tells her: Or

else she'd let him work with her. On the new animal footage from Nairobi, instead of hiring the new assistant she just hired.

After firing the old one.

Who was probably sick of kowtowing to her bossiness. Wasn't that why she fired him? Wasn't it? Wasn't it?

She walks to the window, away from his voice. She doesn't dare remind him of what he knows better than she does: That staring fixedly at a source of light   especially a tiny source of light, like a moveola screen   for hours every day would be a direct invitation to the cyclotaur.

Whose existence he denies.

Although he has, on occasion, taken pride in his kinship with certain great names of the past: Caesar   Alexander   Dostoiewski. Whose otherness he shares.

The centaurs.

The Minotaur. His patron saint, whose beastly half had incidentally   been strictly vegetarian. While the human part fed on yearly supplies of adolescent Athenians.

Which was less barbaric than dehorning generations of adolescent cattle, before permitting them to grow up into beef. He believes in the equality of all that lives. They both do.

It was certainly a lot less hypocritical than the daily sacrifices she exacts from him. As her ritualistic lackey. Her escort service. Her camera-carrying mule.

He knows what she thinks of him: he hisses through clenched teeth: She thinks that he can do nothing. Except maybe sing to her. & sit at her feet. She always makes him feel unworthy.

She won't even give him the benefit of a try, with the Nairobi footage. When she knows that he knows animals. Probably better than her new assistant. Who's probably running her an ego bath.

She knows he spent his boarding school boyhood watching cats & dogs & horses & cows. He knows exactly when they're about to lift a hoof, or prick up their ears. He could cut animal footage better than anybody.

Better than she could, probably. Which is probably why she

won't risk giving him the chance. In case he turns out to be better than she is. Which is fine with him. He understands. He won't be a threat to her ego mirage. He's leaving.

But he continues to sit: in her bathrobe, sex exposed above crossed knees. Coarse, suddenly. All grace drained from body & face. His eyes are dull; opaque. His voice is a leaden drone as he lists more & more instances of her bossiness; her selfish disregard & lack of understanding.

Humiliations inflicted on him by their friends.

Who are her friends, not his.

Their relationship is much harder on him, socially, than it is on her. She may get slanting smiles or a raised eyebrow, because people think she's a hot old bitch.   —Which isn't even true. Not any more. When just the opposite is true.—   But nobody would dream of suggesting that she might be taking advantage of him. Everybody always thinks that he's taking advantage of her.

When just the opposite is true. He's always being treated like an appendage, at the screenings she drags him to.   —To which she can go by herself, from now on. He's leaving.—   He doesn't enjoy playing second fiddle wherever they go.

He's worse off than the female wives, who are at least applauded for playing their second fiddles. But gigolos don't get applause. Or bodyguards. Which is always how he is made to feel. By her friends, who won't even bother introducing him.

Not to mention that adoptive father of hers, who has probably been fantasizing about getting into her pants ever since she turned pubescent.

Which certainly wasn't yesterday.

He is trapped in one of his rages. Which seem to recur in cycles, like menstruation. It's like a bleeding of his soul that keeps filling up with pain. There's nothing she can do but wait it out.

She comes back from the window & sits down across from him.

"Let me finish!" His teeth are clenched. As are his fingers. The loving man who brought coffee to her bed that morning has disappeared behind a wall of hate.

She isn't saying anything. She sits waiting, the round marble table between them. It is early afternoon on a sunny Saturday. They had taken their time having coffee in bed. & cigarettes. Cuddling with her   their   cats. Happily: she'd thought. Leaning into each other, legs intertwined, exchanging the groping esoteric speculations they both like so much. She'd thought he'd hardly noticed   or minded   when she got up to take a bath before their speculations started groping for sex.

He had taken a bath after her. With more coffee, & more cigarettes.   —Which were the ritualistic forerunners of the cyclotaur, sometimes. If she were less self-indulgent, she'd give up smoking.

He'd been lying back in the tub, listening to a tape he'd made the night before, of himself singing & playing the guitar while stoned. He hasn't liked what he heard. He won't get stoned again. He's leaving.

She doesn't know what she dreads more: the dull droning of hatred, or the takeover by the cyclotaur.

Under the table, his toes curl & uncurl. But his mind is hanging on to the mechanized voice. Finally he packs a bag & leaves. In a dead white silence. Dark distrusting animal eyes darting reproaches at her from a dead white face.

She locks the door behind him & returns to sit in her chair. Feeling homeless, in her apartment. & old.

But also released. To her, each departure feels final. She's always surprised   —a gasp of gladness mixed with dread— when he comes back.

An hour   a week   5 months later. She checks his eyes: They're warm & shiny. They hug. They go to sleep holding hands.

Why does she always let that boy come back? asks her adoptive father. Who never knew her to be a masochist before. Nor particularly self-sacrificing.

That boy isn't a boy. He's a man.   & more mature than some older men she knows.

Her adoptive father frowns.

Did her adoptive father think of himself as a boy when *he* was 28?

No. Because, at 28, her adoptive father was supporting not only a wife, but also his wife's 2-year-old daughter. Her 'man' isn't normal.

Probably not. What normal   better-than-normal-looking   28-year-old would love a woman twice his age. Which he does. He does love her.

Which mocks the pragmatic laws of nature. & must therefore come to a bad end. Her adoptive father is concerned: He'd hate to see her come to harm.

He has never hurt her.

Not yet.

She shrugs.   —She has never told anyone what an experience it can be, watching a lover turn into a motorcycle.

Which may be her punishment   she sometimes thinks for having evaded a responsibility once, many years ago, during a bus trip to Florida. When she'd gone to visit her adoptive father & her adoptive father's then-current girlfriend: Grace, was it? Or Lucille?

She had been sitting by a window on the bus, when she'd felt stared at   checked out   by an old couple towing a teenage girl. Soon after, the male half of the couple had climbed on & installed the girl in the seat next to hers. Asking her: PLEASE! to make sure his teenage granddaughter didn't go to sleep. Because his teenage granddaughter had psycho-motor problems, which manifested mainly in sleep.

She had said neither yes nor no, to the grandfather. Feeling presumed upon, because of potential motherliness in her looks, her   already then   responsible age.

She'd stared without expression into the smiling eyes of the old couple who had stood, reunited on the platform, making reassuring gestures to their granddaughter, & responsibility-engaging gestures to her, through the bus window. But as soon as the bus got under way, she had climbed over the girl's outstretched legs, & found another seat way in the back.

She's responsible if she gets hurt: she says. Annoying her adoptive father.

Whom she reminds of an annoying Italian neighbor, who used to go around telling people that they'd be not only responsible, but guilty, if they got themselves murdered: for having kept the appointment.

—An appointment that could last for all eternity, in early-renaissance Provence. Whose laws buried caught murderers with their victims, in a single coffin, the live murderer often tied to the dead victim.—

The annoying neighbor had been a fairly well-known Italian painter of wide-eyed, Greek-nosed women, stringing Vonnegut cats' cradles with fishing nets.

He used to keep a caged canary on his window sill, & a fat white cat that used to sit on top of the canary cage. Forever reaching a six-toed paw through the wires, while the canary pecked at the trailing white tail. Finally, one day, their neighbor had found his cat sitting on top of the empty cage, disconsolately looking at a heap of yellow feathers.

The neighbor had not buried his cat with the canary feathers. In fact, he had not punished his cat at all. Taking full blame for setting up the canary's appointment.

Which may have been his intention: Prodding life to inspire art. Because shortly thereafter he had painted a very large painting of a white Greek-nosed woman with wide slanted eyes, sitting atop an over-size bird cage, inmidst a sea of yellow feathers. Which he had called: The Disconsolate Redeemer of Caged Flight.

Her still annoyed adoptive father shakes his head: He hates to see his mature, level-headed daughter so hung up.

She shrugs.   —Rather than explain that this relationship has less & less to do with sex. At least on her side. They don't make love very often. If at all.

Which he lists as another reason for leaving, when the next cycle comes around.

He has forgotten that they used to make love as often as he'd let her, before the first couple of times he left. After they first started living together. Please: he'd say: I'm tired. Rolling out of reach to the far side of the bed.

Which has become her position: Out of reach of his reaching arms.

It's not that he has lost his attraction for her: she tells him, evading his desire.

Their love has outgrown the need for routine conjugal climaxes: she tells him: the "twice a week," recommended by the rebelliously conjugal Martin Luther.

Her love for him is like a constant embrace: she tells him. Rolling out of reach.

She has been asking herself if she has once again come to the end of a desire span. Based on past experience: 3 years—1 1/2—1 year? Before friendship takes over. Before the all-too familiar body next to hers begins to feel like family. Like a vicariously adopted father. & she feels like wrapping herself in saran wrap before bedding down, to protect her skin from the incestuous touch.

Perhaps she suffers from skin fatigue. Which turns to repulsion when pushed.

But he does not repulse her. Not at all. She loves to feel the touch of his skin against hers. To lie in his arms, quietly, & look at him.   —"Drop": he says, stretching one arm under her neck. He's the tenderest man she knows. & aesthetic to look at. She loves his face, especially from the side. The curve of his nose has such delicate strength.

She has tried asking other women about the length of their desire spans. Do they still feel like making love to the bodies of the men they've been living with for 3—7——20 years?

Of course they do: they tell her. With a quizzical look. A frown of misgiving. It gets better & better: they tell her.

Or else they complain about their man's loss of interest. Never mentioning/always denying their own.

Perhaps it's her age: One day the sex urge simply drops away. With a sigh of relief. Now she can hire her assistants for their professional   rather than their physical   qualifications. It's a great freedom.

Which may not be her conscious spiritual achievement so much as biology. In which case she can't expect his body to be ready for cuddling continence, whether they meditate together or not.

She had hoped that meditation might drive out the cyclotaur. Following the recipe of medieval exorcism, that pitted the positive energy of God against a visiting demon.

& perhaps he had hoped the same. But it hasn't worked. On the contrary: Twice toward the end of sitting side by side, crosslegged in front of a candle for 20 minutes, fixing their eyes on the bridge of their noses, the cyclotaur had appeared in full force.

To her surprise he almost talks about it in front of their friend Malcolm, during a dinner.

Malcolm has come without his brother Bertram, & is telling them why Bertram didn't join them: Bertram had an out-of-body experience during his evening meditation, & upon returning found his body occupied by another entity. He had to fight long & hard to gain reentry. He felt too exhausted to go out.

"The atmosphere is full of disgruntled spirits looking for a body": Malcolm says: "If you leave yourself open . . . unaware . . ."

He nods. "Twice, after meditating . . .": he begins. But he checks himself. The word unaware annoys him. Maybe Bertram is unaware, not he.

Suddenly he has forgotten who Bertram is. Bertram? he asks. What Bertram? Isn't Bertram a cat?

He makes a cult of cats. & quotes a famous painter whose name he can't remember. Who said that: in case of a fire, if he had to choose between saving a Rembrandt or a cat he'd save the cat.

So would he: he says.

In perpetual atonement for the cat he once hanged when he was a 12-year-old boy in a boarding school. When he was the only boy in the boarding school who couldn't go home for the Christmas holidays. Which he was made to spend with the school superintendent & his family because his parents were self-involved in divorcing each other & needed all their psychic energy for getting even.

On Christmas morning he picked up the school superintendent's cat & hanged it from their Christmas tree.

She let me tie my belt around her neck: he says: She trusted me.

His memory comes & goes, remote-controlled by unknown outside forces. Living with him is reference-less. Each day starts from zero.   —The only way Kafka could cope with his unbearable life.—   Each morning she checks his eyes, & again in the evening, when he comes home from work, to see what kind of time they'll be spending together.

But he has left once again. She no longer needs to sit in the cyclotaur's waiting room. She's independently lonely.

Her own age once again: a grey-haired cutter of films, with a studio just off Times Square.

Outside the narrow studio window, a pair of gigantic black-booted legs tirelessly walk along a grey wall. Advertising something. Johnny Walker probably. The window is too low for her to see the total man. Or his message. She sees only the incessant up-&-down movement of the enormous legs. Which look clumsy, out of context. Compulsive. They make her think of the cyclotaur.

She has asked her new Czech   Italian-toothed   assistant to keep the shade pulled down even when they're not working at the moveola.

It's her film-archives memory that makes her think of the new assistant as: Italian-toothed. Although she has traveled in Italy enough to know that average Italian teeth   average European teeth in general   are less limelighted than teeth in America. Besides, the new assistant is Czech. But every time she looks at him, her memory unwinds reel upon reel of Latin lovers, baring remarkable teeth.

He's not her type.

The teeth of the cyclotaur are differently remarkable: They're clenched.

She hopes she wouldn't have hired the new Italian-toothed Czech assistant if he *were* her type. Not at this stage in her life. Especially not if he were her type, & didn't possess the new assistant's surprising eye for cutting.

Which may be congenital. The Czech national affinity with

visual effect in film & theatre. Italians seem to have such an affinity with stone. & Portuguese with flower arrangements. & Anglo-Saxons with suicide.

The new assistant works hard for her approval. He smiles a great deal because he has good teeth & speaks bad English. This is his first job in America. In New York City. It does not occur to him that there might be a private side to her, outside the cutting room. He doesn't think of grey-haired women as women. He is a normal 28-year-old. Instead he thinks of making a film of his own, like other normal   less gifted   assistants before him.

It's an ambition she has never shared. Not once, during the almost 30 years that she has worked with film. Which may be why film makers like to work with her: She thoroughly knows her craft & lets them be   or feel   creative.

Although, for quite some time now, she has been thinking of shooting the cyclotaur.

Which is not an ambition, but rather an attempt at self-justification. She would like to make a documentary of what happens when it happens. To show to him. Afterwards, when it's over.

When he has no recollection of anything. & denies that anything did happen.

Which seems to happen only when they're alone.

She is making it up: he says: to justify not making love any more.

Shaking her reality. Not because she distrusts her senses. & isn't sure of what she has witnessed   15, maybe 20 times by now; 15 to 20 variants of the same dark ritual   but because of the insidious truth that sometimes lurks behind his wildest accusations. Perhaps she avoids making love because her body has grown afraid: seeing itself pinned under a primal motor-cycle.

I am not afraid of cyclotaurs: she overhears a producer's wife say to him after a screening. During the traditional party that follows a screening.

He must have been drinking, to mention the cyclotaur to the fearless producer's wife. After complaining about his sex-exempt second-fiddle existence. He, too, feels like a wife at these screenings: he says: Like an unappreciated backdrop.

He leaves with the fearless producer's wife. Who tosses her a challenging look. & she asks her assistant to put her in a cab.

If he hadn't left, they'd be walking the 24 blocks to the apartment. It's a brilliant night. The kind of perfect weather historically recorded for the starting days of wars, & great depressions.

She's sure this departure is the last: He never had anyone to help him leave before.

But helping a fearless producer's wife get even with her indifferent producer husband   —who smiles fatherly encouragement every time they run into each other, on their respective ways into or out of the producer's apartment building— offends his sense of loyalty.

He comes back, steeped in guilt. He'd had too much to drink, at that stupid screening party. After watching almost 2 hours of mostly sex. If they made love more often...

What has happened to us? he asks: Do I repulse you?

She assures him that he doesn't. & kisses him, to prove to him that he doesn't.

There is that strange smell again   like lead   which seems to come from his nostrils, announcing the approach of the cyclotaur, a couple of hours, sometimes a whole day before it happens.

She would like to tell him about the smell. To warn him. But he's on his way out. She doesn't want to make him feel insecure in the street. At his job. In case it started happening when they're not alone.

For which she wishes, sometimes. Despising herself. Why couldn't he have turned into a motorcycle & run over the fearless producer's wife.

She also wonders if it's maybe her presence that has been bringing it on. Perhaps he's allergic to her. Since it never happened before they started living together.

They had been living together for a little over a year the first time it happened. In his sleep   —when it was supposed to happen also to the old couple's granddaughter whom she had failed to keep awake on the bus to Florida.

That first time he had not awakened until it was over. Shaking his head at her description of what had happened. Asking: If she hadn't maybe had a bad dream.

But believing her, finally. He still trusted her then.

She isn't sure when he started accusing her of making it up. Despite bruises, now. A deep cigarette burn on his inner thigh. It's happening more & more often.

Perhaps he's allergic to her age.

They're lying side by side in the big double bed. The white cat is curled up on his feet. The black cat is snoring on her pillow beside her face.

She wakes up. He is speaking in his sleep. "First we got to get the old woman's leg out of the way": he says, still articulate. Vigorously kicking her nearest leg.

He has kicked off the covers. His toes are clenched. The cyclotaur is revving his motor.

The white cat flies up the flue above the fireplace. The black cat stays to watch:

The slow sideways turn of the head, as though pulled into a different dimension by unseen clamps. Guttural sounds, like a deafmute screaming.

His hands clutch at the lamp for support. It breaks in his grip. The lampshade rolls under the bed.

His body rolls after it. Missing the pillow   her robe   she throws down to cushion his crash.

He is lying on his back, with furiously revving feet & arms. The forehead hitting upward against the iron frame of the bed. His chest is bleeding below the left nipple, where he grinds the broken porcelain stump of the lamp into his flesh.

When it's completely over, the white cat reappears, sooty, ghost-like, cautiously sniffing his toes.

Every return is different. Sometimes there is only exhaustion. Mildness; even a brief muffled song. At others, it seems to take forever for his mind to return behind his eyes, while the raging continues, threatening to bash her face in with the camera she brought home from the studio.

Which she'd been keeping under the bed. In a box, to keep the cats from doing their claws on it. She didn't think he knew it was there.

So far she hasn't been able to use it. She's afraid to turn up the light & shine it on him like a maddening third degree. Besides, she's always throwing pillows. Moving table edges & objects   herself   out of his way.

Which should also be in the documentary she wants to make. To show to him & prove that she hasn't been making up anything. A documentary of the cyclotaur would also serve to prove his innocence in court, in case she weren't able to dodge his onslaught, one day. Or night.

In which case no judge of any era or area could condemn him to being buried with her. In the same coffin. His live youthful body bound to her dead old one. Unable to leave until total disintegration set in.

But he has left once again. This time surely his departure is final. Her adoptive father need no longer be concerned about her safety. She is once again independently lonely.

Her own age once again: a grey-haired cutter of film, with a studio window looking at the back of Times Square.

She pulls up the shade which her new Italian-toothed Czech assistant had quickly pulled down at her entry, & stands watching a screening of the cyclotaur.

He comes walking toward her from the far corner of the grey wall, on tall, black-booted legs.

PETER SPIELBERG

Prognosis

Knowledge came to me in the summer of my sixth year while out on an afternoon hike with my mother and grandmother. It must have been during July, not August, since my father wasn't with us. Early in July, since the trees in our landlord's garden were laden with cherries, boughs bending so low that my sister and I had no trouble filling a large basket for the landlord's wife that morning.

"We'll have cherry strudel for dessert tonight," she had told us. "So don't you go and eat too many raw ones or your stomachs will burst."

That's why my sister wasn't with us on our after-lunch outing. She had stuffed herself in the orchard and then hadn't been able to eat any of her lunch. We left her behind in her room, bent double with cramps. Our mother thought it served her right.

I promised to sneak her a piece of strudel when we came back from the hike, but she shook her head, barely able to keep back her tears. "Next week, then," I said, trying to comfort her since I sympathized with her sense of loss as well as with her passion for cherries. "We'll ask the landlady to bake us another one."

"No, she won't," she explained. "By then the season will be over."

Cherry season is brief. By the end of June, the orchards are picked clean in the lowland. Summer comes later in the

179

mountains. But not that much later, not even in the foothills of the Alps where we were vacationing while my father stayed behind in the city sweating. He couldn't get away from his business except for two weeks in August.

So it must have been toward the beginning of July, not long after we had arrived in Kals—a village in the East Tyrol which my mother's cousin, an engineer by profession but amateur Baedeker by avocation, had discovered and so enthusiastically recommended that he had persuaded my father to cancel our reservations in Semmering, a resort town closer to Vienna where we had spent the summer before.

I used to wonder what would have happened if we had not followed young Kal's advice to abandon the familiar charms of Semmering for the distant and more austere beauty of Kals. (Kals was not his name then, but it's the name I've known my mother's cousin by since, though he didn't formally assume it until his immigration to America some years later. The name suits him. It bears witness to his romantic temperament, his love of the region and perhaps of the local inhabitants as well, despite his having been driven into exile by these very people, or others just like them.)

Or, I used to wonder, what would have happened if my sister hadn't gotten sick on those cherries.... Would she have had the experience instead of me? Would she have reacted in the same way?

Idle speculations. Lately I've come to be a fatalist about such questions. Sooner or later, here or there, I would have awoken from my childhood to learn the same lesson.

It was bound to have happened. In the fall of that year I was to enter the first grade, the official demarcation line between irresponsible childhood and the period when one must prepare for the earnest business of life ahead. Spoiled as the baby of the family—my father laughing till tears came to his eyes when I garbled a word, my mother indulgently applauding my pranks, my grandmother hugging me for no apparent reason—I resisted the overdue end of infancy and ignored the signs which should have prepared me for what is, after all, a common enough experience. My Catholic playmates were better trained for reaching the age of reason since they knew that at a specified age they would be held responsible, their sins counted against them. Yet the signs were there for me to read also. My silliness was no longer encouraged. No one smiled when I bit the ends off my sister's croissant at the breakfast table. They told me to act my age when I resisted going to sleep in a dark bedroom. I must have been particularly naive not to have seen it coming. Or unusually stubborn. Thus, in a way, my afternoon's encounter could be seen as the beginning of my education, although I certainly didn't recognize it for what it was then.

I met the man who led me to knowledge on a footpath that wound gradually uphill toward the "real" mountains.

We had just come around a bend and could no longer see the small town in which our inn (more a restaurant with half a dozen rooms to let by the week, than a genuine hotel) was located. The path snaked its way through a rock-strewn meadow toward the forest. The closest mountain was green to its tip, but behind it one could see the naked purplish tops of the higher peaks rising above the timberline—a forbidding region to which we had never ascended because of my mother's heart condition, where, I was told, the air was too thin to sustain life. If one squinted, one could, on clear days, make out the toothlike shape of the Grossglockner, the highest mountain in the chain, a giant perpetually hooded with snow.

As usual, we had stopped for a brief rest at this point in our walk to look back toward Kals and to exchange platitudes about how, if one didn't know, one wouldn't guess that a village, a warm, friendly place with all the comforts of home, was just around the corner, an easy half-hour downhill trot.

"If a traveler, weary from a day-long trek through the high mountains, were to arrive at this spot," my mother speculated, pointing to a miniature wooden altar by the side of the path, "he might fling himself down in despair, not knowing that another ten, twenty steps would have revealed the achievability of his goal. The poor man! To have come so close to finding shelter, to being saved, only to fail because he didn't have the strength for the final effort."

"Poor man, indeed!" a stranger's voice coming from the

meadow surprised us. "They buried him right where you're standing, right on the spot where he gave up hope."

With his final word, he appeared, somewhat out of breath, to stand beside us: a ruddy-faced individual dressed in green from head to foot, from his pointed Alpine hat to the tips of his boots, an outfit that made him look like a hunter out of a picture book and helped explain why we had not seen him coming out of the forest and across the meadow, which was the same shade of green as his suit, while we were standing there admiring the absence of a view, so to speak, sighing about the sudden disappearance of our corner of civilization, listening to my mother's little sermon. (That's how I interpreted her 'romance,' an offhand lesson aimed at my ears—she couldn't resist the opportunity—an early attempt to shake me out of my lack of perseverance. Yet in all fairness, I probably misinterpreted her intention since my defeatist attutude didn't surface until later, until after our meeting with the stranger in green.)

"I trust I haven't startled you, honored ladies." He bowed from the waist and brought his heels together in a parody of a formal citified greeting. "Or scared the little fellow." He pointed his walking stick at me.

He hadn't, my mother assured him with a simper; which makes me think that he couldn't have been a big man because my mother was afraid of tall men and of stout men and, especially, of tall, stout men. She came from a family of short, fine-boned people, she had told my sister and me numerous times, as if it were a special honor, hinting at, though never laying formal claim to, ancestors connected to the nobility. There wasn't a waspwaisted woman over five feet in height among my maternal relations or a male over five foot six. The only tall, stout man she was not afraid of, it seemed, was my father who was well over six feet and weighed close to one hundred kilos stripped. But he wasn't there to offer us his protection had the stranger been a large man. He was an overnight's railroad journey away, back in Vienna, sweating, and wouldn't be joining us until the end of the month at the earliest.

Thus, he had to have been smaller than average, our nice

hunter. Otherwise my mother wouldn't have encouraged his familiarity. Also, I don't believe he was a hunter at all, despite his costume. He carried neither gun nor game-bag. Instead he held a book under his arm, a large one, the size of an illustrated children's book or a deluxe edition of the Bible, though not as fat.

Short though he must have been, he wasn't as short as a dwarf since I had to bend my head back to look him in the face.

"You'll get a crick in your neck if you stare at me like that," he told me.

My mother apologized for me, but he waved my rudeness off with his free hand as if he were shooing a fly.

"I like your son," he announced, then added—unnecessarily since no one had challenged his statement: "I mean it!"

My mother smiled and my grandmother nodded.

"Yes, I can see that he's a sensible lad," he nodded his head in rhythm with my grandmother. "I pride myself on my ability to read character. I haven't been wrong yet."

"He's a good boy," said my grandmother.

"Especially when he's asleep, right? Then he's an angel." He laughed at his joke. "Well, to show you that I mean what I say, I have a present for him. A very special present."

My mother, thinking that the man was going to present me with the extra large book under his arm, started to protest, but ceased—her open mouth pursed in a tiny oh—when she saw the object he was offering me.

It was a dark green pencil stub, no bigger than his pinkie. Its end had been chewed ragged, but its lead head was whittled to a fine point.

"Mind you," he bent down as if he wished to speak to me in private, "this is no ordinary pencil. Indeed not! It was given to me by a famous writer on his deathbed. A youngish man he was, with a weak chest and a wicked cough that made it difficult to hear him talk. Yet I haven't forgotten his voice although he died more than a decade ago. He knew his days were numbered, but he couldn't rest easy until he had settled his worldly affairs. Not that he had much to dispose of. He ordered that his manuscripts be destroyed; not a scrap of paper was to escape the flames. But his pencil—the special one that he clutched in his bony hand— posed a problem. It was not his, he confessed. It had merely been lent him, and now it must be passed on to a worthy successor. Being without issue..."

He stopped in the middle of his recitation to ask me if I was following him so far. "Do you know what that means?"

"Yes, I think so," I lied, so that he would get on with his story.

"It means having no children of your own, you little fibber!... So, being without issue,the mortally ill writer begged me to take on the task. 'You'll recognize him the moment you meet him—my heir,' he assured me. Then he turned his head to the wall and died. I had to break a couple of his fingers in order to get at the pencil, so tightly was he holding on to it. And let me tell you, I was as surprised as you to discover that the famous pencil was worn down to a mere stub."

He rolled the green pencil between the fingers of both his hands as if he were trying to make it grow longer. "Like the way the landlord's wife kneads the strudel dough before stretching it on the kitchen table," I thought.

"Never mind your silly strudel! It's the last wish of a famous author that I'm concerned with. He knew whereof he spoke, all right," the pompous little man continued. "The moment I laid eyes on you, I realized, as surely as if he had given me your name, that you were his destined beneficiary. Though I must admit, I had forgotten all about him and his pencil until today; but as I came out of the forest I felt a sharp pain in my side, as if someone had stuck me with a pin. I cursed the tailor who had patched the moth-holes in my hiking suit, I haven't worn it in ages, for having left his needle in my back pocket. Yet instead of a needle I found the pencil! And I remembered my promise. A quarter of an hour later I spotted you. Funny, isn't it, but that's how fate works. What do you say to that, my friend?"

I had long lost interest in his story, but having been trained to be polite to grownups, even if they were longwinded and undergrown, I shrugged my shoulders and mumbled the requisite "Thank you, sir."

"You're welcome," he responded as he slapped the stump of a pencil into the palm of my right hand and folded my fingers closed around it. "Go on, take it. It's yours."

The pencil was so short that only its lead point poked out of my fist.

"Do you know how to write?"

I grunted yes.

"Why of course you can! Even a blind man could see that you're a smart fellow. That's why I'm going to tell you something else. But it's a secret."

He looked left and right to make sure that the others were out of earshot. They were, having wandered off to pick a bouquet of wild flowers. To make doubly sure, the man in green turned his back to them so that no one could read his lips.

"The pencil is magic," he told me. "It will grant you three wishes. Anything you want. But three times only. After that it won't be anymore use to you than an ordinary pencil. Less. Look how short it is already. Not much lead left. But enough for you. More than enough to give you your three wishes."

Although so far I had not been impressed by the gift, his revelation of the pencil's special qualities aroused my curiosity. Not that I was so credulous as to accept any old yarn, but there was something about the man's manner and about the pencil itself—now that I held it in my hand—that invited, if not trust, serious attention. This was no simpering auntie who was patting me on the head, but a stranger who would brook no nonsense, whose voice was on the edge of irritability. And the pencil, which looked so ordinary, so insignificant, was no child's toy. It was a genuine stump, which anyone but a miser would have thrown into the dustbin, its green paint scarred by teethmarks, as intricately etched as a piece of scrimshaw.

"This is how it works," he explained. "When you're ready to make a wish, go off into a corner by yourself and write down what it is you want. As simple as that. But be sure you've thought it over carefully first. Once you've written it down, it's too late to call it back. You can't erase the wish. And you only have three chances, so don't waste any of them on some foolishness like a bowl of cherries, or on something as dangerous as being a writer.

"And when you've had your three wishes, don't throw the stub away. You musn't!" He raised a finger in admonishment. "Listen to me: although the pencil won't do *you* any good after you've had your chances, it will work for someone else.

"Not for your sister, oh no!" He had read my mind. "It will only work for a stranger, someone you meet unexpectedly on the road. Pass it on to him and he'll have three wishes also. That's only fair. Right?"

"Yes, of course," I saw no reason to argue.

"Let's shake on it."

We did. He seemed happy at having palmed off the pencil stub and pumped my hand with such exuberance that I let out a squeal of pain.

"Thank the nice man for his gift," said my mother who had finished gathering flowers and wanted to resume our afternoon hike. She bade the stranger good-day and, linking arms with my grandmother, started off at a lively pace. I made ready to follow.

"One other thing," the man in green held me back by the suspenders of my Lederhosen for some final instructions. "You mustn't think of a crocodile when you're making your wish. Do you understand? If you do—if you as much as begin to think of a crocodile—the magic won't work. Have I made myself clear?"

"Yes."

"The gift will be wasted! We don't want that to happen, do we?"

"Of course not!" No longer having any doubt about the genuineness of the pencil and anxious to put it to use, I repeated after him: "I mustn't think of a crocodile."

But he wouldn't let it go at that. To engrave the image of the forbidden word on my mind, he sang a verse from a children's ditty in a rather unpleasant voice:

Auf der grünen Wiese
Sitzt ein Krokodil
Hat 'ne lange Nase
Wie ein Besenstiel!

"Don't forget to forget," he called after me. "Never think of that crocodile floating down the River Nile! If you do, the pencil will lose its magical power."

I've never forgotten.

A week later I flung the pencil stub across the room in a fit of frustration because I couldn't write a word without seeing a *Krokodil*. There was no way in the world I could get that smiling green beast out of my mind. I tried humming the Austrian national anthem while I worked on my wish, hoping that the words would make me forget. I recited the names of other animals from aardvark to zebra, but that terrible crocodile kept popping up.

It's been the same ever since. For a while I believed that the green man was a sorcerer who had been waiting to waylay me, who had appeared expressly to put a curse on me. I asked my mother about him, but she didn't take the meeting seriously. My grandmother shook her head sadly and told me that perhaps it was for the best I hadn't gotten my wishes since only God knew which of our desires should be fulfilled.

Yet it wasn't the unfulfilled wishes I was complaining of; it was the fear of the crocodile.

Years later, as a cynical college student, I dismissed the little man as a shrewd but nasty psychiatrist of the old Viennese school on his summer vacation who hadn't been able to resist practicing his craft when the opportunity presented itself. A sharp judge of character, he had instinctively spotted my problem.

"That boy is a weakling," he must have reasoned, "a dreamer who doesn't have the guts to face reality, a coward who'll back away from any challenge. And a potential compulsive. Yes, that's in the cards. You can see it in the way he walks, by the way he lifts his feet rather than scraping them against the pebbles as others kids his age do. I'll prove it too. Test him with the old three-wishes-*but* trick!"

Now I suspect that he was a little of both—psychologist and evil spirit. Whichever, this hunter who wasn't a hunter turned out to be my particular devil. Once awoken, the fear of failure never left me. The crocodile has stayed with me all my life. I play the game—which wasn't a game—in earnest.

"If you don't think of 'crash'," I say to myself every time I'm up in a jet, "the plane will land safely.... If you don't think of 'no,' the woman you're hopelessly in love with will say yes. If you don't think of 'never,' you'll finish that task in no time. If you don't think of 'fizzling,' you'll be able to...."

RONALD SUKENICK

At This Very Instant

While waiting for a LOT airliner to Warsaw in a lounge at JFK, Piotrek and I were playing frisbee in the Sheep Meadow in Central Park. This will be explained. Meanwhile, I was also walking up 72nd street toward the Dakota with beautiful Magda. She was staying there with a rich, old surrealist poet who had found her standing at the entrance like a lost puppy and invited her in. She accepted immediately of course, since this was a fantasy trip for her from its conception. Magda, like most of the people in the world, comes from a country where one is not free to do many ordinary things, so that a journey like this one to New York had required a certain amount of imagination. A certain amount of imagination and a certain amount of faith. All the people in this story have maintained an innocence in face of the hopelessness of events that allows a certain amount of faith. All of them except me who has maintained, however, a certain amount of stupidity that permits, at least, a temporary suspension of the irony required by impossible contradictions. And so the impossible becomes possible again. Iwona could watch her seaside sun setting over the Atlantic, as she had so long longed to do, from the boardwalk at Coney Island, while Ewa 2 finally realized her ambition to be in a Broadway play with a one night walk-on in a production at the Morosco, picked up next day as a human interest item—FOREIGN STUDENT LIVES DREAM—and both of them were careful to avoid the riot police patrolling the pleasant campus in the middling city

189

where, during the war, their parents could smell burning flesh from the camp at the edge of town.

But that was a different time, Malgorzata thought as she walked down Fifth Avenue in her blue dress, the one she bought yesterday at Bloomingdale's. "A time when they picked you right off the street, put you on a train, and suddenly you lost your health," she explained to me. "A different time without rhyme or rhythm, all gone now. I wasn't even born then. Now in Lublin, walking through the medieval gate to the modern city with its trams and sullen queues, you feel time come down like a lid, final. You feel it does not belong to you."

"But everyone knows you can't keep time," Irek objected. Irek was slim and noble looking, like a Round Table Knight, and very idealistic. He spoke with a slight accent. "Time is something everyone shares. This is a very selfish attitude."

"What, then, can you keep?" complained Malgorzata. "I want some time to myself. I would think that in a capitalist country you would be allowed to keep some things, and what more important than time?"

"No," said Agnieszka, who played jazz piano, "only musicians can keep time. Even here."

"Let's eat lunch," I said. It was wonderful walking with them down Fifth Avenue. Everything was new to them, and marvellous, even Chock Full O' Nuts. Even shrimp salad sandwiches. Even the subway, which we caught down to 34th Street on our way to the object of today's excursion: Macy's. Their country suffered from a severe shortage of things, basics like shoes, meat, toothpaste; even soap was scarce because, according to the indigenous humor of despair, the regime was trying to repopulate the Jews. But despite the demands by the regime that its citizens work harder things continued in short supply. Which explains why I was rumbling along in a jammed car of the Lexington Avenue local among a group of Polish students heading for an internationally famous emporium of things, though it does not yet explain why I was rumbling through the night on a train in southern Poland, in a region that was part of Germany till the fall of the Third Reich, trying to get through Czechoslovakia to Hungary, trouble with my visa, border guards pounding at the door of my Pullman compartment. It does not explain but I will now explain it. I had gone to Poland presumably for professional reasons but I had really gone there to look for Ronald Sukenick, and I had found him. What I mean is, given Jewish grandparents from Poland, I had always suspected a Polish component of my personality absent to my consciousness, whose analogue was apparently not to be found in Buffalo or Chicago. I needed to go to the source. So when the opportunity arose, I accepted a lecture trip that would take me through Rumania, Bulgaria, Poland, Czechoslovakia and Hungary—the whole Gulash Archipeligo—just so I could get to the Medieval/Renaissance cloth market in Krakow called the Sukiennicce. And there I found the absent Ronald Sukenick.

It was not an auspicious night to be on a train rumbling through the cold fog of Eastern Europe, harassed by heavy-handed border police. That day I had followed the railroad tracks into Auschwitz-Birkenau, and the less said about that place the better, it is a black hole defined only by an absence, the absence of about three million people. Especially Birkenau, where most of the killing was done, the name might otherwise have a certain delicate charm to it, a summer camp for slender pubescent girls. But I kept thinking about the sign over the entrance to Auschwitz, which was the showplace of the complex for organizations like the Red Cross—odd to think there can be a showplace among death camps: "Work Makes You Free." When I saw that sign I decided to give up irony forever, it was never my thing anyway, I've always been a kind of plodding literalist. And actually, I've always believed in the slogan. Work, after all, was what gave me the chief clue in my Polish odyssey— I think I can call it that—because as it turns out, Sukenick is an unusual but traceable trade name. In Warsaw a lexicographer, surrounded by dictionaries, had worked it out for me. *Sukno* is a kind of fine, woolen cloth used for overcoats, something in the direction of loden, perhaps, and a *sukennik* is one who makes it. Simple as that. My grandfather came from Bilsk and was engaged in cloth manufacturing; my grandmother's family, from Bialystok, owned a cloth mill. I knew the trail through those two towns was void, through any Polish town since 1945, so my destination remained the Sukiennicce.

But first I had to go to Lublin, not that far from Bialystok, they are both near the Russian border, which was the focus of my professional trip whose purpose was to give what intellectual and moral support I could to the increasingly oppressed but quixotic intelligentsia. Solidarity. With this country and its new death camp saint whose Auschwitz cell is the only one decorated with fresh flowers. It was another Jew who mentioned that the martyr priest, Kolbe, had sacrificed himself for another Pole in the camp and had run an anti-semitic periodical before the war. But the status of Jews had improved recently since the regime tried to persecute them as the instigators of Solidarity, because everybody knew there were almost none left.

In Lublin the patrons of the restaurant where I was eating were toasting Brezhnev's death, while in Macy's the others had joined us, including Monika and Ewa 1, in harvesting toasters and hair dryers and calculators, before our appointment with the president of the establishment who was to welcome us— PREZ PALS POLES—since the visit of the students had become a moderate media event of some promotional value. A certain amount of free merchandise was expected to demonstrate the bounty of the free world. On the campus of the university, students walked about sullenly under the eyes of the brutish ZOMO security police which had just suppressed riots in Gdansk, Warsaw, Katowice and Nowa Huta, adjacent to Krakow. The only news about the strikes and demonstrations was coming through on BBC, Radio Free Europe and Voice of America, when they weren't jammed.

The odd thing about the group of students I encountered in Lublin was that we had much in common. When I came to Poland I had expected a lot of fat people and babushkas, but there was not a peasant in sight and the women were very stylish. What I found was a Western country with Western ambitions, habits, styles, with an alternate dollar economy using Polish-version dollars, whose kids started rock and roll bands in every vacant basement, but whose dreams were in bondage to a quasi-feudal power bloc. Every time one made a phone call the ring signal was punctuated by a message that said the call was being recorded. "I took a trip to Czechoslovakia," said one of my young friends, "and people there are very nervous about police spies. We have them here too, but we don't care." These rebellious students and I had no trouble with rapport, but for me something was missing. They had no sense of the contradictions involved in rebelling against a society of which one above all needed to be part. Their situation seemed difficult, but not impossible. A young Jewish intellectual, in contrast, told me how, during the government's post war purge of the remaining Jews in the country, an old Jewish revolutionary walked into a Party meeting and was confronted by a misbegotten anti-Zionist banner declaring, "JEWS BACK TO SIAM." I was haunted by the absence of Siam. So even at the very moment, in a cafe in Lublin, when I was agreeing with my nine young friends who would never visit New York, to put them in a story about it if they told me what they wanted to do there, I was feeling a degree of distance. But that was before I had visited the Sukiennicce.

According to my snapshots, the weather of the Sukiennicce is damp, grey fog condensing on grey stone. The old cloth hall is very large and bordered by a graceful arcade on whose pillars the weight of the massive structure seems to rest. It is set in the center of an immense plaza with the Baroque tower of the old town hall on one side and a small Byzantine church on the other, so ancient it is partly sunk into the ground. The people hurrying across this great space are hunched over and have their hands in their pockets. Inside the Sukiennicce cloth is still sold in the stone stalls where I feel sure that in the 1870's my grandfather sold his. And there I found the absent Ronald Sukenick. It was not simply that she had my father's green eyes, a trait common to many Poles. Though she was emphatically Slavic and I am distinctly Semitic, I felt I had found my Siamese twin.

We met by appointment in front of the monumental statue of Adam Mickiewicz, Poland's liberation hero poet, off one side of the Sukiennicce. She had told me she wanted to meet in a public place because that was the only situation where privacy was possible. She was one of the few writers publishing in the underground press under her own name, though I can't tell you what it is. She hardly spoke at first, staring dully at the ground as we walked around the square. The adjective that occurred to me was morose. I knew that she had been interned for many weeks after the military coup and when released had been fired from her job as a journalist. She now wrote on farm animals for an obscure veterinary magazine which had suddenly developed an allegorical level in the manner of George Orwell, along with a new audience. I supposed that, like many of her compatriots, she was suffering a profound depression because of the political situation, but I was wrong. As soon as she started talking about that situation she became energized, animated, almost gay. Her tactics, she said, were different from those of many Solidarity people. The underground must not hide itself, she said. That was why she used her real name in underground publications, and why she wanted the underground press and magazine she had helped start to be openly defiant. "We are not subversives. We are fighting a war for our own country. It belongs to us."

"Many think it's a war you can't win."

"Of course we can't win. Not now. Maybe not ever."

"Then why fight?"

"Because we're stupid. Stupidity is our means of survival. It is what you call a Polish joke. I have heard people say that Walesa was stupid. Sometimes it takes some really stupid people to change a situation the smart people know is hopeless."

When she started talking about stupidity I suddenly felt right at home, back in Siam, so to speak. I had always disliked those smart people who know what it's all about, the wise guys born to succeed, who are skeptical about everything and always wind up on top. Now I know why. It's because I'm stupid. I'm stupid because I want to be stupid, obstinately stupid like my friend in the Sukiennicce. With her help I bought a piece of cloth in one of its stone stalls, and went to pack for my grim train ride out of Poland through Czechoslovakia, and back to my desk. So here's a stupid story, kids, for you in Lublin and for stupid people everywhere. While you are in Macy's, with Agnieszka playing jazz on a piano for the customers and TV news crews, accompanied by a guitarist the store found somewhere, and the others, especially Ewa 1, wait for the president who is going to take the group to dinner, I leave with Monika to show her all over New York in a yellow taxi in the rain. As promised. At the same time we are at JFK waiting for the LOT airliner that will take you back to Poland, at the same time I finish writing this story in New York, at the same time you, in Lublin, finish reading it at this very instant.

CURTIS WHITE

Howdy Doody is Dead

An Apocryphalyptic Fairy Tale

In the Peanut Gallery, the children boiled. Loaves of Wonder Bread, Hostess cup cakes, Tootsie Rolls like tidy feces spilled out from beneath the bleachers. A side stage door strained and trembled. That was the last day. I, Doctor Ditto, a simple toymaker and one of Howdy's innumerable fathers, was left the sorry task of relating just how it had all come to pass. This, you must take my word, is a true story, although none remain to bear me witness.

It was once upon a time and it was December 27, 1941. It was in a faraway land that was once known as California. Another Howard was born to parents. I am able to show you many photographs of the boy, taken with the family "Brownie." The edges are serrated, someone's idea of decoration. For in the '40's whatever was not grossly functional, baldly machine fit, was ipso facto decorative. Let me tell you, even children's toys acquired a charmless generality. No more could you take a leg of wood and stout knife and whittle until a great pal, a hero, or the shifting self of the devil surfaced. This fact we should have known to be a sign. Searching the depraved void in the "Barbie's" eyes, seeing there that cruel and sterile lust, we should have understood, we should have been able to see more clearly the shape of things.

Nevertheless, there is something for us in these early photos of Howard. They are crisp, glossy, black-and-white, precisely what I need in my effort to make what is nothing in the world less than the facts seem at the very least plausible. Here, for example, is one of our boy on his tricycle. The cowboy hat hung behind the head is a nice touch, don't you think? There's Cisco Kid in that. And look here, he's smoking a pipe with his dad. Or making the stranger dance with his six-shooter. But what in the world do I expect you to make of all this? Why, it's the chemistry! Add together a driveway, a concrete sidewalk, a newly planted lawn, a nice quiet suburb, a boy who thinks he's the son of Hopalong Cassidy, who hasn't a clue that he's not a real boy at all, and above everything a queer half-light, as if the sun were the light bulb in a refrigerator. What the poor boy doesn't understand is enough to make you weep, and Doc Ditto has seen a thousand such cases.

But, you say, am I not a bit ahead of myself? What about Howard's mom and dad? Who were they? How did they bring Howard about? How does this information help to explain his tragic character? Well, I'm sorry to say that I'm not sure what needs to be known about his parents, since they were out of his life by the time he was six. Sure! He had his own show by then, 1947.

LET'S GIVE A ROUSING CHEER, 'CAUSE HOWDY DOODY'S HERE.

I will say, though, that if his father had known that he carried the germ of such a one as son-Howard, he might have given another thought to what he was about as he clambered over Mom's nice big backside, sturdy as baking soda biscuits.

When Dad met Mom, it was April of 1941, the last spring before the war, and it was San Diego, California, the naval facility there. Dad was a strapping lad of a man, born in wheat's home, Kansas. He played varsity sports in the public schools, learned to smoke Lucky Strikes while walking the long country roads to class, and when a lightning storm was near, and the ozone in the air met with the Dixie Peach in his hair, he seemed to radiate. He was a "plumb enchanted guy," so the girls all said.

But Kansas couldn't hold him. A month after graduation,

he was off to join the navy and see exotic ports of call: Pearl
Harbor, San Diego, Alameda. That's how he came to meet
Wanda, Howard's mom, some three years later, near the end of
his hitch, in palpable, palmy, remorseless San Diego. Now,
Wanda too was a child of the farm, but she was also part of a new
American type. She had rejected the ground worn bare by the
scratching of chickens, rejected the sparse shade of an oak,
rejected finally, utterly the misery of a clapboard house. She
came to San Diego to take a job in a parts factory in war related
industry. But she would stay because of the life which flowed
from the folds and flounces which San Diego kept beneath its
tropical skirt. San Diego acted on her as if it were the most
acceptable hand come to hunch permanently at her groin. It was
a change of life as different as a yawn from a moan, and it was
something she would never willingly forsake.

   Wanda was a May Queen with a lunch box. She was an
eyeful that knew it. And she was a meat eater. Learning the
various purposes of a wrench had changed her; it had changed
the way she approached a pork chop. To see the way she held the
t-eed bone and plucked the gray meat from it, a man had to be
completely cocksure to ask if maybe there wasn't just one bite on
it somewhere for himself.

   But a country boy like Howard's dad didn't know enough
to be daunted by Wanda. So one warm spring night, at Uncle
Chuck's Bar and Grill, where Wanda ate her chops and drank
plenty of vodka in grapefruit juice, Dad pulled up a chair. But,
jeez, he was something special himself. He took off his sailor's
hat and puffed on his Lucky, made it blaze in that dim space like
a tiny red eye. Then he reached across and gripped Wanda's
hand, which gripped the greasy pork chop. Then he brought the
whole thing, hand, chop and all, over to his own lips and sunk
his teeth into the meat firmly, painfully, splendidly. A correla-
tive chunk of Wanda's thigh trembled, felt the sweet nip of it.

   It was not very much later that they were in the backseat of
a 1936 Buick, convertible, stars overhead, Dad over Mom,
larding each other with kisses, comforting each other with juices
that this poor toysmith can do no justice to. And you know

what? Something special happened, too. Little Howdy was conceived that night.

Soon the war was over (or over for Dad, who had the good fortune to be gettin' out when the gettin' was good, just when a million others were having to join during the very scorch of it) and Mom and Dad got married. Dad found a job adjusting claims that a world of people made against his employer. Eager to better himself, provide for his family, buy ball bats for his boy, Dad went to night school where he learned about engineering, geography, the basics of accounting and field tactics. On the weekends he took apart radios, planted lawns, cleaned the Buick's carburetor, and threw baseballs which always came caroming off of Howdy's dense hands. But never, never did he look in Wanda's eyes, for very fear of what obscure thing he might find fermenting in that bright liquid.

* * * * *

If it's possible for five years to be a moment, Wanda spent 1941-46 in one long, slow startle, in which painfully, gradually she demanded, "Hey, Buster Brown, what's happening here?" What had happened was that she was now a wife and mother and no longer responsible for her own keeping. It seemed to her that getting married had been a trade. In exchange for a son and a TV set, she had given up her tough hungry life of busses, sandwiches made with Bob Ostro luncheon meats, the smell of machines, the exciting smell of men at work, men jitterbugging, men hot and hepped with Burgermeister beer and Old Crow whiskey. But now, after all, she could watch TV.

One day after watching a program on which a woman won seven Amana gas ranges and a weekend for two in Oakland, she took the front door off its hinges, dragged it out into the yard, buttered it high and low with Sterno and set it on fire. Little Howdy went teetering after her on his uncertain legs, trusting that there was something to be learned in all this. The door was still smoldering when her husband came home. The fire captain was not happy and talked to Howard's dad man to man.

The next day Wanda took all of the canned goods and produce and frozen meats and cartons of milk, put them in the Sears' Best Kenmore oven and turned it on Broil. Later she said she would have done something, would have tried to save the day, but her fingers had gotten tangled in her hair. This time the fire captain took Dad aside and laid it on the line.

The ultimate day, the fateful day was hung with a suspicious ordinariness. When Dad came home from work, Wanda greeted him at the new, green enameled front door. Her hair was combed, she was neat, she wore a house dress open nearly to her waist, she had a Chef Boyardee genuine gourmet Italian dinner prepared. Dad didn't like the looks of it. It was like in the cowboy movies when things are quiet, too quiet.

"Where's Howard?" he asked.

"He's all right. He's in his bedroom."

"Why doesn't he come out to give me a kiss?"

"I've hung him up in his closet."

Dad ran down the hall. He'd save his boy if he could. But when he reached the bedroom, sure enough, there was Howdy, strung up, dependent from a noose of stiff box-cord suspended from a hook for hanging garments high up the closet door.

Coming up behind, Mother said, with some annoyance, "Now look what you've made me do."

It was this awful experience that demonstrated beyond doubt that Howdy was not like other boys. He survived his own hanging because he was a wooden-head, a puppet, a marionette; and as everyone knows, a puppet cannot be hung, except in the sense that puppets are routinely be-strung.

As for murderous Mom and mortified Dad, Howdy's last memories of them are of a distant, indistinct wrangling. Howdy was systematically orphaned. That is, as his parents willed themselves to eternal mutual recrimination before an indefinite series of drowsy magistrates, Howdy was—for his own well-being and protection—taken off and put in the mothering care of programs, organizations, funds, resources, out-reaches, etc. And, the truth be told, things didn't go badly for the youngster.

Buffalo Bob Smith was appointed as his guardian, and within just a few months a Saturday morning television show, on which he was the star and host, was on the air. Best of all, in 1958 a love relationship, which had long been growing, declared itself. Howdy and the Story Princess announced their engagement and a sensible marriage date for the spring of 1962. The Princess was a longtime member of the Doody cast, but, unlike most of the paltry, painted things of that time, she was so delicate, so reserved, that it took years for Howdy to notice her, years more for him to recognize her for the charming, perfect thing she was. But when at last the scales, the crust fell from his eyes, he found himself so in love that nothing in this world or the next would ever hold any pleasure for him without her.

The perfect sweetness of their love renders itself in my memory in a simple scene. I see the two of them on a Saturday morning, still in their pajamas, splayed before the TV, holding hands chastely and watching their favorite shows: Brother Buzz, Crusader Rabbit, Beany and Cecil, Andy's Gang.

Ah, but memory won't let me pass that last so breezily. There was, after all, Andy's gang, and the simple, raw possibility of such a show goes a long way toward explaining the woe that is in this world. For if nothing else could convince you, Andy's Gang could convince you that there was evil, was malice, essential as marrow, flagrant as a footstone, and wholly without motive. So sinister was the show that Howdy often had to lead the saddened and confused Story Princess from the room, just to spare her what little he himself could see that she was spared. But Howdy was fascinated by Andy's "Mob," as he called it, fascinated as by something so real and yet so foreign he could hardly understand it. Officially, he thought the show was artless, and he suspected Andy Devine of being a child molester. Yet he watched it worried and rapt, seeing in it a threat to the popularity of his show, and a menace to the health of the beautiful kids who filled his Peanut Gallery. Andy's Gang was for Howdy the discovery of an ugliness that made his own daily beauty somehow corrupt. Or, worse yet, stupid.

"Hi-ya, kids. Hi-ya, hi-ya, hi-ya."

That was Froggie the Gremlin, how he'd welcome us to the show. A presence as dark and deep as buried children, as the base purposes of animals. But how he'd rouse 'em in the gallery! The kids would lift from their ordinary lives and begin to storm. Some of the little girls would even rise up in the air, the boys clawing at their legs, panties, buttocks. And then Andy himself, every week's witting victim, would come on stage and sit in his chair—avuncular, doomed. At a certain point in every program he and Froggie would have a talk with the kids about things like "daily duties."

"Ya know, kids," Andy would say, his voice broken, whiny, bathetic, "When it's time to go to bed at night, help your parents out. Put your toys away, put on your pajamas, and. . ."

"AND THROW YOURSELVES DOWN THE STAIRS."

". . . and throw yourselves down the stairs. Wait a minute, that's not what I mean! Now, Froggy, cut that out!"

Kids: "Ahhh, haaa, haaa, haaa." A little eight year old girl had quietly removed her panties altogether.

"Where was I. Oh, yes, put on your pajamas, go into the bathroom and clean yourself up. Don't make your parents nag. Get a nice warm washcloth and clean your face. Take a toothbrush and the toothpaste and. . ."

"SMEAR IT ON THE TOILET SEAT."

". . . and smear it on the toilet seat. Ah, no, now doggone it, Froggie, not one more time."

Kids: "Ahhh, haaa, haaa, haaa." Now she took the hand of the little boy beside her and brought it up beneath her charming, pleated skirt.

"Twang your magic twanger, Froggie. Go away."

"AND PISS ON THE FLOOR, KIDS. PISS ON THE FLOOR."

"Froggie!"

Poof!

Now even Andy laughed, as if laughing and having a seizure, *grand mal,* were the same thing.

When this episode was over, Howdy's mouth hung open,

his face was gray in the thin light of the television. He raised his hand to his face and felt there the rigid contours.

* * * * *

But not even here, in this tale to end all tales, should it seem that Howdy's life (or for that matter our own dismal, discredited lives) was one long disease. How could he have lived as long as he did, how could his show have prospered over thirteen years, how could he have so cozened fate to allow him his Story Princess, if life were but an affliction? I can give you an example of the happiness he sometimes found. For there were days when Howdy's commitment to his art, his devotion to his own ideas of puppet beauty and life were pleasant to the point of ecstatic, were what any of us bother to breathe for.

For instance, there was once an afternoon in the studio at NBC which we spent shooting many segments, trying to cushion our production schedule. Well, we'd been there for hours, we'd done some damned good work, some fine work. The Peanut Gallery, those wonderful kids, had been patient and enthusiastic and happy. We were done for the day, we were tired, and yet there was that clarity, that elation, that energy we could hardly stand to part with. When, after all, might we again come together in such joy? So, Buffalo Bob took out his harmonica and pulled up a stool and started laying down this happy foot stomping line. Before you knew it, Clarabell Hornblow had picked up the rhythm and Doctor Sing-a-Song had joined in with that perfect tenor of his. Soon, what the heck, there we all were, the Flubadub, and Dilly Dally, old Sandy McTavish, Ugly Sam, Phineas T. Bluster and even Tim Tremble, dancing and holding hands. Then Howdy himself went into the gallery and started scooping the children up in great armfuls of hugging flesh. Those kids! And soon we were in a fine unbroken circle, laughing, falling, hurtling through the studio as though through all time and space. Howdy's head was thrown back, his arms and legs spun about the pins in his joints, he opened his eyes, the ceiling vanished, the gauzy stars spread like a blanket. . .

* * * * *

As you know, I am a simple toymaker. And in my time I have made many puppets both for the Doody people and others. But there is no doubt that the peculiar puppet I carved in the summer of 1960 was the most momentous of them all. I discovered, in going through a pile of scrap, a block of wood I hadn't noticed before. How I had missed it I don't know. For it was a stunning piece, one of those that virtually speaks to the puppet-maker, that cries out, "I am here! Find me!" It was a handsome piece of wood in the ordinary sense—a thick, dark walnut. But it had an extraordinary beauty— perhaps I mean an unworldliness—that attracted me. Across its upper quarter, just where I knew I would have to cut his face, ran a dark flaw, almost maroon, a burl, a moan, a black snake.

I fell to work with my knife and tools, and soon had carved the hair, the top of the head, and then the eyes. But no sooner had I smoothed the little bubbles of light than this gruesome doll began to move them and stare at me. Practically the whole length of this block was bark that clung like a reptile's scales, but I had already cut the windows to its soul and what I saw there made me afraid.

Next I made the nose, but no sooner was it made than it began to grow. It grew and grew. I cut at it with my knife, I broke it with my hands, I bit at it with my teeth, but the more I fought against it, the longer it became, the more assertive. So I let it be and began the mouth. But the mouth was hardly half done when it began to tremble, the lips swelling like buds.

Then, arrogant, drunken, this half-made boy began to mock me. "Old fool! Old toymaker! Hurry up. I have business to attend to."

As I worked, it made faces. The great dark flaw, the apparent scar which cut diagonally across its face writhed allowing him to appear as a grizzly, groundling, great auk, grayling, hurdy-gurdy, hermaphrodite, Hecate, and even Herbert Hoover. I pretended not to notice and went on with my efforts. Soon the chin, the neck, the shoulders, body, arms and hands appeared. Finally, the legs and feet were done. Then he leaped from my work bench, landed unbelievably on both feet, put his arms akimbo and announced, "I am Howdy Doody."

"You are not Howdy Doody," I replied.

"I AM HOWDY DOODY." And off he ran, out the door, down the street. I collapsed to the floor, shaken, humiliated and ashamed.

Hours, days, perhaps a lifetime later, I was awakened by the telephone. It was Martin Stone, producer of the Howdy Doody Show. "Doc," he said, "Have you seen Howdy?"

"No," I said, afraid of what would follow.

"But you've heard what happened at the studio?"

"No."

"He came in today and tore up the set. Then he locked himself in Princess Summer-Fall-Winter-Spring's dressing room and beat her up pretty good. She still won't talk about it. What the hell is going on?"

"I really don't know," I lied. God, how afraid I was of the truth, of the implications for myself.

And then began that awful prelude. This gross caricature, this seem-alike, tried to take the place of Howdy Doody. And he actually had people fooled. You had to look closely at the mere Mortimer Snerd-ish quality, a sort of cruel stupidity, in his eyes, the trembling sneer in his lips. How he strutted about, laughing maliciously, asking people to do the ugliest things, threatening them if they hesitated. But, of course, the big question was. . . where was Howdy, our Howdy? I mean, Howdy-himself?

For weeks and months this went on. If I hadn't known better, I too would have supposed that Howdy himself had simply undergone some monstrous change. But there was always that mark—the purplish scar, the moan, the snake—that cleft his face like an axe stroke.

Don't ask what took me so long to act on what I understood of this deceit. If it helps any, I will simply confess that I am guilty. Guilty, guilty. Before and after. Guilty of a monstrous creation, guilty of a shameful tolerance. Sure, there were extenuating reasons for my indecision although they seem even to me woefully lame. There were, as a matter of fact, two enormous dolls, thugs, Frankensteins, assigned by Doody-the-hideous to follow me, to see that I caused no trouble. There was also a strange warp, the kind often found in a dream, in which one means to act but just doesn't ever quite get around to it until the last shocking moment when it is clear that the world is about to collapse. What did finally move me would have moved anyone.

Of course I was aware, as everyone was aware, that the saddest aspect of this very sad situation was the effect it had on our own Story Princess. She was heartbroken by the apparent change in Howdy. It was all she could do to force herself through the show. She cried often, her memory slipped, she complained of the cold, she seemed out of touch. And it was rumored that Howdy misused her. It was said that there would be no pleasant discoveries on their wedding night. It was said that disreputable sorts, people outside of the Doody circle, pimpish "Plowboys," men more eager for corruption than Pinocchio's Lampwick, visited them at all hours of the night. There was even a rumor that a sudden "vacation" taken by the two was in fact a visit to an out-of-state abortion clinic.

But none of this did I allow myself to understand, until one day as I passed Howdy's dressing room I saw that the door was part open. I will not try to tell you that "courage" made me enter. I am not such a hypocrite. Let's just say that I entered. What I saw there was terrible: a woman, a small woman, nude, chained by a dog's collar to a bed. On her face she wore a mask, simple and plastic, of the ever-cheerful Bugs Bunny. When I walked to the figure and removed the mask, I found that beneath it was the Story Princess. She was not dead, but there was in her eyes no sign of life.

The bruised, bitten, brutalized body of the Princess which the very hideous soul of irony had placed beneath the Bunny mask had at last made finding the real Howdy important to me. It was easy to find him. He was at his own little apartment and had been the whole time. He was alive, but I won't say he was well. I had to force open the front door to his apartment. When I walked in the livingroom, I saw him in the opposite corner, broken. It was a sad thing to see because his arms and legs were collapsed grotesquely this way and that. Already he was layered with dust, cobwebs, brittle roach bodies. He really did look like some doll which had finally bored a child and now paid a doll's price, neglect and disintegration.

I went to him and began to take his pulse, but instantly the little body whispered to me. "Doc, Doc," he said, "Is it still there? Look at my left arm." I looked and saw there something I can hardly describe. On his forearm was a pale bubble of skin which, when I looked closer, I saw to be more like a flexible scab or crust. And then looking even closer, I saw two eyes, the protruding snout, the darting tongue of something like a tiny, squat crocodile. This thing lived on his arm! What monsters this world breeds!

"Doc, take it off. Pull it off."

The beast seemed to sense it was in some danger. It had withdrawn entirely within its bubble. I felt for its tail and pulled, slowly ripping it through the skin. Then I held it in my fingers where it dangled impotent and vicious. I found a jar and dropped it inside. Closed the lid down good and tight. I hid it on a kitchen shelf, back among the pickles, ketchup and jars of Best Foods mayonnaise. But I can hear it to this day moving against the glass, lifting itself and falling on the sheer walls.

Once this creature had been removed, it was not long until Howdy began to stir. I explained what had happened, that an awful homunculus, dybuk, satan-spawn, changeling, had taken his place and was, it seemed to me, in something like the process of destroying the world. He replied that he understood and feared as much. He said it was his hungry brother, Double Doody.

He said there wasn't a moment to lose.

* * * * *

We caught a taxi outside of Howdy's apartment and told the driver to hurry to the NBC studios. As we drove, Howdy provided me with what he understood of this situation. Some months before he had been attacked in his own apartment late at night by this perplexing puppet who claimed that he was the real Howdy Doody and that he (Howdy-Howdy) was an imposter who had unjustly enjoyed his (Double Howdy's) success, and that matters would be set straight now. Howdy was then disabled in the mad, terrifying manner I have already described: the incapacitating leach, the very toad of the unconscious, was attached to his arm. From that time, Double Doody returned only to acquaint Howdy with his most recent outrage.

"I know all that he has done with my sweet Story Princess," Howdy acknowledged.

Here, he could not take it. His head dropped and he began to cry. For the first time I felt sorry for the little face, frozen by craft into the brightest smile. The tears ripped along the slope of his grin.

But because Howdy was brave, he didn't indulge in this suffering for long. Suddenly he lifted himself and smashed his forearm against the window which separated us from the driver. "A bloody curse on your children if you're not faster, driver." He turned to me. "But there's worse to come, Doc. Today he plans to make the children mad, ruin the Princess and end forever our show. Unless we can get there to stop him."

We arrived at the studio and Howdy jumped from the car and sprinted across the street, myself not far behind. At the set, Howdy was stopped by a security man.

"Not so fast, mister, the Howdy Doody Show is on the air."

"Why you fool, you blockhead, *I'm* Howdy Doody."

The perfunctory, galling man stared in bewilderment. Then with a roar of impatience Howdy knocked him aside and broke through the studio door. And there it was, the last installment:

In the Peanut Gallery, the children simmered, rising and sitting, rising and sitting, their eyes fixed on an atrocity. On the stage Double Doody romped and bucked astride the Story Princess, a nifty stetson hat (ten gallons if it was a drop) in his hand, his hand high over head. "Eeh-hah, call me Howdy! Call me Pecos Bill! Give me land, lots of land, under starry skies

above! Don't make me stop!" His creaseless, dovetailed buttocks rose and fell mechanically, his hips rolling on pins.

Howdy leaped across the room, nothing but rage, grabbed
devil-Doody from behind, spun him and with one immense,
poetic, Jim-dandy of a roundhouse, punched him right on the
jaw. The gallery, the crew, everybody leaped to their feet,
cheering, glad at last. Howdy lifted the fallen form of the Story
Princess and took her in his arms. The audience began to weep in
happiness. She recognized her true lover and fell onto his chest.

But my gaze was elsewhere. The Other Doody was, after all,
my creation, and I knew his strengths and weaknesses better
than anyone else. I saw for one thing that the force of Howdy's
punch had caused the seam in Double Doody's face to split. His
head now hung together only at the neck and his eyes stared
singly from two sides, like a hammerhead shark's. Dead, you
say? You forget, he was a puppet. What was it to him if his head
forked at the neck? So, as Howdy comforted the Princess,
Double pulled from some fathomless resource a dirk. He had
one intent.

You know how in the old Saturday afternoon cowboy
movies at the moment where the bad guy was about to shoot our
hero—Gene Autry, Roy Rogers, Hopalong, the Lone Ranger—
in the back, the sidekick would yell, "Watch out, Roy!" and
Roy'd turn, shooting precisely from the hip? Needless to say, this
was the moment at which Howdy needed the fortunate warning.
But who was there to shout?

It was Double's turn to spin Howdy. He forced the dagger
squarely into the gut. When he removed it, fuzzy kapock clung
to the blade. For a moment it seemed funny. It was so much
what you don't expect in a stabbing. But it was only seconds
before we realized that this wound was like puncturing the bag
of the world. A bubble in which we had long found our comfort
had been perforated. A terrible, sucking force ripped the smiles
from our faces.

In the Peanut Gallery, the children boiled.

Notes on Contributors

RUSSELL BANKS, an early member of the Fiction Collective, is the author of eight books of fiction, most recently *Continental Drift* (Harper & Row) and *The Relation of My Imprisonment* (Sun & Moon). He lives in Brooklyn, New York, and teaches in the Writing Program at Princeton.

JONATHAN BAUMBACH is the author of twelve books, including *Reruns, Babble, Chez Charlotte and Emily,* and *Return of Service.* His stories have been widely anthologized, appearing in *The Best of Tri-Quarterly, The Best of Esquire, O. Henry Prize Stories,* and *Best American Short Stories.* He directs the graduate writing program at Brooklyn College.

JERRY BUMPUS, whose stories have appeared in many literary magazines, is the author of four books: the story collections *Heroes and Villains, Things In Place,* and *Special Offer,* and the novel *Anaconda.* He is currently teaching in the People's Republic of China.

GEORGE CHAMBERS teaches at Bradley University in Peoria, Illinois. His work appears in recent issues of *New Letters, Chicago Review,* and *Northwest Review.* His novels *Vain Repetitions* and *The Sentiment of Home* are now ready for publication. In 1980 he was awarded a fellowship grant from the National Endowment for the Arts. In 1983 and 1984 his stories won the PEN/NEA National Syndicated Fiction Award. His story collection *Null Set* is available from the Fiction Collective.

MOIRA CRONE's short fiction has appeared in *The New Yorker, Mademoiselle,* and many quarterlies. Her latest book, *A Period of Confinement,* is forthcoming from Putnam in 1986. She teaches at Louisiana State University at Baton Rouge.

211

B.H. FRIEDMAN was born in New York City in 1926. He is the author of six novels, of which *Whispers* was recommended by William Gass for a National Book Award, and *The Polygamist* was optioned by Columbia Pictures. His other books include the story collection *Coming Close*, two biographies, *Jackson Pollock: Energy Made Visible* and *Gertrude Vanderbilt Whitney*, and many art monographs.

RAYMOND FEDERMAN's novels include *Double Or Nothing, Amer Eldorado, Take It Or Leave It, The Voice in the Closet*, and *The Twofold Vibration*. He writes in both French and English. His new novel, *Smiles on Washington Square (A Love Story of Sorts)*, was published by Thunder's Mouth Press in the fall of 1985.

THOMAS GLYNN's short stories have been published in *Paris Review, The New Yorker, Playboy, Fiction International, North American Literary Review*, and other literary publications. He has written two novels: *Temporary Sanity*, and *The Building*, which was published by Knopf in 1985. He has produced and directed a film documentary called *God Bless The Child*.

MARIANNE HAUSER was born in 1910. Her seven published novels include *The Talking Room* and *Prince Ishmael*, which was nominated for a Pulitzer Prize. Her latest novel, published by Sun & Moon Press, is *The Memoirs of the Late Mr. Ashley: An American Comedy*. She has published essays and literary criticism. Her short stories have been widely anthologized and were collected by University of Texas Press in 1964 under the title *A Lesson in Music*. At present she is finishing a novella and working on a new novel.

FANNY HOWE is a poet and novelist whose two most recent books are *In The Middle of Nowhere* and *Alsace-Lorraine*. Two additional books will soon be published by Sun & Moon Press and by Alice James Books. She lives in Brookline, Massachusetts, with her three children. She teaches at MIT.

HAROLD JAFFE's "Pelican" is from a forthcoming volume called *Beasts*, scheduled for publication in 1986 by Curbstone Press. His other fiction includes *Guatemala*, a new novel, *Mourning Crazy Horse, Dos Indios*, and *Mole's Pity*. He is co-editor of *Fiction International* and lives in San Diego.

STEVE KATZ's books of fiction include *The Exagggerations of Peter Prince, Moving Parts, Saw*, and, most recently, *Stolen Stories*, published by the Fiction Collective, and *Wier & Pouce*. He lives in Boulder, Colorado.

NORMAN LAVERS has published monographs on Mark Harris and Jerzy Kosinski, a collection of short stories, and a novel, *The Northwest Passage.* This year he is teaching as a Fulbright Lecturer in Bangkok, Thailand.

MARK LEYNER's collection of stories *I Smell Esther Williams* was published by the Fiction Collective in 1983. He is currently working on a new book of fiction entitled *My Cousin, My Gastroenterologist,* excerpts from which have appeared or are forthcoming in *Fiction International, Rolling Stock, Between C And D,* and *Guest Editor.* He lives in Hoboken, New Jersey, with his wife, Arleen Portada.

LARRY McCAFFERY is the author of *Anything Can Happen: Interviews With Contemporary American Novelists* and *The Metafictional Muse: The Works of Coover, Gass and Barthelme,* and he co-edits the journals *Fiction International* and *Critique.* He is a professor of English and Comparative Literature at San Diego State University.

CLARENCE MAJOR has, in recent years, lived for extended periods in France and Italy and has travelled extensively in other parts of Europe and in Africa. He recently completed a novel about the Southwest and a romance set in Venice. His latest published novel is *My Amputations,* forthcoming from the Fiction Collective.

URSULE MOLINARO is the author of six novels, two books of non-fiction, a collection of poetry, and three collections of short stories. She has published 80 stories in a wide range of magazines, and ten of her one-act plays have been produced on off- and off-off Broadway. She is the recipient of two CAPS grants in fiction, a National Endowment for the Arts grant in fiction, and a MacDowell fellowship. Her story, "The Historical Week of Charlotte Corday d'Armont" was recently selected by the PEN Syndicated Fiction Project.

PETER SPIELBERG is the author of two volumes of short fiction, *Bedrock* and *The Hermetic Whore,* and two novels, *Twiddledum Twaddledum* and *Crash-Landing.*

RONALD SUKENICK is the author of several books of both fiction and non-fiction, including the novels *98.6* and *Long Talking Bad Conditions Blues* and the story collection *The Endless Short Story;* a book on the theory of fiction from the writer's point of view; and a study of Wallace Stevens. Raised in Brooklyn and educated in California and Boston, he has lived in Paris, Jerusalem, and the American West. He is currently tenured at the University of Colorado, Boulder.

CURTIS WHITE is the author of *Heretical Songs*. He teaches creative writing at Illinois State University and serves as Series Editor for the Illinois State University/Fiction Collective Award series.